The Bangka Inquiry

Dave,

Hopefully you'll enjoy!

Tony

By

Tony DeMarco

BLVRCA

Copyright © 2007 by Tony DeMarco
All rights reserved under International and Pan-American copyright conventions.

Printed in the United States of America
First American Edition
1 2 34 5 6 7 8 9

Thanks to Carol and MaryLou

Special thanks to Roy for the recipe

For them and the scions

The Bangka Inquiry

Tony DeMarco

CAST OF CHARACTERS

Ahmed	Driver assigned to the CCG consultants
Amulya	Wife of Marapani, the dredge captain
Angelina Fatori	Attorney for Catherine Prendergast
Archie (Alfred Archibald	CCG's project manager in Indonesia
Budi	I-Tin translator assigned to the visiting consultants
Catherine Prendergast	Joe Prendergast's wife
Chu	Managing partner of CCG's Jakarta office
Curtis Morgan	Local partner from CCG's Perth, Australia office
Dadang	Waiter at the Parai Beach Hotel on Bangka Island
David Prendergast	Son of Joe and Catherine Prendergast
Deirdre Cowen	Guest at the Parai Beach Hotel; friend of Archie
Diva	Waitress at the Parai Beach Hotel on Bangka Island
Effendi	Owner of the Wisma Jaya
Fiona	Fiancé of Troy Eastward, the Perth staff person
Greg Manning	Worldwide partner in CCG; Archie's boss
Hans Glos	Shrimp farmer; friend of Archie
Hayward	Randy friend of Troy Eastwood
Helen Wortley	Wife of Russ Wortley; government's consultant
Irene & Lynette	Randy friends of Troy and Hayward
Joe Higgins	Current managing partner of CCG's Chicago office
Joe Prendergast	Employee of Chicago Consulting Group (CCG)
Kevin Buscombe	Staff person from the Chicago office
Mahmood	Minister of Transportation
Marapani	Captain of the dredge where Joe Prendergast died
Marty Sauer	Future managing partner of CCG's Chicago office
Michael Manning	Corporate Council for CCG Worldwide
Michael Power	Head of another consulting firm
Monica Prendergast	Daughter of Joe and Catherine Prendergast
Richard (Richie) Rowland	Staff person from the Perth office
Russ Wortley	Indonesian government's consultant
Scott Jefferson	President of CCG Worldwide
Subroto, Bambang	President of I-Tin
Suradi	Head of Security for I-Tin on Bangka Island
Thobrani	Minister of Economics; I-Tin President's boss
Tim Snyder	Staff person from the Chicago office
Troy Eastwood	Staff person from the Perth office
Wiranto	Manager of the Parai Beach Hotel on Bangka Island
Yono	Supervisor of the Nais Workshop on Summatra

Major characters in bold

Map of Indonesia
...with Bangka Island Inset

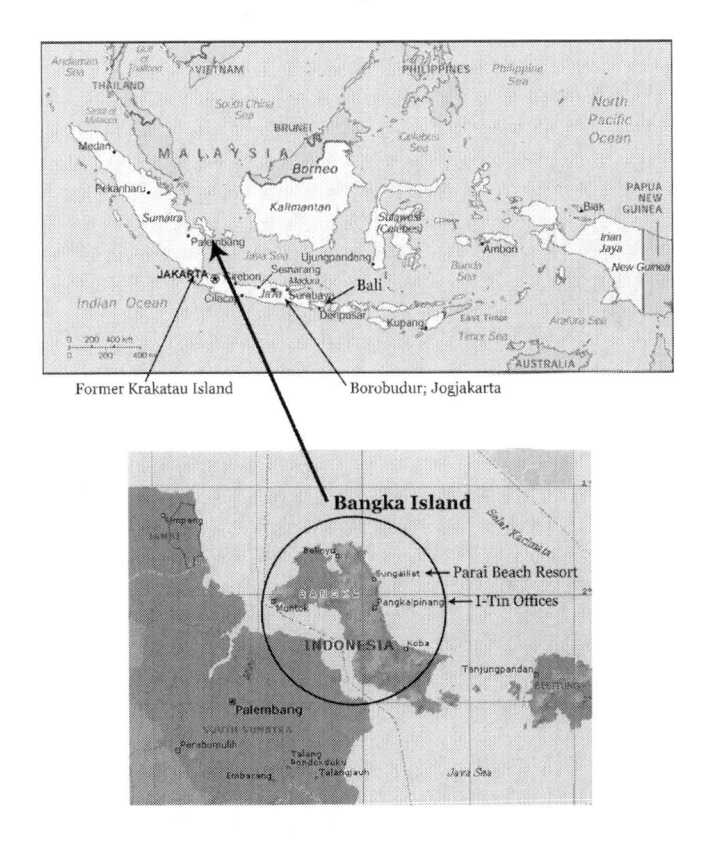

Preface

They said he died instantly, but everything, including death, has a beginning, a middle and an end. It took Joe a long moment to realize he was at the beginning. He felt an excruciating pain across his chest, like someone drawing a sharp blade from one armpit to the other. In that same instant he saw his right arm fall away, shatter, and even though it was no longer attached to him he still felt it, not pain so much as surprise.

Then he heard a sharp "crack." Was that what caused the pain in his chest? He drew a breath. Nothing. Just the sound of air rushing into the open hole, then he felt the warm liquid spill out. He was peering into a long blue tunnel. It had a black ball in the center that was spinning toward him and as it got closer and larger it became a ring that turned white on the edges.

Too quickly he was at the middle, saw Catherine, his wife, spinning helplessly in the tunnel. All of a sudden there was a loud sound, though not in his ears, in the middle of his head, deep inside; it caused a flush of dizziness.

Oh Catherine, what have I done? I promised nothing would happen to me.

They often discussed what they would do in the event one of them died. They were usually in bed, the discussions took them over the edge, into sleepiness; it was relaxing...and seemed so far off. Now Joe was sorry he'd said that if Catherine died first he'd find some rich, eighteen year old, oversexed nymph.

Of course I was kidding...of course! Please God, one more moment...please? I have to let her know I was kidding.

While they were playing at this game Catherine would counter:

"A big Italian stud who will take care of me forever; he'll be a mobster, tough, always saying he'll kill anyone who even looks at me."

But when they got more serious Catherine announced she'd never remarry; couldn't fathom going through all the games...at her age, with two kids to see through high school.

The Bangka Inquiry

"Anyway, where would I meet someone who wasn't damaged goods? Besides, you'll outlast me, no question about it, long life runs in your family, not in mine."

The end was coming too quickly. There was so much more he wanted to think about...but everything was becoming blurry. He felt so tired he could no longer think.

I...I don't want to sleep yet...I must stay awake or I won't see Catherine anymore. I... have so much tell her....

Catherine, wait, I have more to tell you, but now she was spinning down the tunnel, away from him.

If I concentrate, yes...that's it...I'll concentrate harder. What...what was I just thinking about? I can't remember.

Mom, what are you doing here?

I feel dizzy...everything's whirling...I can't stand up. What's happening to me? I'm so tired... I'll just sleep for a second...then I'll be able to think...I'm falling asleep...slee....

Joe fell into a lasting sleep. It only took a moment.

Joe Prendergast was a powerfully built man thirty-four years old. He looked happily married with that look of satisfaction when everything is going great—like it's supposed to.

I've married my high school sweetheart who's my favorite person in the whole world. I've got my two kids, I love my job, what more could anyone want?

This is what the little squint on his face told you. His light, sandy colored hair was short and cropped. What wasn't on his head was on his muscular arms that supported his large hands and long fingers.

Even his fingernails told you, this is a man who takes care of himself, not because he is vain but because he should, everyone should. The Indonesians noticed him immediately; they are generally quite short, small, and hairless. But he was not forbidding, it was the smile, even when he wasn't smiling his face was built that way.

"Sure I'll help you, what do you need?" Joe didn't walk, he moved, like the pope going through a crowd, looking at people rather than things. "Bless you, bless you." You had to love the guy.

2

Suradi met the plane as usual. His is one of the typical faces of Indonesia, a constant smile, whether meant or not, and like most Indonesians, he was wary from years of having to be on guard. He had a beautifully crafted, light brown face, crowned with jet-black hair that looked shiny and new.

Suradi was always crisply dressed, always in a light tan shirt, always perfectly creased tan trousers; a black leather belt, and matching shoes—which looked suspiciously like army issue. His cap looked army as well and had no insignia. He always stood erect, fully spit and polish.

"Suradi, you look very nice today, did you have an inspection this morning?" Archie could not resist pulling Suradi's chain.

"What is inspection, Mr. Archie?" Suradi threw his head back and stiffened just a little bit more, but ever so slightly. Either he did not understand English that well, or had no sense of humor...or both.

"Suradi, I don't understand, you are in the army and you don't know what inspection is?"

"Yes, I do not know what inspection is. I am not in the army. I am head of security for all of Bangka Island...for I-Tin." He had to accentuate his built-in smile of course, but the eyes said,

I do not know if you are joking. If you are not joking, if you are serious, how did you find out I am in the army?

"I understand, Suradi, you are not in the army, you only look like you are in the army."

"Yes, I am not in the army." He gave that look of satisfaction that comes with deciding that Archie was joking. These Americans, yes, they are very strange, was Suradi's final take on the subject.

Suradi did not deviate from his story that he was not in the army; he was head of security for I-Tin, the large Indonesian tin company whose headquarters and most of their operations were concentrated on Bangka Island, situated in the southern part of the South China Sea between the islands of Sumatra and

Kalimantan. The other half of the latter is the exotic and better-known Borneo.

Bangka Island is medium size as islands go in Indonesia—there are some fourteen thousand of them, about six thousand inhabited, stretching across three time zones and scattered near the Equator—and back in the early nineties, was not where you'd find a lot that was modern. The flight to Bangka Island from Jakarta normally took fifty minutes on Garuda, the Indonesian National Airline, in a DC6 that was old when they bought it.

But Archie, Alfred Archibald Glendenning III that is, had no other choice. The consulting firm he worked for was doing a project for I-Tin, and Archie needed to get back to work. The only good thing about the flight, other than it was the only way to get to Pangkalpinang Airport and the omnipresent Suradi, was that you flew over the renowned Krakatoa.

Archie, of course, had seen the movie when he was a kid but just recently found out that the correct name was Krakatau...at least according to the locals. On August 26, 1883, Perboewtan, the northern most crater on old Krakatau Island erupted in one of the largest explosions ever recorded; it was heard four thousand miles away.

The next morning a tsunamis, thirty meters high, hit the coasts of Java and Sumatra killing thirty-six thousand people. Now you can only see the remaining two volcanoes, smaller but very much alive.

Krakatau blew itself out of the water so to speak, but looking at the spot and knowing the devastating power of it, was a chill-producing experience for Archie. He made it a point to request a window on the left side going to Bangka and the right side returning to Jakarta.

How lucky I am to be looking straight down at it, he never failed to mumble to himself every time the weather was clear enough to see. Who'd ever thought I'd get to see this in real life. I *am* lucky!

But he wasn't looking out the window this time. He wasn't looking forward to seeing Suradi either. There was something sinister about him that put Archie and the others on guard. He had a subtle way of finding out things that were none of his

Chapter 2

business, and when he answered one of your questions, he would move his head back as far as it would go without moving his shoulders back. Then he'd begin talking with a slight, nervous laugh. Of course he was in the Army! His job was to report everything the visiting consultants did. He did a poor imitation of a Colombo type character, who acts dumb, but as we will see, was really very clever. Diabolically clever.

Even though I'm dead tired I'll have to be very, very careful, Archie warned himself.

* * *

Archie had been in Indonesia for the past eight months and had looked forward to getting home for his week of rotation. It occurred every three months. This time however, the previous afternoon, only minutes before he left for the return trip to Indonesia, he'd gotten a call from his office informing him quite matter-of-factly that Joe Prendergast was killed in a freak accident aboard one of I-Tin's mining dredges.

It was just too bizarre, how could it be?

No, they got something wrong, what with the communications gap from Bangka he didn't get killed he just got hurt, maybe not even hurt, probably involved somehow but certainly not dead. Archie couldn't think about it. The report from the Chicago office came so matter-of-factly. It had to be messed up.

He was traveling with Greg Manning, his boss, friend, mentor; person Archie looked up to. Greg and he hadn't really talked about the accident. All during the trip they just sat there in business class, quietly thinking to themselves. About what, who knows? Obviously Greg hadn't fully processed his phone call either.

It too came just as he was ready to leave for the airport. Besides, the office intimated that the short message was either all they knew, or all they were going to say for the moment.

"Please don't call anyone now or when you get to the airport. Least of all Joe's wife," was the gist of the message.

The Bangka Inquiry

Archie and his wife knew Catherine well; she and Joe had two kids. The boy, David, was fourteen, and Monica was eleven. The two couples weren't best buddies, but they enjoyed each other; thought alike about life, work, and family. It was not unusual for the two families to see each other at the Christmas party, the summer picnic and, for the parents, the frequent tickets to the opera or symphony or for black-tie dinners.

Archie was told not to contact her; they'd do it. He should wait until the firm's management had a chance to find out exactly what happened, wait until they got back to Bangka; get the facts. Then, later on, either he or Greg could fly back to Jakarta and phone Catherine.

The phones on Bangka Island were mostly for local calls. You could call the local operator if you wanted to phone Jakarta. You'd give her the number and she'd call you back when she got through. The same went for calls to the United States, only most of the time if you did get a connection you couldn't understand each other through the static. To make a call to the United States it was better to fly to Jakarta. Sounds like it would be an expensive phone call, doesn't it?

Well it wasn't really. Garuda flew two round-trips a day, one in the morning and one in the afternoon, for just a few American dollars. So you could leave in the morning, do whatever you had to do, and catch the return flight. All in all it was a nine-to-five ordeal. Archie and the big shots from the tin company did it all the time; like taking a taxi downtown.

If the communication wasn't personal and you didn't care who and how many people read it, you could send a fax to the tin company engineering office in Jakarta and they'd fax it to the United States. This wasn't as simple as it sounds however, most of the time the fax to Jakarta didn't work either. And, like I said, everyone read it.

Archie wasn't looking forward to landing at the Pangkalpinang Airport. Suradi, the guy you didn't want to know too much of your business, or to annoy, took your passport right at the door as you walked into the little terminal building. He said he was taking it for "safe-keeping" but Archie knew having it stolen was not an issue, at least among the Bangka Indonesians.

Chapter 2

"You could leave a twenty on the table and it would be there when you returned," Archie mumbled to no one in particular.

Because you couldn't leave Indonesia without your passport, Suradi said he didn't want to see anyone misplace it or over-stay his visa. Archie and the team suspected that he sent detail accounts of everything they did to the army's police headquarters. They wanted to know when you arrived and when you left the island; to keep track of everyone; where they were and what they were doing.

As for holding on to everyone's passport all the while they were in Indonesia, and certainly as far as Bangka was concerned, it was a joke among the staff. Wherever you were in Indonesia you were on an island. There was very little chance of anyone "escaping" the country.

Archie maintained that it always made him uncomfortable traveling within Indonesia and not having his passport.

"Suradi, I'm going to Denpasar for the weekend, can I have my passport?"

"I get it for you and have it when you are ready to board the plane." Of course he showed up fifteen minutes before departure and forgot to bring it.

"Suradi, what if something happens to me, like I have a heart attack and need to go directly home, I won't have a passport and I'll die before you can get it to me in Bali."

"You worry too much about things I take good care of. I make sure of everything when you are here helping us...yes," said with that ubiquitous Indonesian smile, which could sometimes drive you nuts.

End of conversation, it just went round and round. After numerous weekend jaunts, which Archie and the others took to visit places like Bali, Surabaya, and Jogyakarta, it didn't make sense to even ask any more.

Suradi did perform a valuable function, however. The visa to Indonesia was good for two months, not one second more, and passport control was very strict about it. It was issued on the spot when you arrived, so Suradi let Archie know whenever any of the consultants on the team was close to the expiration of his or her visa.

Then you could take the afternoon flight from Bangka to Jakarta, on to Singapore, have a much appreciated western-style dinner at the Le Meridien, stay overnight, fly back early the next morning and arrive at work by ten—good-to-go for another two months.

Archie came to rely on Suradi to let him know when one of the staff was in danger of overstaying his or her visa. Suradi, who was always and everywhere being helpful, took care of the reservations, maintaining that he had a great deal of influence with Garuda Airlines so it was better if he made the reservations for everyone—no matter where they were going.

Actually, he got the travel agent's commission. Seems his wife or son or some other convenient person just happened to have opened a new travel agency and Suradi got the commission from the airlines and the hotels. Suradi was the type of man who prided himself on being able to be in control, to take charge, but was uneasy when anything out of the ordinary happened. He was a constant challenge.

Now Archie was ten minutes from landing on Bangka to bad news, horrible news.

Poor us, we're the ones who have to stay here on earth...to suffer; this is what was going through his mind.

It only took a moment they said. How could your world so completely turn around in a moment?

* * *

Earlier that morning, before boarding the flight to Bangka, Archie and his boss Greg had breakfast at the Jakarta Hilton's beautiful dining room. They'd arrived in Jakarta the previous evening. Both of them had the night to ponder the strange, depressing, incredible news that confronted them. It was so unbelievable. Joe Prendergast was the last person Archie spoke to before his trip back home.

There weren't many instructions Archie had to leave with Joe, everyone knew exactly what had to be done; they were professionals, not like you had to check up on them every day. But there were a few housekeeping chores and Joe was Archie's right-hand man. After eight months of working closely together they became good friends. Now he was dead. What could possibly have happened?

"Greg, have you met Mr. Jefferson or Mr. McMillan?"

Scott Jefferson was the head of Archie and Greg's consulting firm. He was from the headquarters in New York and Archie had never met him. It turns out that Greg had but just briefly. Michael McMillan was the senior of the two full time lawyers the firm had on staff.

Archie had met the lawyer just once, they happened to be on the elevator going up to the Chicago office and Mike introduced himself. It was a long time ago, and probably Mike wouldn't now recognize Archie if he was floating in his soup.

During the brief phone conversation just before he left for Indonesia, the person from the Chicago office who called Archie with the news about Joe, said that Jefferson and McMillan were going to leave the next day for Indonesia to look into what had happened. Archie was told not to discuss anything with anyone until after he talked to them.

"I don't really know Jefferson," Greg answered, "but I've had a few occasions to be in meetings with Mike. He's a nice guy, very savvy and knows what's best for the firm."

Greg had been with the firm just over eleven years and made full partner more quickly than most people did. He was very smart, able to look at a problem, a consulting problem that is, and boil it down to just a few simple terms. But he was stumped with this news, couldn't, like Archie, believe it.

"I suspect the firm is very worried. As you know, Archie, our relationship with Indonesia is not without problems. There are lots of people who make lots of money on tin and we're putting our noses into their business. They don't like it and if the firm in any way is responsible for the death of an American, they'd have a good time with that. That's why I think Jefferson and McMillan are wasting no time getting over here."

"Do you have anything set up with them?" Archie asked Greg.

"I'm going to meet them here in Jakarta while you go on to Bangka. Find out what you can from our folks but I suggest you not talk to anyone else, especially Suradi. From what you tell me, he'll want to find out everything you know as soon as you get off the plane."

"I've already thought about that and have my story ready. Knowing the staff, I suspect they too have been careful, they know what Suradi is like. When do you think you and the honchos will arrive in Bangka, I'll want to meet you at the airport?"

"I'm not sure. I don't even know what time they'll arrive in Jakarta. The only thing I was told was to wait for them here at the Hilton. But I'll get a message to you when I find out. Tomorrow probably, depends on what Jefferson and McMillan want to do."

3

"We will arrive in Pangkalpinang in five minutes," the pilot announced, "please make sure your seat belts are fastened." The cabin attendant repeated the directives in Indonesian.

How did we get to this? Archie pondered, this isn't supposed to be happening. His firm, CCG Consulting, had a project with the tin company to help them through a crisis. Brazil, one of the largest producers along with China, Malaysia and Indonesia, was cutting the price of tin ingots by flooding the market.

The price had gotten so low it was almost impossible for I-Tin to cover its expenses and needed to be bailed out by the government. Not that there was anything more than a transfer of funds from one account to another; I-Tin was owned by the government. But it was the biggest presence on Bangka, the biggest employer.

I-Tin ran the airport, the schools, the hospital and clinics, produced the electricity, was responsible for the telegraph system, and even the roads. Oh, and the Pangkalpinang Golf Course.

CCG Consulting's charter was to come up with a plan to privatize all the many entities that were not the core business. The objective was to reduce costs so I-Tin could again become a low-cost producer. There were two other pieces to the project. The next was developing a RFP (Request for Proposal) to overhaul the dredges I-Tin used to mine the tin from the bottom of the South China Sea.

The final piece was to design a program to increase the productivity of the workshops—there were several of them on various nearby islands where the dredges and other capital equipment were repaired.

To make matters difficult, about seventy percent of the total Indonesian tin output was from inland mining by small, illegal miners who destroyed their property in the process and sent the tin ore in small quantities to private smelters, mostly in Malaysia. Talk about low-cost producers!

We know tin as pewter, which is about ninety-five percent tin, soft and pliable, smooth to the touch and quite pretty in its industrial kind of way. Copper is added to the tin in varying amounts to harden it, and on Bangka you can buy some pretty things made of pewter by the local artisans.

One, for example, which Archie has at home, is a miniature golf bag on a golf cart with six individual golf clubs, in addition to a putter, each carefully crafted. The little wheels turn and the golf bag can be detached—Archie had it engraved with his firm's logo and bought it for ten American dollars.

It went well with the saying he was known to repeat often enough:

"It's comforting to know that every hour of the day, somewhere in the world, someone is playing golf, therefore I don't have to."

But Archie wasn't looking out the airplane window this time; he was holding his head in his hands, elbows on his knees, thinking back to his first time on this very flight. It all started back in April on a very rainy, gray, overcast day in Chicago. The dreariness of the day should have been a foreshadowing of what was to come—if, in fact, you believed in such things.

"Now I wonder," he mumbled, almost too loudly.

The huge man in the seat next to him turned slightly, probably wondering what was wrong with this miserable looking, morose person sitting in the window seat.

Yes, on that day, Greg called Archie into his office and said, with the same tone of importance as "What are you doing for lunch—"

"I have a huge project for you, it's in Indonesia, it will take about nine months and, if you want it, we will leave next Tuesday to meet the client, set up logistics, and be back here on Friday.

"Our office in Jakarta sold the project but they don't have the personnel to manage it. What do you think? I'd like you to go."

Archie didn't exactly know where Indonesia was and never gave a thought to an office being in Jakarta.

Chapter 3

"I didn't know we had an office in Jakarta," he responded; surely with the dumbest look possible. "What's the project?"

"It's not really an office, we have an arrangement with them and I don't know too much about the project as yet. If you want to go, I'll phone Jakarta and find out more," answered Greg. "I got the call from the New York office and apparently this is a high-profile project. It would mean a lot to both you and me."

Put like that, Archie reflected, how can I refuse? But instead he asked,

"How long did you say I would be there?"

"My understanding is nine months, you'd be back by Christmas. Naturally you'd be back in-between, but you need to pass it by your wife. Unfortunately I need to get an answer back to New York right away, so you and your wife don't have much time to discuss it. Do you think you could call her and run it by her?" Looking back now, Archie believed Greg knew it was a done deal, that Archie would quickly see the potential from managing a project that the firm considered "high-profile."

In this case, "high-profile" for Archie was code for "big promotion" if he saw it completed at or under budget. He had his eye not only on the promotion to partner, with its big jump in prestige—there were only sixty in a firm with four-thousand consultants—and, of course, the increase in compensation that went along with it, but on being appointed manager of the firm's Asian sector.

"The current partner is due to retire shortly." Greg added this little sweetener, knowing full well that Archie would get its significance. They worked well together and had a language of a sort, a way of understanding each other that conveyed more than the spoken words.

Just think, Archie picked up on it, first of all I never gave Jakarta or Indonesia any more thought than the hole in my ear, soon I could be running the show there, the main man.

This could certainly be the horse to ride in on. The possibility for anything less than an outstanding success never entered his mind.

"I think I'm good to go," Archie said to Greg. "My wife and I knew when I took this job there would be the possibility of

The Bangka Inquiry

transfer, overseas engagements, long days and crabby bosses, so she'll be cool," in an attempt to show Greg he was excited...which he was. "The first thing I'll have to do though is look up where Jakarta is."

"While you're at it, look up Bangka Island—that's where we're going. I figured you'd accept so I have our travel agents already working on arrangements. No one seems to know too much about accommodations on Bangka Island, so we'll stay in Jakarta, go to Bangka in the morning, find a place for you and the team to stay, then back to Jakarta that same day. That much I know is doable.

"Supposedly," Greg continued, "the client will have a few hotels picked out in Bangka; you'll just have to decide which one you want. You're the one who is going to live there."

Archie's wife had lots of questions; Archie had no answers, even though Greg briefed him after he called the Jakarta office and talked to the soon-to-retire partner who sold the project. Greg passed on the name of the client to Archie along with a quick overview of the project's deliverables, and little else, other than they were to meet the client Wednesday morning at their offices on Bangka Island.

"I don't think Jakarta wanted to tell us too much; doesn't want to give us a reason to not want to go," Greg added, kidding of course, but clearly if positions between him and Jakarta were reversed he would have done the same thing.

Is doing the same thing, thought Archie...to me—not telling me everything.

Before Archie knew it, it was Tuesday and a lot had happened from the time Greg offered the project. They were both on the flight to Amsterdam where they would change planes to Singapore, then on to Jakarta—a long flight so Archie could concentrate on the real issue: where were they going to stay for nine months, out near the end of nowhere.

He was very nervous about it. There had been several phone calls between Greg and the partner in the Jakarta office about details.

Chapter 3

He had sent Greg the project scope which outlined exactly what deliverables were expected, fees, due dates, staffing requirements, the fact that the client would provide office space, supplies (even a copy machine), cars with full-time drivers—and so forth, but interestingly, no mention of accommodations.

"Doesn't that seem odd?" Archie asked Greg but didn't get a satisfactory answer.

When the plane landed at the Pangkalpinang Airport there was a welcoming party from the tin company, five of them plus Suradi who was smiling in the background, even though Archie didn't know at the time who he was—very quiet, trying to make himself invisible, with his little, "I'm watching you" grin...even on that first trip to the island you didn't miss him.

The group got into three lime-green Volkswagen vans, the ones with the sliding passenger door. Each was in perfect condition with air conditioning and a bottle of perfume on the dashboard.

Archie soon figured out why the perfume: there was a pervasive smell of mildew almost everywhere. It was a bright, sunny day, the humidity just short of falling rain...and hot.

Each in the welcoming party was dressed in black or brown slacks and the typical business dress for Indonesians throughout the islands: a batik, open collared shirt, which hung loose over the waist, and was the same height from the floor all around; no shirt tail, it was like a suit coat. With their bright colors, one was more beautiful than the next.

One in particular had a series of ornate peacocks intertwined to make a pattern you had to look carefully at in order to see that they were peacocks.

It was an exquisite design, the nicest looking of the bunch, and the man who wore it looked very important. He was. He was the tin company president.

The vans took off on a quick tour of the part of the island where the headquarters were located: the main buildings, the main school, the main hospital and, of course, the golf course. They were very proud of their golf course.

The Bangka Inquiry

Considering that they were inches from the equator wouldn't you expect it to be lush green? It was except the grass looked more like thick, sharp, juicy blades.

Not what I'd want to walk on with bare feet, thought Archie.

Finally they went to visit the first of three "hotels." In Indonesia there are hotels like the beautiful Jakarta Hilton, the even more spectacular Melia Sol in Bali, but nothing of the sort on Bangka Island.

Instead there was the next level of lodging called a wisma. The first one the group visited had a series of twelve by twelve rooms with a bare light bulb hanging from the center of the ceiling, a bed, desk and overstuffed chair that was ninety-five percent mildew and a TV bolted up on the wall above the desk. Against one of the walls was a small armoire, hardly enough room to hold the nine months worth of clothing Archie was planning on bringing.

The community W.C. was down the hall: two rooms...sort of. One side of the room had a metal plate on the ground with two embossed footprints so you could line up with the hole in the center. There was a hose hanging from a faucet on the wall next to it. No toilet paper, so guess what the hose was for? It hung on the left side; they never used their right hand for such things.

The other side was really the "bath" room. In Indonesia it is called a mandi. This one had its large, waist high concrete tub filled with room temperature water. Most of the water came from the roof but could be supplemented using a faucet. There was a small, gray fish swimming in it.

On the ledge of the mandi was a long-handled plastic ladle and it was obvious that you stripped, stood over the same hole you pooped in and ladled water over yourself. You then lathered up and scooped water again to rinse off. Archie assumed that you were probably not supposed to scoop up the fish.

The second wisma was somewhat better.

"Hopefully they are saving the best to last," Archie whispered to Greg. "That first one was absolutely unthinkable. Greg only nodded. This second was called Wisma Jaya and run by a rotund man with a jet-black mustache and a long ponytail,

Chapter 3

named Effendi. It was quickly pointed out that he was Chinese, for whatever that meant. He seemed nice enough. He was exuberant about the gardening, and understandably so, it was quite pleasant.

There were flowerbeds throughout with one flower more colorful than the next. Interspersed among these were seven birdcages with red, blue, green, yellow, and white birds. What were they, large canaries, parrots, or some other indigenous bird? In front of the garden, facing the road was the parking lot; meticulously raked white gravel with a stone walk through the garden up to the main entrance.

The entire property was surrounded by a white fence with flowering bushes that kept the traffic noise from reaching the rooms in the building at the rear of the property. Behind the rooms was another garden, though not as big as the one in front, with a patio and a small western-style pond and some lawn chairs. You could enter a few of the rooms, the nicer ones, from their private entrance at the rear, just off the patio.

The rooms were a little more spacious but not by much, and all but a few had a private bathroom, although the basics were the same: hole in the floor, hose on the wall, water in the tub—but no fish.

It's passable, Archie thought, but where does the rest of the group stay. The Wisma Jaya didn't have enough rooms for the expected staff of eighteen. In good conscience, Archie could not picture himself facing someone in Chicago saying, "you'll love the accommodations."

By this time, one of the men on the tour was identified as the English-speaking staff person who would be assigned to the consultants full time. His job would be to help with translating, logistics, dealing with local customs, and so forth. He was a nice guy named Budi. Since they had to work closely with each other, Archie quickly glommed on to him.

Both places were dismal, such that Archie convinced himself that there was no amount of money in the world that could tempt him to stay in that first place even one night. The second would be a challenge, but for nine months? By now it was

The Bangka Inquiry

noon and off to an open-air restaurant that eventually became one of the consulting team's favorite places.

The building had a very high ceiling, open all around, with a tile floor that gave it a feeling of coolness. It was open, as in no windows or even walls. Its basic shape was similar to a Greek temple with three steps up, steep red-tiled roof; the height making it feel cooler.

The beams holding up the roof were huge round timbers roped together and stained dark, almost a reddish color; exotic architecture. The tables were black wood as were the chairs, constructed with dark hemp twisted around the various pieces that back home would either be glued or screwed together.

The seats were a beautiful batik design, wine colored—the entire ensemble went together to create a cooling effect that made you hungry even though just outside the restaurant a few minutes earlier, Archie mumbled to no one in particular,

"How can anyone think about eating, it's too freaking hot to eat...but I could go for lots of water with lemon in it."

The restaurant was so inviting it changed all that. The cover of the menu read Watergarden Restoran and inside was listed all the ways you could have the ubiquitous cumi cumi—squid that was served in various forms for breakfast, lunch, snacks, hors d'oeuvres, dinner and evening treats in a myriad of ways, each, to Archie at least, surprisingly good.

After the lunch it looked like there were going to be some speeches. By this time Archie was wondering when they'd get to accommodations number three. The afternoon plane back to Jakarta left Pangkalpinang at three and they could not afford to miss it...God forbid, they'd have to stay in one of those wismas.

"Where's the third hotel we were supposed to visit," Archie asked his new buddy Budi.

I think that is what I will call him, Buddy Budi, Archie could not resist this internal conversation with himself and he cracked the first smile of the day.

"It is far away," Budi answered, wondering what Archie was smiling about. "But you can stay there on weekends, for get-

Chapter 3

away, it has a swimming pool and music. It is very beautiful but very expensive and too far away from here to visit today."

"How long does it take to get there?" persisted Archie.

"Too long, you would miss your plane." Archie had an idea. He whispered to Greg that he was going to the third hotel and if he missed the plane he'd stay there, assuming from what Budi had said that it was the most acceptable of the three.

He'd take the morning flight and catch up with Greg in Chicago. The firm popping for an extra night at the Jakarta Hilton was cheaper than finding someone else to manage the project, because there wasn't a chance in hell that Archie was going to spend even one night in those dismal accommodations he'd seen so far—he didn't say this last part to Greg, but his demeanor showed it.

Greg agreed with the plan. He was so wrapped up in conversation with the tin company bosses it probably didn't register anyway.

"Let's go, Budi, and tell the driver to go as fast as he can, I have a plane to catch."

The trip to Sungailiat was harrowing the first time. Eventually it became a normal commute. Here's what happened. It took forty minutes to get to Parai Tenggiri Beach just outside the little city of Sungailiat on the eastern side of the island. The road was narrow, winding, and full of potholes. Generally the traffic drove down the middle of the road until they saw someone coming from the opposite direction.

The beach had huge boulders surrounding a small cove with an island jutting out into the sea and connected with the shore at low tide.

"It's the ideal place to relax and laze in the sun," says the brochure.

The Parai Beach Hotel stood on the beach and was exquisite. It had a large pavilion that served as the dining hall, the music stage, and the cinema. There were ten cottages each containing two units; white, concrete buildings with blue tile roofs. There was a larger cottage with four units.

Inside each unit was a regular bed with a whorehouse-pink bedspread, same color god-awful taffeta curtains, an armoire, desk and chair, TV, and a real bathroom.

There was even a shower that, although it resembled a mandi, it didn't have the water filled tub. In spite of the pink colors it was heaven. And, the sink and shower had hot and cold running water.

By this time it was two o'clock and there was a forty minute trip back to Pangkalpinang in order to catch the last flight of the day. The flight to Chicago left Jakarta at ten the next morning and Archie wanted to be on that plane. The next hurdle however, was negotiating the room rate. The posted tariff was sixty dollars per night for each person. It would be inconceivable for two or more to room together for nine months. However, the firm had allocated only thirty-five dollars per person per night. Time was running out.

Archie asked for the manager and was told he was not available but would return shortly. Arrangements were made to telephone him from the Pangkalpinang Airport and Archie, Budi, the driver and the little green VW van hightailed it back to Pangkalpinang.

There was just enough time to call the Parai Beach Hotel when they got to the airport. Archie rapidly proposed that he would purchase twenty-five hundred nights at thirty dollars per night...American dollars were more desirable than rupiah.

That would cover most of the staff and Archie speculated that some of the younger ones might prefer the action in Pangkalpinang instead of being isolated on one of the most beautiful beaches in the world!

"I think it was only because that manager knew my plane was leaving in five minutes that he agreed; he knew there would be no time to haggle," Archie told Greg while flying back to Jakarta.

"But I'll bet the prices for the food will triple."

So what, Archie continued—but to himself. No one set a dollar limit on food, liquor and entertainment. They had a deal.

4

In Greg's eleven years with the firm he made partner quickly. At CCG it comes to those who show executive level promise, or by bringing in a lot of work. He was married to a beautiful woman, about two inches taller than he, and more educated. He earned his MBA from Stanford; she had been working on her PhD. at the University of Chicago—until she got pregnant. They decided they did not want any children so she had an abortion.

While working on her PhD., and throughout the pregnancy ordeal she continued to work for a financial company in downtown Chicago, and still does. They live in a big expensive condominium in a high-rise in downtown Chicago. She drives a huge white van that one wonders what the reason for it is. She never leaves the city and uses it only to go to their frequent dinners at one of the better restaurants.

Greg also likes nice things. Occasionally the tailor would come to his office with samples for next week's suit. The first time Archie witnessed this meeting he was stumped.

The visitor (unbeknown to Archie at the time that it was Greg's tailor) was dressed in a natty, pin-stripped suit.

Come on, thought Archie, who is this guy? Certainly not the usual client, looks like a hit-man. Archie knew that not minding your own business was one of his character shortfalls, but he couldn't resist. He walked over to the secretary they both shared and asked,

"Who's the suit?"

"His tailor," she rolled her eyes upward, and answered as she exhaled her breath. "Greg is a clothes-horse, haven't you noticed, he never wears the same tie twice."

"I've been here several years, how come I've never seen him before," Archie answered with his own question."

"Because he doesn't come very often. Usually Greg goes to see him, not the other way around. But I know who he is because I pay Greg's personal expenses. Besides, I was introduced once...how should I know why you've never seen him before? Now that we are on the subject, you could use a make-over yourself, want me to tell him to stop in your office before he leaves?"

"No, I don't think so. Besides, I can't afford it, I'm not a partner and *my* wife doesn't work." He was sorry he said that after it came out; it didn't sound right, but he figured he could only dig a deeper hole by apologizing, so he said "thanks" and returned to his office.

Like all of us, Greg had habits—some good, some not so good. The annoying one was when he contemplated out loud he would repeat certain phrases several times so it took double the number of words and twice the amount of time to get it all out. If Archie asked,

"Greg, what is the fee arrangement with Jakarta?" Greg would reply, "It ah... it ah... normally they charge less per, ah...normally they charge ... umm...less per... ah... man-hour than we do...but ah... since we will bill the same rate for... ah...since we will bill the same rate for everyone on the project...umm...umm...they get ...ah...they get a little bonus, that's... ah...that's the arrangement."

But Archie wished he could make digesting the Wall Street Journal every morning a habit...like Greg did. No matter what was on his plate for the day, the first thing he did when he walked into his office was scan that newspaper. He wouldn't necessarily read the details, perhaps he did that later, at home, but he knew the jest of what was going on in the world. He especially looked for articles about his or the firm's clients.

No wonder everyone thinks he is so smart, so sharp; he knows what is going on. I have *got* to get into that habit...duh!

Often Greg would pick up the phone and call Archie's office next door.

"Archie, could you...ah...come in a moment?" A conversation would follow about something interesting in the paper or something on Greg's mind. He wasn't hesitant about speaking his mind about anything, not even the inner workings of the firm. Archie liked these impromptu meetings, he liked and respected Greg and he believed Greg liked and respected him.

Several days earlier, Greg called Archie into his office and said,

Chapter 4

"Yesterday I got wind of a major shakeup at our New York headquarters. It seems that we in this office might be reporting to someone else, not Joe Higgins any longer."

Archie knew Joe Higgins was the managing partner of the Chicago office. Greg continued,

"Joe is due to retire, but it's going to be earlier than he planned. Seems the big guys in New York want to give it to Marty Sauer—not one of my favorite people."

"Why's that? I didn't know you had feelings for Marty one way or another," Archie put in.

"He's a good trooper but I am not entirely comfortable with some of his methods. I've had to call him on a couple of things in the past; wants to take what I refer to as the 'economic' way out; whatever will show in his numbers. He squeezes the tomato when it comes to holding firm to our values." This was one of Greg's sayings when he drove through a traffic light that was yellow but on the verge of turning red—he referred to it as squeezing the tomato.

"Well, Greg, you've always said the firm is a hungry tiger and needs to be fed."

"True, Archie, but of course it shouldn't come as any surprise to you that most of us in the firm are more concerned with doing what is best for the client regardless of the outcome for us individually. And that includes selling projects the client truly needs, not what we need."

"And Marty...?" Archie probed.

"I worry about Marty's ethics. Although it may only be a rumor, started by someone who doesn't care for him very much...but you know the old saying, 'where there is smoke there is fire.' Well, Marty has some smoke about him. The story is he gave one of his clients a kickback on the fee to assure he was awarded the project. It's a rumor mind you, but just the same...in any case Archie, keep it to yourself but be careful."

"I understand, Greg, and as always, what is said here stays here."

"You know I've—no we've—lost clients in the past because we told them things they didn't want to hear, and when it is up to me I don't hesitate, if it's the right thing to do."

The Bangka Inquiry

This philosophy suited Archie just fine. He liked the idea that he was associated with a firm that had high standards; he liked the status of working with the best. And Greg was the best.

* * *

It was on a similar morning that the call to Archie's office was about the project in Indonesia. The two of them met throughout the next day in order to put the staffing together. There were no idle staff waiting around for assignments; they'd have to be pulled off whatever they were doing.

In true Greg fashion, he left the final decision up to Archie. After all, it was Archie who had to work with them. That's how Joe Prendergast was recruited for the Bangka project. He and Archie had never worked on the same project but they viewed things the same way. Neither had an advanced degree and although Greg was not Joe's official mentor he constantly counseled both of them to get going, sign up for grad school...

"Get it over with, what are you waiting for?" Greg would drone daily.

"Weird, Greg, you've been pushing Joe and me to sign up for grad school this semester, now you're sending us for nine months to some place we've only heard about in passing. Even the firm's library doesn't have much, only a state department advisory and that gives exports, the per capita income, and other stuff I don't particularly care to know about right now. Should this make me worry about your motives?" Archie and Greg were at ease with each other and could banter about almost anything.

"Archie, there are two hundred fifty million people in Indonesia, with the largest Muslim population in the world; they survive beautifully. You will too, especially if you convert...just don't get friendly with any mosquitoes and you'll do fine."

"Doing fine is not the thing I worry about, Greg, I'd like to do it but I have to consider my future, my career."

"You do this right and your career will be mighty secure, I'll see to that...what does Joe's wife think? You know her pretty well, don't you?"

Chapter 4

"We've certainly spent enough time together. According to what Joe told me just a little while ago, she wasn't too happy, but I know they eventually want to live in France for a while and to do that he needs to get promoted to there—hint, hint, Greg."

"I hear you. Joe's a quality guy, he'll get there whether I push for it or not. You know it isn't mine to promise, but I *can* promise to do whatever is possible."

"I know," Archie responded, "it never hurts to keep it in the forefront of our minds though, does it?"

Archie and Greg settled on two additional staff from their Chicago office, Kevin Buscombe and Tim Snyder. Neither was married so that eliminated one potential problem. Tim was engaged, but the date was a year and a half out.

"Archie, I got a call awhile ago from the New York headquarters. Seems this is like I thought, a high-profile project. So high they want to staff it with some folks from Australia. Seems: a) the Australians need the experience. Nice to know we here in Chicago have a worldwide reputation, and b) costs less. Australia to Indonesia is like New York to LA.

"There will be a partner named Curtis Morgan and two staff guys, Troy Eastwood and Richard Rowland. I don't know anything about Curtis Morgan, never remember meeting him although I'm sure we were at one of the partner's meetings together. You've got your work cut out for you since he's a partner. However, New York made it crystal clear that all direction comes from this office, not Australia. With Curtis outranking you it will be a challenge, but I'll back you up."

The next Tuesday, Greg and Archie were on their first flight to Bangka where they met the client and Archie arranged for the accommodations at the Parai Beach. They returned to Chicago the next day and a week after that Archie was packed and ready to go to Indonesia for the duration.

The second flight over was relatively uneventful. Being by himself was a nice respite to get his mind in order.

The plan was for him to go first and get things set up for the rest of the team. Curtis and his crew from Australia would be the next to join him and shortly thereafter the remaining Chicago staff would fly over. There would eventually be additional consultants from specialty firms to round out the total team—accountants, and metallurgical and mechanical engineers.

Meanwhile, I-Tin selected office space for them that was quite nice, just down the street from the I-Tin president's compound. The office building was built as a regular house, apparently put up by the Dutch when they controlled everything in Indonesia. Some years earlier it had been converted to office space and no one ever thought to ask who got kicked out, obviously to a lesser office, in order to make room for the consultants, or had it been vacant for a while?

The house/office was one-story stucco with a brown tile roof, jalousie windows with shutters. It was air-conditioned, so the shutters were kept closed during the day to keep out any direct sun, but still, a surprising amount of light got in. It had three smaller rooms, bedrooms in their previous life, and three large rooms that had been a living room, dining room, and office or library.

There was a room with a sink, refrigerator and electric hot-plate, probably a butler's pantry at one time. There were two bathrooms with regular toilets and a sink with hot and cold faucets. One of the bathrooms had a mandi that was now used for storage; the water input hole had been closed up.

Out back there was a huge, three sided garage that held four cars and a workshop and had two attached rooms where the drivers hung out; one room was formerly the main kitchen, Archie was told. A small W.C. was on the other end of the building; used by the drivers and other staff of which there were currently two full time servants and two full time gardeners.

The entire property was neat and tidy. In true Indonesian fashion however, there were finger and handprints all over the painted walls—especially in the bathroom. The toilets were western style but the locals were accustomed to the traditional hole in the floor so they perched their feet up on the toilet seat, holding on to the wall in the process. They conceded to the use of toilet paper however…or at least one would hope so.

Chapter 4

"Mr. Archie," it was Suradi. He just walked in since the door to the office Archie had staked out for himself was open. "Mr. Richard Rowland from Perth arriving this afternoon, yes. They telephone Suradi until your telephone is in working." Suradi was delighted, some news he could forward onward and upward.

So, the Australians would arrive piecemeal; not what Archie had been told but so what. He looked forward to meeting his new buddy at the airport. Even though it was only three days since Archie arrived in Bangka, it would be nice to have a compatriot.

Richard was in his late twenties, very white, with blond hair and striking, azure-blue eyes, which would surely be of great interest to the darker skinned, black hair, dark eyed natives many of whom, Suradi warned Archie earlier, especially away from the I-Tin compound, were not used to seeing really-white people.

First impressions were that Richard was capable, had a quick mind and was there to do an outstanding job—you know the type, for no other reason other than that's what he was there for. He had an accent that came from rounding his lips when he spoke so that everything came out slowly, crisply and distinctly. With the accent, the words rolled out very round, which gave him an immediate endearingness that together with his genuine smile gave the impression you'd enjoy his company.

There was never a thought to where he would stay, the assumption was that the firm's staff, Australian and American, would stay at the Parai Beach Hotel and when they ran out of rooms there, whoever was left—most likely the British engineers who were scheduled to arrive last—would stay at the Wisma Jaya in town.

Brits are used to staying in out-of-the-way places anyway, figured Archie.

Any managers visiting from Chicago, Jakarta or Australia would have to stay at the Wisma as well, unless any of the rooms that the Parai insisted on reserving for other guests happened to be available.

That isn't what Suradi had in mind, however. He apparently had directed Ahmed, Archie's driver, to go directly to the Wisma, intending that Richard would check-in there. Suradi wasn't hard to read. Clearly he planned to lean on Effendi, the Wisma Jaya hotel's owner, for a few rupiah for steering a customer his way.

Fortunately, Archie recognized that the direction they were driving was wrong and got Ahmed pointed toward Sungailiat and the Parai. Suradi never learned. At every opportunity he'd try that trick again. Interestingly, Archie asked Ahmed about it later but it was obvious it was making him uncomfortable so Archie just dropped it.

Same situation, not too long ago, in New York, when Archie was coming out of Penn Station and some low-life offered to take his bags, expecting you'd think he was a porter and give him a tip.

"No, I'll carry them myself…be funny if he just ran off with them," Archie chuckled to himself; a not unheard of trick for unsuspecting visitors. It didn't stop there however, the guy followed Archie to a cabbie who had just pulled up to the curb.

"That'll be one dollar," the low-life said as Archie got in. He was holding the door open.

"For what?"

"I got this cab for you."

"Beat it." Archie said, and then to the cab driver, "take off." But when the cabbie just looked straight ahead and Archie realized he wasn't going to move, he quickly put his foot in the low-life's crotch,

"Close the F—door!" The guy got the message, let go, and a few seconds later, when they were moving, Archie asked the cab driver,

"Why didn't you take off when I told you?"

"You don't have to live here, buddy, I do," was the answer.

Once Richard saw the Parai, he made it clear that the accommodations were just fine with him and he reverted to speaking Australian.

"Apples she'll be, this is like being at a resort on an all expense-paid vacation," was how he put it. He was obviously excited about the long, white, sand beach and crystal clear water. "I'm a jogger, you see and every morning I'll be taking a run in me bathers, then jolly into that water."

Chapter 4

However, Curtis had other arrangements in mind. On Monday, now that Archie's phone was working, he received a call from Jakarta. Curtis Morgan, the partner from the Australian office and Troy Eastwood, the third Australian, announced they were on their way to Bangka and could "Richard" meet them. Fortunately, Archie decided to go along.

When they arrived Curtis asked where the hotel was and when he discovered it was a forty-minute drive from the office asked about alternative accommodations. He decided he wanted to check out the Wisma Jaya, which was all right with Archie, and after he saw the nicer room with its own entrance off the rear patio, decided he'd stay there. Troy seconded the decision and they checked in.

By now it was early evening and arrangements were made for Archie and Richard to wait while the newcomers got settled. The plan was to then head to the Parai Beach for a welcoming drink and dinner. Afterwards, Ahmed could drive them back to the Wisma Jaya. It was close to getting dark and in Indonesia, since it is essentially on the equator, the sun rises at six a.m. and sets at six p.m.—every day. If you are used to living in the United States, it becomes unnerving to have such a short period of sunlight every day.

During dinner, Archie experienced the initial challenge that Greg warned him about. With an unmistakable "I'm in charge here," Curtis told Richard he should pack his bags in the morning, check out of the Parai and move to the Wisma with him and Troy.

"I want all of us to stay at the same place," which of course was meant to be interpreted as "there are two of us in charge and I want the people who are going to report to me to stay at the same place I do."

This toenail had to be clipped—

"That's okay, Curtis. Since Richard's already at the Parai it's up to him where he'll stay. If you want the Wisma, it's fine with me, but everyone will decide for himself where he'll stay, and that goes for Troy as well."

Curtis, Archie deduced, was going to pick his battles and this was not the time nor place; he'd wait for something more

37

substantive. Clearly, Richard wasn't intimidated by Curtis like Troy was. Richard just sat there looking like he wasn't the person being discussed. On the other hand, Troy looked like milk toast, poor guy.

Curtis quickly got on Archie's nerves. He didn't like the Parai because it was too far from the office, yet most nights he appeared for dinner. It wasn't hard to figure. Curtis was accountable to the Australian office for charges to his expense account. If he and Troy ate at the Parai, it showed up on Archie's—Chicago's—expenses, so Curtis got credit for coming in below budget. I-Tin supplied cars and drivers but Curtis had his own, which he rented, along with a driver, and that he charged to Chicago as well, maintaining it wasn't a personal expense.

"I can't be at the mercy of *my* entire team; when I need to go somewhere, I need to go now!"

He frequently took a bottle of "free" vodka back to the Wisma with him. He'd tell, not ask mind you, the waiter whose name was Dadang,

"Bring it out to my driver."

As Richard put it, speaking Australian,

"He's boggy! He's taking advantage of Dadang. The dunny rat knows he's putting him in a difficult position but he does it anyway."

However, for the same reason—not wanting to chance getting Dadang in trouble—Archie never said anything. It wasn't worth it.

One of the sports to help pass away the evenings was playing euchre. Those who didn't arrive knowing how to play were quickly taught. It got competitive, the boys did some serious drinking and, as you would expect playing cards, the language got a little earthier.

They quickly learned how to say gutter-words in Indonesian but it was kept in check, however. They were careful not to use them when Indonesians were in hearing distance. Everyone was conscious of the decorum the Indonesians showed. Whether they used foul language among themselves? Almost certainly, but they were uncomfortable hearing it from others.

Chapter 4

Not Curtis, he'd come up with crude statements that clearly made the Indonesians stiffen up. When he addressed them using choice words they were too gentlemanly and ladylike to bend to his level but they were obviously embarrassed for him.

"You can tell I don't like him," Archie wrote to his wife on more than one occasion.

5

"Catherine," Joe had a discussion with his wife before his initial trip to Indonesia, "we've been through this a hundred times, I do what I've got to do. We both made that decision when I took this job. It's not like 'surprise' you have to go away for a while."

Joe was packing his suitcase, getting ready for the trip that would last nine months, trying not to get angry; realizing it was an ordeal for his wife; it all came so fast.

Catherine Prendergast should have known he was right, they had agreed to take the good with the bad. Joe made more than a decent living now and back in Iowa when they were young lovers in high school, their goal was to get married right after graduation, him to finish college, move to wherever, work hard and smart and become financially successful, and have kids when they were young enough to enjoy them.

They both agreed it was "work like hell" while you can, tuck enough away so you don't have to worry about being poor, but enjoy life while you're doing it.

Now she was being difficult. It made her happy that she could be a stay-at-home mom but it was just that, according to Catherine...

"The kids will be going through a formative time in their lives and their father will be in Indonesia; home three times in nine months." She was directing all this at Joe.

"You're going to miss both of their birthdays, I hope you realize. You told me you can't even telephone from there, what are you going to do, send a card?"

It was so unlike her to be like this.

"Catherine, what's going on, you're acting a little strange. This isn't like I'm leaving forever; its three months then I'll be home for a full week. We can celebrate birthdays, report cards, hell, I'm even thinking we'll take the kids out of school for a week and go off on a trip. By the time I'm ready to go back they and you will be sick of me."

"Don't be fucking cute, I don't think you are funny one bit. I'm worried; something inside me says this is not a good move. You know it's unlike me to worry about the future but I am. Your dad's ill, your mom's worse and what if something happens to them; where will you be? What if something happens to you...go ahead, laugh...but I'm worried. There's malaria; you could get appendicitis out in the god-fucking jungle; one of the natives might be a cannibal.

"And the kids, have you even noticed? They've been very upset since this came about. Have you noticed? Of course not, just the thing to send them into dressing like Goths or Monica going bulimic. And you living in la la land, 'Oh, how neat, this'll be good for my career.' I don't like it one bit."

Joe continued packing.

She's being weird, best to just keep quiet, and she'll get over it. She has had a tough time with my parents...with the kids...with me. But she'll be all right, she's tough, was Joe's response to himself. The kids will be fine. The only thing David thinks about is "what if I get a pimple?" Monica, "Suzie Q likes the same nerd I do."

By the time the four of them went to the airport everyone calmed down. Joe and Catherine even figured out how they could get the nun who was the principle of the kid's school to stay with them for two weeks while Catherine went to Indonesia. They'd take a trip to Bali; it would be exciting, visiting a part of the world one only hears about. Sister Joselda got all excited when Catherine asked her.

"It'll be a chance to see what it's like from the mother's side," was her response. "Perhaps the experience will help me be more understanding of what moms go through; might help me sympathize with them." Much to a mortified David and Monica it was settled; Catherine even picked the two-weeks.

* * *

Now he's dead. Archie could think of nothing else. Although no one could ever know for sure, it was as if Catherine's prophecy came true. How had she put it?

You know it's unlike me to worry about the future but I am.

Chapter 5

Fortunately Mr. Chu took care of the arrangements. Joe was already heading home when Archie arrived back on the Island. Apparently there weren't too many facilities. When Muslims died they were buried within twenty-four hours; Archie didn't want to know the details. Mr. Chu was the managing partner of the firm's Jakarta office; the person Greg first talked to about the project, the partner who was soon going to retire. I-Tin was his client so he felt it his responsibility to come over to Bangka from Jakarta and handle the arrangements himself.

By the time Archie saw Chu he was visibly worried, the old man's face showed it. Worried about Joe's family? No question about it. But understandably worried as well about what this would mean for the project.

"Lots of people realize," Chu said to Archie, "that they are going to be, let's say inconvenienced, by the work of the consultants and this might be all they need to create an incident."

Mr. Chu was at the Parai when Archie met up with him.

"I remember," Archie recalled while he and Chu were having a drink of tea at one of the pavilion tables looking out over the South China Sea, "Joe's first ride to the Parai. He was fascinated the way families take their bath in the river each morning. Moms, dads, kids; they soap up, then dunk themselves to rinse off, get out, dry off and walk home. Meanwhile there are other folks washing clothes, beating them on the rocks, wringing them out and carrying them home to hang out to dry."

"They've been bathing like that for hundreds of years, I suspect," Mr. Chu responded. He said it in a way that told you he was genuinely upset about the accident, you got the feeling he knew Joe as well as Archie, but in fact they had only met once.

It was just a month earlier, at Mr. Chu's club in Jakarta. He invited the entire consulting staff, the executives of I-Tin and some government folks to what Archie decided was probably the most memorable dinner he'd ever had. There were a dozen courses, one more spectacular than the next even though, for some of them, Archie didn't really want to know what he was eating—served with sterling silver chopsticks that rested on an ornate, sterling silver block. It was more than First Class; it was Royal Family!

"I remember Mr. Prendergast well," Mr. Chu continued. "How could you not remember him? He had a magnetism about him. My first impression was, 'this young man is going far.' When you meet a lot of people at one time you usually don't remember most of them, but there was something about Mr. Prendergast. I wish I could have spent more time with him, he made that much of an impression on me. I'm so sorry this happened."

He's being genuine, thought Archie. It's the impression everyone got when they first met Joe. I can't imagine what Catherine is going through, how is she going to tell the kids. I just can't imagine. And his parents.

Archie pondered while he and Mr. Chu sat there.

Yes, Joe had a way with people, made them feel like they were the most important person in the world. Loved watching them bathe in the river; he'd wave, they'd wave back. Look at Dadang over there, with his weird inch-long fingernail and the way he always puts his left hand in the crook of his right elbow when he hands you something, to show he doesn't have a weapon, at least that's what I was told, they all do it—the service class that is. And Diva, she looks thirteen yet she's married with a couple of kids. Couldn't be more than four feet tall. And of course Wiranto, Mr. happy Parai Beach Resort manager.

"We always gave Joe the job of asking Wiranto for special stuff; getting more vodka, getting charcoal so the Australians could have a 'bit of a barbie', getting bikes," Archie mused, not exactly to Mr. Chu, even though he was still sitting there.

"Wiranto would laugh and in his indubitable way tell me how he couldn't resist when Joe asked for something; in a way letting me know that he wouldn't be so accommodating if anyone else asked.

"Mr. Chu," Archie came back to the present,

"The Indonesians are difficult to understand. All the while they are talking about Joe, how sorry they are about the accident, how much they liked him, they still have that same smile on their face. I'm not sure I've ever seen one of them frown. On the rare occasion when you see two of them get into a tussle, you know they are annoyed with each other, yet if you didn't know what

Chapter 5

they were saying you'd never know they were arguing—at least not by their expressions."

"Yes, it does take some getting used to. You have to be very careful you don't raise your voice or embarrass an Indonesian in any way. However, I'm happy you brought that up, Archie. While we are on the subject, Mr. Curtis Morgan is becoming a problem and you may need to talk to Greg about him. He is not well liked by the Indonesians. You know Mr. Subroto and I are friends and when he was in Jakarta a few weeks ago he told me about the dinner party he had for you and your staff to brief the government minister.

"Mr. Curtis insisted on sitting at the right side of Mr. Subroto, only because he is the president of I-Tin and he apparently wanted to impress him with his knowledge of the project's status. Mr. Subroto tried in the Indonesian way to let Mr. Curtis know that protocol demanded that that was the place the minister should sit. It was very awkward for Mr. Subroto and he had to apologize to the minister; an embarrassing thing to have to do."

"I understand, and now I apologize for Curtis," Archie responded. "You probably know that Greg is in Jakarta with our firm's president, Mr. Jefferson and general council, Mr. McMillan. This is the time for you to do things the American way, be right up front, tell Greg exactly what you told me; it would have more of an impact than me telling him."

Mr. Chu gave a slight nod of understanding then continued, "I just recently heard that Mr. Jefferson and Mr. McMillan are coming here. It is because of the accident, is that correct? I came here immediately myself to take control of the situation and only heard from my office this morning. I am here because I do not want rumors to start. Some of the islanders are very superstitious and they are concerned already about what is going to happen with I-Tin. It is important for me to be here, I hope you understand."

"Of Course I do, Mr. Chu, and I appreciate everything you have done. It would have been impossible for me to arrange getting Joe back home. I have no experience in these sorts of things. I am not sure which flight from Jakarta Greg, Mr.

Jefferson, and Mr. McMillan will be on, but perhaps you can stay on the Island until they arrive?"

"Of course." Then Mr. Chu said something that took Archie by surprise.

"Greg will be having a private meeting with Mr. Subroto today as well, so it may be tomorrow before they all arrive. Yes, I can stay through tomorrow."

Why would Greg be having a meeting with the I-Tin President...in Jakarta...at the Hilton? He specifically said he was waiting for Jefferson and McMillan, he would have told me if any of them were planning to meet with the president. So unless Greg knows something he's not telling me...no, he certainly would have told me if he knew he was meeting Subroto. I'm sure he'll tell me all about it when I see him.

6

From the airport Archie went directly to the Parai so he had not seen Curtis. Aside from his meeting with Mr. Chu, what few details he got about the accident had come from Kevin Buscombe and Tim Snyder, the staff from Chicago, and from Richard Rowland, the Aussie. None of them had been on the dredge where it happened, so there wasn't much they could tell.

"Curtis told us to stay here at the Parai and not talk to anyone, not even to discuss it among ourselves."

"Of course he was very upset," added Kevin, "almost angry so I...I mean we," he looked at the others, "we...thought it best to get out of his way. It was such a shock. In fact I still can't believe it. God this is terrible. His wife and kids..."

Here was this big galoot with tears welling up in his eyes. Archie next looked at Tim but it was evident he didn't have any more to add. All three of them looked pale, they looked little and weak, little boys standing there stumbling for words to say, what to do.

"I'm going to the Wisma Jaya. I think it best you three stay here and I'll let you know as soon as I get back."

* * *

To get the tin from the floor of the sea, I-Tin uses bucket-chain dredges, dinosaurs floating just off the coast of the beautiful South China Sea, devouring the seabed ahead of them constantly in search of tin.

The bucket-chain at the head of the dredge scoops up sand, roughly twenty-five feet below the surface, like the mouth of a beast, while the stacker at the end looks like its tail where the sand, minus its tin, is discharged.

Dredges are elaborate. They are self-propelled vessels built with a longitudinal well in the center almost the entire length of the deck and open to the water beneath. Mounted and hinged over the well is a long steel frame that can be raised or lowered depending on how deep the water is. The frame is equipped with a string of buckets passing over sprockets at each end. The buckets, operating through the well, turn along with the chain they are attached to and dig into the seabed.

When the full bucket gets to the top of the arm, it tips over, emptying the sand-tin mixture into a chute that carries it to a series of sluices where the tin is separated from the sand. The bucket then moves around the sprockets at each end of the frame, endlessly scraping, emptying, scraping, emptying. The tin is captured in tubs and transferred to a barge that travels back and forth to the smelter on Bangka Island.

After the sand goes through the sluices, it is returned overboard, leaving a long trail of dirty water in an otherwise clear blue sea. At the smelter the tin is heated to high temperatures and ends up as beautiful ingots of pure tin.

I-Tin had commissioned a film, which was produced about ten years previously. Its purpose was to train the workers in safe practices. A dredge can be a dangerous place. There are many huge moving parts, everything is always wet, slippery and noisy, the inside is relatively dark during the day and since it works around the clock it gets really dark at night.

Most of the I-Tin dredges were rust buckets, with railings rusted through, stairs with holes in the steps, tenuous electrical connections—many of the light fixtures included—and since the crew worked twelve hours on, twelve hours off, there were some not-so-alert folks working onboard.

The safety film was pretty good but outdated. Indonesians enjoy their movies. Along with every thing else on the Island, I-Tin ran the cinemas. These were large permanent screens mounted in open-air places scattered around the neighborhoods. An I-Tin truck would show up just after the dinner hour and show films to a capacity crowd. This safety film was occasionally shown either before the feature or during an intermission—a perfect way to get the message out.

However, the film needed to be updated. Its audience had seen it so often it lost its allure. Besides, they liked more action. Recently, there had been a steady increase in the number and severity of accidents. Most entailed lost fingers, toes (many of the workers wore flip-flops), as well as limbs. But it was only May and there had already been four deaths since the beginning of the year

Chapter 6

from accidents on dredges. The film needed to be updated and the task was included in the consulting project's scope of work. Curtis was the producer.

The script and storyboard were written in the UK, where the dredges were made, spiced up with heroes and villains in a saga the locals would enjoy seeing over and over. It would be filmed in Indonesia, sent back to the UK where they would produce four sagas—for variety—each with different characters but with the same safety scenes interspersed. It was decided that local people, along with some of the consulting staff, should be included as actors. Curtis had plenty of experience producing films—in fact it was the reason he and Troy were there. Back in Perth, in Australia, they'd made a series of documentaries that were well received.

Archie had seen the original film but Curtis suggested the others on the team not view it.

"I want this remake to be fresh and it won't be if everyone sees the original," Curtis said. "What? Would you expect them to be creative? Of course not, seeing the original they will have formed mindsets...just repeat the same boring scenes...with a new script." Curtis was adamant.

"Curtis, aren't you exaggerating? This is an entirely new crew of actors and the script is different. True, the message is the same but like plots, there are only a handful of them...with variations."

"Archie," Curtis slipped into his "creative director" mode and continued, "I do not want to take the chance. This film has to be exciting...new...or the audience will lose interest. I know films, if the actors are boring then the film is boring. This has to look like it is the first time, you know, like your first fuck, it can only happen once. Same with these actors, they ain't as creative as you might think."

"I think you are exaggerating, Curtis," Archie responded, "it's a safety film, unlikely to win the academy award, so let's not get carried away. My bigger concern is the safety of our folks and the Indonesians who are going to be in the film. But if you feel that strongly, go for it."

The original was okay as far as safety films go; the format was reminiscent of the old newsreels.

Hey! Pay attention...this is big news.

Most of the safety tips were what you'd expect, but since a dredge is noisy, and since many times we sense danger through hearing as much as seeing, there were important messages about how the equipment worked and what to listen and look out for.

For the locals—most of them did not grow up around machinery—the first time on a dredge could be scary, so the film was reassuring. The safety program, introduced along with the original film, must have worked. According to the records they kept, accidents dropped significantly when it was first rolled out and were kept in an acceptable range for most of its early life.

"You are not missing anything," Archie relented and told his teammates after he saw it, "the new one will be a lot better."

The dredge where the accident occurred was captained by an Indonesian named Marapani. His dredge was selected for several reasons.

First, and probably most important, Marapani spoke English, one of the few captains and perhaps the only one on board his dredge who did.

Second, his dredge was considered the worst in the fleet so Curtis thought it offered an opportunity to demonstrate the importance of safety since there weren't many safety features built in.

A third but lesser reason Marapani's dredge was selected was because of his wife. Her name was Amulya, which meant "priceless" in her native Indian language. She was a beautiful woman, a Hindu goddess, while Marapani was a Muslim. This caused some friction among the locals. However, her personality as well as her beauty overcame any misgivings, at least among the men.

She also worked at I-Tin, and because her English was exceptionally good, she was assigned to the consultants, specifically to work with Curtis and Troy—more often than not dreary Troy who seemed to brighten up when she was around.

Chapter 6

The actual filming consisted mostly of local Indonesians as the actors. One of Amulya's jobs was to translate the script and pass on the acting instructions for each scene.

Troy was a strange one, Archie thought. He was definitely intelligent, no question about that, but he never had much to say and if Curtis was around always looked to him first, as if to clear that it was okay to speak.

He was average height, on the slim side and had rough features, with what Archie's wife would have described as, "no gift to women." His skin had a gray pallor, which with his constant five o'clock shadow, made him look dirty. It was an in-joke among the staff that there were three Troys: Curtis's, Amulya's and Fiona's.

Troy and Fiona were engaged and planned to married in Bali. In the pictures of her that Troy showed around she looked stunning and everyone concluded the same thing—she had to be hard up to marry this lump.

One time when Troy wasn't there Richie Rowland launched into Australian and explained it this way.

"You perves don't understand, when that Jackaroo cracks a fat he's got the bigger boomer."

For whatever the reason and since neither Troy nor Fiona had much family to speak of, why not take advantage of Bali, the Hawaii of Southeast Asia and get married there. Thus she was due to arrive on Bangka Island in a couple of weeks.

* * *

Archie had talked to Marapani on several occasions and felt he knew him reasonably well. He was the darling of the fleet of dredge captains, relatively young, in his early thirties and was known throughout I-Tin to be on a fast track to become manager of dredge operations. Archie thought him a little timid, not unusual for Indonesians in the company of anyone of a perceived higher status, but Marapani always seemed a little too unsure of himself. Strange, since it was not a secret that he was being groomed for a higher position.

The Bangka Inquiry

Now, as he was heading towards the Wisma Jaya, to find out from Curtis exactly how the accident happened, Archie was deep in thought.

What could possibly have gone wrong, especially with Marapani on-board. He's so overly conscious of the dangers. His dredge has the best safety record of the lot, and even though it is a rust bucket he runs a tight ship.

He's constantly attentive to safety, knows where everyone is at all times. I don't understand. And I find it strange that no one seems to know exactly how the accident happened, like it was a secret or something. When someone tells you an accident occurred, the first question is "how did it happen?" and they tell you. It's part of the horror message that is passed from person to person; it's as if "thank God it didn't happen like that to me."

They arrived at the Wisma Jaya. Ahmed dropped Archie off at the entrance gate, then parked the van. Archie got out and saw Effendi sitting as usual on his lounge chair in front of the lobby. He seemed to be directing his caged birds to sing, to produce the perfect tropical effect for his guests. He loved his Wisma and made sure everyone who visited was made to feel that no one was more important.

On the other hand, he always knew exactly what was going on. He was a little busybody. You couldn't keep a secret from Effendi yet no one knew how he managed to find things out.

"I am full of unhappiness hearing about your good friend Joe," Effendi said as he got up from his chair and bowed to Archie. "And no one feels more sorrow than Marapani. He holds himself to blame since it was his dredge where it happened," he continued, "this is not a good thing for all the people who know Joe and love him so much."

"Thank you, Effendi, I am here to find out how the accident happened so whatever you can tell me will be helpful. Joe's wife will want to know everything and, unfortunately, I am the one who will have to tell her."

"You will have to talk to Curtis...and to Troy. It was a last minute decision that afternoon to go to the dredge, Curtis was in a great hurry; he usually stops to talk to me when he is leaving here.

Chapter 6

That is how I know. He just walked to his van. He was upset about something."

"Thank you, Effendi. Is Curtis in his room?"

"Yes, I believe so," Effendi bowed again.

Archie knocked on the door. Curtis opened it slowly, saw it was Archie and opened it further, a signal to step in. Curtis's room was the best in the Wisma Jaya, which was not saying much. A book was open on the small table, Curtis had been reading.

"I suppose you heard what happened?" which was a stupid thing to say, thought Archie.

Of course I heard what happened, you ignorant fuck, why do you think I'm here. And no one wants to give me the details, seems you've effectively shut them up. Archie didn't say it out loud but certainly the expression on his face told Curtis how despicable Archie thought he was.

"Yes, I got a phone call from someone in the Chicago office just as I was leaving for the airport to return here but they didn't have much information only that there was an accident on a dredge and Joe got killed. How did it happen… were you there…was Troy…where was Marapani… was Amulya there?"

"We were re-shooting one of the scenes about the buckets, what to do if there is a jam. It happens a lot and they are very careful because it is so dangerous. Troy was on the camera and Joe was making sure the lighting was just right. We were shooting lead-up scenes and all of a sudden there was a 'real' bucket jam; made to order. We were going to fake it but here it was, a real situation…I had to take advantage of it, but needed better lighting. That's what Joe was doing, setting up the lights.

"As the workman was freeing the bucket a cable that supports the bucket shaft, someone probably stretched it too tight, snapped and struck Joe across the chest. It happened so fast there was nothing I could do, nothing anyone could do…*he died instantly*. The floor was wet, it was horrible, the wire cut across his chest with such force it tore his arm off. We tried to find it but it was gone, it went down the bucket shaft so quickly we couldn't get it.

"Marapani sent a few men out in a dinghy but it was getting too dark, they couldn't see anything and came back with nothing. We tried, Archie, we tried, but we couldn't find it. Marapani looked the next morning too, but it was gone. It was a horrible accident. I can't get it out of my mind, he lost his arm. What will his family think when they see him without an arm? It was an accident, a horrible accident. Whoever stretched that cable too tight..."

Archie couldn't believe what he was thinking.

This guy is full of shit, an actor. Of course you are to blame, you stupid, blithering son of a bitch. *He died instantly!* Are you crazy? No one dies instantly. Joe felt it, he felt pain, he felt searing pain; he saw what was happening even if it was just an instant. Don't you know? It must have felt like eternity, there had to be horrifying pain in the beginning. Then, in the middle, when he realized he was going to die, his whole life flashed before him. Then came the end...he died.

He didn't die instantly, no one does, you idiot, there's a beginning, a middle and an end.

7

The drive from the Wisma Jaya back to the Parai Beach Hotel in Sungailiat took forty minutes, some days more, some days less. There normally wasn't much traffic this time of day, but the roads were narrow, and if a slow car or truck was going the same way and there was no way to pass, you didn't have much choice but to wait it out.

Since Ahmed did the driving, Archie could look out the window at the unusual and, he thought, quite beautiful sights. Not the vegetation, although that was unique to a Chicago boy, but the people, the way they lived, their universal smile, the comings and goings of their daily lives.

I can see why they are called "beautiful people," it's the combination of their looks and their simple but proud nature.

Yet don't be entirely fooled, he concluded after further deliberation, they have been known to be brutal to each other in the not so distant past.

He looked at the neighborhood he was driving through. Back home a manicured lawn with trees and bushes planted just so is the sign of a careful homeowner—an owner who takes pride in the way his property looks. Back home, the yard you notice has a canvas of colors, textures and symmetry. All of it well taken care of. Naturally it depends on where you live, a front yard in Phoenix is quite different than one in Upstate New York.

But even in Phoenix, a well-tended yard has manicured plantings of whatever will grow, be they cactus, evergreens, lemon trees, or just rocks and stones. Not on Bangka Island. Since it is essentially a jungle, a beautiful yard is a dirt yard. The less trees, stones, shrubs and any other growth, the more manicured. An obsessed homeowner has a yard that is devoid of even pebbles; the flatter, smoother and more bare the dirt the more pride the owner exhibits to his neighbors. Instead of mowing the lawn they sweep the dirt.

Their homes come in all sizes, shapes and types of construction. Some are brick while some have tin roofs. Many are without glass in the windows, and most homes have, of course,

The Bangka Inquiry

the ubiquitous motorbike. The air stinks with their smell and their noise takes some getting used to.

Between the two major cities, Pangkalpinang on the east and Mentok on the west side of oval-shaped Bangka Island there are hundreds of acres of palm oil farms, rubber tree plantations, pepper farms, mineral fields and so forth, owned by large conglomerates who rape the land in the process of producing their product. The result is that the huge population is concentrated on the coasts.

Interspersed between the plantations there are areas of jungle where you occasionally see some monkeys but, surprisingly, not many birds. Archie speculated that the natives must have killed them years ago for food or, more likely, that the chemicals that help the products grow are disastrous for the birds. They were noticeable in their absence.

Archie was sure there was an explanation but he never troubled to find out. It was strange, especially since Sumatra, just across the straits, has many birds and butterflies—it also has less people per square mile. Later on he regretted not knowing more.

Other than the monkeys, there were very few animals except skinny dogs and there were thousands of them. The domestic animal population consisted of, besides the dogs, butt-ugly black pigs with their bellies hanging down to the ground, chickens, and pet civets, a furry animal that looks like a big black mink. Ahmed's family called theirs Moonson.

It was around noon now and Archie had just left Curtis; he didn't want to spend any more time with him than he had to.

His face showed what he was thinking: everything will become more clear.

Effendi will be sure to find out each painful detail from the others on the dredge—he has his network. And Marapani...I'll talk to him as well.

As the van traveled toward the Parai it was as if there were two thoughts in Archie's head competing for brain time. The first was about what Curtis had told him, what Effendi said, how Curtis looked, how Effendi looked—whatever the horrible truth was.

Chapter 7

I am not satisfied, I have to know more, I want to recreate what happened, like I was actually there. Archie's brain also wanted to think of more pleasant things. A nicer thought tried to shoulder its way to the front of his brain and for the moment it succeeded.

Archie watched the school children as he passed the schoolyard. The girls wore red skirts with white blouses, the boys dark blue pants and white shirts; some younger ones wore red shorts. Like kids everywhere, they were running around the dirt yard making a lot of noise. How did they keep their white tops so clean? It was amazing when you considered that for most of them their mother washed their clothes in the river. Very few houses had running water and even fewer had a washer or dryer. How did they get those shirts and blouses so white in the first place?

As he drove along, Archie contemplated the answer. This wasn't the first time he thought about it, it happened every time he drove by the river. The simplicity of these people and how they did things was comforting. The clothes washing process was easy but the work was hard. The women would soap up the clothes, make a ball and beat the ball on a boulder in the river. They'd rinse the clothes out, soap again, roll into a ball and beat some more. This would be repeated until they were satisfied each item was clean. They did what a washer does; agitate the water through the clothes to release the dirt.

The kids in the schoolyard were oblivious to their white clothing and the effort their mothers put forth. However, they managed to look like they just arrived at school, clean, not sweaty like you would expect from kids who are in the midst of their playtime.

Muslim girls wear the traditional headscarf, and at the Muslim schools they wear a long, light-gray garment that reaches to the top of their sandals. In the United States it might not be unusual to see young girls holding hands as they walk down the street—but boys, never. In Indonesia boys and even grown men hold hands as they walk and talk. It goes along with their smile, their good nature and their ability to live in close quarters with each other.

They are a very tactile people. It also is not unusual for two men to be sitting at a café with one having his hand on the other's knee. They are very pleasant to each other.

The nice thoughts won out, they stayed at the front of Archie's brain, wouldn't let the horrible ones take over. It was in Archie's nature not to dwell on bad stuff so it made his brain's job easier.

Regardless of what happens, you can't undo the past so why dwell on making it go away. Archie realized how ignorant and childlike this kind of thinking was but he couldn't help it. The good thoughts always captured his meager brain time. Besides, thinking about their time together, his and Joe's, in some strange way was like he was still alive. Archie was in the middle.

Every event has a beginning, a middle and an end. The beginning was when he first heard of the accident, the horror of it, the unbelief. Now the middle, thinking about everything that had to do with Joe, their time together, what he'd say to Catherine, how he'd have to finish the project without him. The ending would come soon enough and Archie knew he'd recognize it when he got there.

His brain refused unpleasant thoughts. Instead he remembered an incident Joe told him about. It happened to him a few days after arriving on Bangka. Archie didn't think the episode was that unusual but Joe was so excited to tell Archie about it. He loved everyone, it showed, and they loved him back.

"I was standing on the seashore down the way from the Parai and all of a sudden this guy touched my shoulder from behind, ever so gently." Joe had just returned from his morning run and stopped to visit Archie who was sitting on his porch.

"It came as a shock because I didn't even hear him come up behind me. The guy just touched my skin, probably to see what white skin felt like. He couldn't speak English but now we are best friends just by using sign language," Joe laughed at his own absurdity.

All the staff experienced the same thing. They soon found out that it was not unusual, when taking a walk on what you thought was a secluded beach, thinking there was no one within miles, to suddenly have an assembly of people appear a few paces behind, looking intently at the unusual white person stripped to a bathing suit. It was a little unnerving, certainly annoying, but Joe was the only one who turned each encounter into a friendship.

Fortunately for Archie, who was trying hard to keep the unpleasant suppressed, there were a great many more nice things to think about. For instance, the time he and Joe spent one of their weekends visiting Borobudur.

They flew to Jogyakarta, over on the island of Java, taking the afternoon flight and after a nice dinner at a western type hotel, left early the next morning with a hired car to see the monument. It was incredibly hot. By the time they returned that evening, Archie's undershirt and whites were so wet he could wring them out over the sink.

Borobudur is a wonder of the world; the spectacular scene came back to Archie. A Hindu shrine bigger than a football field and nine stories high, built of huge blocks of stone chiseled to interlock so the entire structure looks like a huge, rectangular unfinished pyramid with a flat top.

Most of the stones have scenes carved on their facing side. As you climb, every level has a walkway around its perimeter with a low wall to keep you from falling off.

Each of the four sides has a stairway in the middle that goes from the ground level to the top, quite dramatic looking as you climb it. The steps are tall, steep, and not wide, so it is a little scary if you are afraid of heights.

As Archie and Joe found out, it is a classic Buddhist ritual for pilgrims to carry out the stages of a visit by walking clockwise, so the right hand keeps in contact with the wall of the shrine, and gradually upwards until reaching the top level.

Buddhist implications at Borobudur are complex; it takes a whole series of levels of varying awareness for a devotional person to reach unity at its summit.

Fortunately Archie and Joe purchased a guidebook, which described the first level as the most intricate, adorned with panels depicting the joy and despair of the world of desire. The carvings of the next five levels are teachings from the life of Buddha and depict the world of form.

The next three levels above that are less intricate and contain seventy-two stupas, which are round, bell shaped, lattice-walled structures. You can see the statue of Buddha inside through the latticework. These represent moving from the world of form to the world of formlessness. Crowning the entire structure is the great stuppa, which is empty; it represents nirvana.

When Archie and Joe arrived at the base of the monument, as soon as the car stopped there were twenty kids begging for money. With so many it would be impossible to help them out. Furthermore, the driver discouraged it.

"They will get used to it and begin to act nasty when you don't give them enough. We discourage people from giving them money or anything else." It seemed so out of character for Joe to agree with what the driver said, but he promptly did.

"Damm, it's hot," Archie heard Joe saying. It was like he was alive and sitting right next to him. And it *was* hot as they started to ascend the temple steps.

"We should have purchased an umbrella, like the peddler warned. Man that sun is hot."

"We'd probably still sweat, but the sun wouldn't sting so bad," Archie responded, "anyone with average intelligence would have at least worn a long-sleeve shirt and left the shorts at home."

"Yeah," Joe continued, "the worst is the top of my feet...from wearing sandals...another brilliant move." They both chuckled at their common sense,

"Or lack thereof," Joe added.

That night they went to the huge outdoor theatre in close by Prambanan to see the fabulous epic play *Ramayana*. There were perhaps a hundred in the cast and the story was told through dancing and music.

"I love Siamese dancing," Joe whispered, "I love the way each dancer strikes a pose, the way their torso, head, fingers and toes are bent just so. See it Archie? Damn, I've never seen anything like it." Joe tended to get enthusiastic about everything, but he was beside himself with this.

"Of course I see it, what do you think I'm looking at?" Archie answered lightheartedly. He was happy for Joe's enthusiasm, "and look, look how they sway, ever so gently, and how they move their eyes from side to side. It goes perfectly with the gamelan music."

"Yes, it's spectacular." Joe was like a little kid witnessing his first circus. "Look at the men, how they rock from side to side, their arms, hands and toes telling the story. I'm fascinated by the extreme positions of their eyes, fingers and toes. Look, that one, the guy with the arrows in his quiver, the hero, he has his feet on the ground with his toes pointing straight up. How does he do it? It's what tells the story...so very artistic...I love it."

They whispered so as not to disturb their neighbors. Fortunately the seats were like sofas, and spaced pretty far apart. The sky was clear and you could see the stars. The temperature was perfect—no wind, no mosquitoes.

"I don't know how they do it," answered Archie, "and the costumes, look how ornate. It all works together to tell the story."

Their program book described how this wondrous tale of cosmic adventure immerses the audience in a world of heroes, gods, and demons. The play tells the story of the Lord Rama, the seventh incarnation of Lord Vishnu. At about 50,000 lines the original *Ramayana* is one of the largest epic poems in history—as well as one of the world's most important literary and spiritual masterpieces.

The story of Lord Rama, Archie and Joe learned, is both a spellbinding adventure and a work of profound philosophy, offering answers to life's deepest questions. It tells of another time when gods and heroes walked among us, facing supernatural forces of evil and guided by powerful mystics and sages. The play ends with a very real and spectacular bonfire at the rear of the huge outdoor stage, signifying the triumph of good over evil.

I remember how enthralled Joe was when it was over, Archie reminisced. We both were. He must have repeated to me a thousand times that no matter what, Catherine is going to see...*no, she's going to experience*—was how he put it—this play.

Unlikely now. Joe's gone and the chance of Catherine ever wanting to visit Indonesia, the place of her husband's death, is unthinkable.

"I know Catherine enough that she does not want to ever think of this place," Archie mumbled softly, "no less to visit."

Ahmed heard and turned around but didn't say anything. He knew what Archie was thinking. It is strange how when we lose our friends and relatives the loss is deeply felt. But there are some people that when they die, even though they may not be related or never even seen face-to-face, a President Kennedy or Princess Diana, the feeling of loss is even greater. Joe was one of those people, even to Ahmed, who had seen a lot of sorrow in his life, among people much closer to him than Joe.

They were passing where the I-Tin President lived. It stood out among the houses and businesses along Jl. Jend. Sudirman, the main road between the offices of I-Tin and the Parai Beach Hotel— Jl stands for Jalan, which means road in the Indonesian language. The compound had several acres, perhaps ten, with a white concrete wall surrounding it. Four full time gardeners tended the manicured grass lawns.

There were seven servants in the house: maids, cooks, butlers, cleaners, man-servants and a stable of little lime-green VW vans with a suitable number of drivers. It is part of the economy; give jobs to as many people as possible even when there is not enough work to go around.

The house was a single story stucco building with separate kitchen and garage. The furnishings looked like something you'd expect in a Park Avenue apartment, older yet stylish and nicely kept. One never got a tour of an entire house in this part of Indonesia, it was considered bad form for guests to go anywhere except the living room, dining room, porch or, if they were overnight guests in this house, the guest wing with its own western style bathroom.

When Bambang Subroto, the President, invited the consultants for dinner usually every few months or for holidays, the dinner was very nice. There were several courses of typical Indonesian food, several rice dishes prepared in various ways and, of course, cumi cumi. Executives from I-Tin were usually invited as well.

Chapter 7

The dinner was an opportunity to discuss the project in a less formal way. Mrs. Subroto never appeared during any of these dinners and the company executives did not bring their wives. Of course liquor was not served.

It was at a dinner like this, with a government minister as the guest of honor, where Curtis made a fool of himself, embarrassed his teammates as well as his host, by taking the seat reserved for the minister. It wasn't a mistake, Curtis knew what he was doing, his desire to act important got the better of his judgment. This was the situation Mr. Chu was referring to when he asked Archie to speak to Greg about Curtis.

Several months earlier, when Archie's wife had visited Indonesia for two weeks, Mrs. Subroto invited her to a luncheon along with the wives of the I-Tin executives and she was shown around the house. That's how Archie knew about the guest suite. The Subrotos had a son and a daughter who were currently studying in London, which naturally led to the two mothers nose-to-nose in conversation.

They discussed how Indonesians' teeth were deteriorating at an alarming rate—one of the wives was a dentist—because of the influx of American fast food and sugary snacks.

They entertained themselves playing dress-up, dressing Archie's wife in Mrs. Subroto's native costumes and taking pictures.

As a gift from the wives, she received a bolt of batik cloth, two scarves and a beautiful wall hanging.

Ahmed continued driving while Archie reflected on his wife's visit and, while she was there, the long weekend in Bali. They stayed at the Melia Sol, an exquisite hotel on the South China Sea. What a magnificent structure, with gardens full of flowers, several swimming pools and waterfalls everywhere.

They hired a driver who took them to see the sights of Bali, one of which was a play in an outdoor theatre that was next to a Hindu temple. While waiting for the play to begin, Archie and his wife took a stroll through the temple gardens. Above the entrance gate was a sign, "Menstruating Women Not Permitted."

Archie's wife was currently in that situation.

But who'll ever know? Was the position they took. Well, they shouldn't have. She became violently ill and was confined to her hotel room for a day.

"Someone knew," Archie said to her later on, but she was not amused.

Something you frequently see in Bali are the bigger than life figures of the Garuda bird—one was standing guard in front of the Melia Sol dressed in a black and white cloth sarong. You see them standing guard everywhere, skirts flapping in the breeze. On the ground in front of each statue is a plate with rice, flowers, either a piece of vegetable or fruit, and a few incense sticks...*plates for the gods*, the same ones that punished Archie's wife for going into the temple.

They managed to enjoy Bali in spite of it all, and once they returned to Sungailiat and the Parai Beach Hotel, the illness was forgotten. Naturally everyone wanted to hear about their trip.

"Denpasar is the 'city', Nusa Dua is the Fort Lauderdale and Kuta, where the airport is located, is Miami's South Beach," was how Archie described it.

"Australians especially like Bali; it is *their* Florida—and one other village bears mentioning, Ubud, up in the mountains, and famous as an artist colony. The general impression you get is that these towns and villages are a platform for hotels, restaurants and tourist shops," Archie continued.

"And you do see some strange people along the way."

Archie recounted how he and his wife saw a few of them: the first was a totally naked Indonesian man with long dreadlocks.

"Was he just out of the bush, from the Stone Age?" Archie reminisced about the night he was telling all of this to the guys at the Parai.

"Another was a short elderly woman, more wrinkled than I've ever seen, most of her teeth were missing, her cheeks were painted with bright red circles...but she looked very happy.

"Then there are the visitors. Australians can be a strange lot. They appear to be still living in the fifties, but they *do* like to have a good time and they *are* friendly, especially the young newly-weds who befriended my wife and me, and who seemed to have the same schedule for breakfast, dinner and sightseeing as we did, so we saw a lot of each other."

Archie whispered most of this out-loud, never noticing that Ahmed kept looking at him in the rearview mirror. Ahmed was concerned for his friend; it was so unlike him to appear emotional and seemingly powerless.

Archie snapped back to the present, the newlyweds reminded him of Troy and Fiona who were making their wedding plans.

"How unfortunate for them," he mumbled, "I hope this doesn't ruin their wedding. It's difficult to begin a life together with a horrible accident looming over your head. I wish them well, they'll need it." Archie leaned his head back against the rear seat, closed his eyes and stiffened his jaw.

"Fuck it, fuck this fucking place."

8

When Archie arrived back at the Parai he was surprised to see that Troy had driven over from the Wisma Jaya; they could have passed each other on the road earlier when Archie was on the way to the Wisma and not known it. He was sitting at a table in the pavilion talking with Richard; odd because the two Aussies didn't usually spend that much time together. From the looks on their faces Troy was doing all the talking and Richard was doing all the listening. As he passed them, they looked up, Archie acknowledged them with a nod and continued to his room.

It was another beautiful day. The light breeze coming off the South China Sea was constant, which kept the mosquitoes away and brought with it the narcotic smell of the tropics. The sound of the gentle waves breaking up over the rocks that stood out from the beach created a consoling sound.

Before he left for his trip home and before the accident, Archie loved this place, even daydreamed about buying some land, building a small villa to visit from time to time. It wasn't a pipe dream. Property was cheap as was the labor and materials to build a nice one story, three-bedroom house. Upkeep costs were minimal. With the temperature and humidity constant throughout the year, a brick house covered with stucco and with a tile roof was the way to go.

He figured that with his promotion into the league of big bucks and his probable appointment as manager of his firm's Asian offices—both of which he fully expected—would require frequent travel to Southeast Asia, he'd be able to visit his island home enough times a year to make it worthwhile. He pictured his wife and kids spending a few weeks during their summer break.

Today, however, Archie gave a quick notice to the tone of the sea and the tropical scent but his mind was racing elsewhere. The fragments of information he had gotten so far were too scattered and it troubled him. What was it? Archie couldn't help thinking there was more to the riddle...which he had to find out.

From his window he saw Troy get up from the table and walk toward the parking lot.

"Probably to go back to the Wisma Jaya," he mumbled.

He made a quick decision to walk out to the dining pavilion where Richard was still sitting, tracing circles on his ear lobe with his forefinger and thumb, staring out to the sea. Archie sat down and asked him if he could talk to him for a few minutes.

"You and Troy were nose-to-nose. You look troubled, anything you care to share with me?"

"Sure," Richard answered willingly, "Troy was telling me about their wedding plans. It seems his phone call to Perth got through to Fiona this morning and he told her about the accident, they argued. 'A lot,' is what he said. Said he was annoyed that she didn't understand, so he needed to talk with someone."

Richard raised his eyebrows, grimaced, and twisted his palms up.

"I was surprised he picked me of all blokes to talk to," he continued while sliding his chair in to get closer to Archie. "He's very upset, wouldn't spit the dummy, but there's something going on I'd say. I'm afraid there's more to this whole thing than sunshine. Being as how he said they argued a lot."

"Arguing with your fiancé isn't all that unusual," Archie had to say something, "what makes you think there is something going on, he must have said something to give you that impression?"

"Well, he told me how Fiona couldn't understand how Joe's accident has changed things...with the wedding plans that is, even after he told her he was worried. That's how he put it, 'worried.' Then he told me about getting married in Bali, even about the chapel she picked out from back in Perth. Told me he wanted to cancel the buck's night, didn't think it appropriate with the accident and all, but she said she couldn't, it was too late because she'd already set everything up at the hotel and invited all the male friends who planned to come to the wedding. Even ordered all the grog."

Archie inched his chair in slightly as well, wanting to find out if there was anything else Troy was worried about since Richard thought there was something more going on. Richard continued.

"Troy told Fiona he thought no one from here would attend the party anyway, 'they'd only go to the wedding, seeing as

Chapter 8

what happened,' is how Troy put it to me. I can see Fiona's point though, but I didn't say anything...not my business, I just listened. Besides, only Curtis, you and I were invited, and Curtis, he's going to attend no matter what," Richard continued, "I didn't say that to Troy, but I bet I'm right." He looked Archie in the eye perplexingly.

"Troy then told me he got furious when Fiona said it was too bad about the accident but she'd lose her deposit if she cancelled.

"He said he told her to fuck the deposit, he'd made up his mind. Then, for some reason, he started in about his parents and her mom going to be there and Fiona has a brother but he's in Denmark and won't be able to attend. Got the impression Troy doesn't like him, said he stands out like a dog's balls whenever they get together.

"He sure spent a long time and used up a mighty lot of words telling me about the brother that isn't coming to the wedding and he won't see but every five or ten years...didn't fit."

"What do you mean, it didn't fit?" Archie asked.

"Like I said, spent a long time describing the brother, how when he's around you can't miss him, not because he's saintly, just the opposite. He said the brother always wants things his way, orders Troy around, makes him feel like shit, 'just like Curtis does,' is how he put it.

"He never looked at me though," Richard added, "just down at the table. Strange, don't you think?"

Archie put his forefinger to his lip and said, "I figured that he didn't like Curtis all that much but I'm surprised he'd admit it to anyone. Strange is right. Strange comparing the brother to Curtis." There was silence, both of them apparently dwelling on the word strange.

"Yes," after a moment, Richard went on, "told me about a time when he and the brother were talking on the phone about the wedding arrangements and Troy told him he thought they were spending too much money, but the brother disagreed, said it was very important to his sister to have a big wedding, she didn't want to hear stingy talk and neither did he.

"Then Troy said, 'it was like he was threatening me, come over and break my legs if I brought it up again,' that's exactly how he put it."

"Fiona's probably right," Archie agreed with Richard, "the wedding is a month away, life must go on. The brother, that's something else again. Yes, Troy's worried...about something. Although Troy knew Joe I'll wager the two of them never spent more than ten minutes in conversation on anything other than what was necessary to do the film, right?"

Richard gave a grimace of agreement.

"And Joe wasn't invited anyway," Archie added, "I'm curious though, why did you say you thought there was something else going on, what was it? His expressions?"

"A little, didn't look at me, hardly ever, looked down at his coffee cup all the while he was talking, kept looking around as if to see if anyone else could hear what he was saying. He just looked nervous. He's not my good friend and I don't know him real well, but I've seen this in others, means they're holding something back.

"I tried to get it out of him but he insisted nothing was wrong. Except the argument with Fiona."

Richard paused a second then continued.

"I think Joe's accident really got to him. Actually," he went on, "I think Troy is giving Curtis's domineering, blood-sucker characteristics to the brother and venting to me because talking about the brother is safer than talking about Curtis. I've watched those two, here as well as back home, and at home Troy is like Curtis's lackey, his gofer, his little puppy."

Suddenly Archie's interest perked up. Putting together the strange behavior of Effendi and now what Richard told him about Troy wanting to cancel the stag party that beside himself only Curtis and Richard had been invited to attend.

"Something is wrong. Does Troy have a reason to be troubled?"

Richard only shrugged.

Archie decided right then to visit Marapani, the only other person on board the dredge when the accident happened—aside

Chapter 8

from the crew, that is, and certainly Marapani had already talked to his crew.

I'll have to find out when he is available, Archie thought.

"I'd better get going, I'll see you later," to Richard, "and thanks." Archie went back to his room.

Earlier, while Archie was at the Wisma Jaya getting the details of the accident from Curtis, Greg was at the Jakarta Hilton meeting with Mr. Bambang Subroto, the president of I-Tin. It was only through Chu's offhand remark earlier that morning that Archie became aware a meeting was going to take place.

Why didn't Greg say something to me, the thought of the meeting came back to him as he was walking to his room, before I left him in Jakarta? He must have known, it must have been planned, otherwise how would Chu have heard about it, like he said, from his office?

I should have asked Chu what time he got the message. Could someone at his office be involved in setting it up? How else? Certainly not a coincidence that Subroto happened to be at the Hilton; besides, how would Chu's office know in advance about a coincidence? There is something going on here and I am out of the loop for some reason and I don't like it.

* * *

Before the consultants came, all of I-Tin's management lived in Jakarta. I-Tin had a modern, six story building that held their comfortable offices along with sales, marketing, purchasing, accounting, and engineering. When the consulting project began, Mr. Thobrani, the government Minister who authorized the project, insisted the top executives move to Bangka so they could be closer to the action. In Jakarta they arrived at any hour, took three-hour lunches and usually found something more "important" to do during the late afternoon.

Jakarta is a bustling city, especially if you have money, with lots of nice restaurants, entertainment, shopping, plenty to do. But on Bangka, there was little else except work. Given the condition of I-Tin, Archie agreed it was a good idea to move the offices and figured the minister was a no-nonsense guy.

Archie had only met the minister twice, once at the president's house, the time Curtis sat at the place reserved for him and then at the fete given by Mr. Chu at his private club in Jakarta. Both times they hit it off, if you can call it that. The minister was important, knew he was important and carried himself with an air of importance. Even though he was an ordinary looking guy, he carried himself well, bowed when he met you, not out of subservience, but to enhance his own position—he didn't bow that far down!

His greeting made you feel he was genuinely happy to make your acquaintance. He sized you up. However, he didn't seem to be full of himself. He got to his position because he was smart and personable, not only because of his lucky birth.

He came from an old royal family from near Surabaya, a large city in central Java, and with his MBA from Stanford, had an easy time working his way up the government ladder. In Indonesia you are either rich or powerful or both. Minister Thobrani was both. He was married to an equally distinguished wife and, like the I-Tin president, had a boy and a girl currently in university, both working hard at Boston College—the minister accepted no nonsense.

Although the I-Tin offices relocated to Bangka, the top executives still maintained their houses in Jakarta and returned to them on the weekends. It wasn't that the accommodations on Bangka were dismal; to the contrary, the houses were nice. Very nice, with lots of servants, but without the social life there was in Jakarta.

The I-Tin president met Greg in the breakfast room of the Jakarta Hilton. Jefferson and the corporate counsel wouldn't arrive from New York until later in the afternoon.

"Greg," Mr. Subroto started the conversation, "I am sorry to hear of Joe Prendergast's death. Please accept my condolences to you and please relay them to his family. It must be a difficult time for all of you. One doesn't think of young people dying, so when it happens it is a great shock. Under the circumstances, and

Chapter 8

on such short notice, I appreciate that you could find time to meet with me.

"I am troubled about this terrible accident," he continued.

"As you are aware, your firm has a future here in Indonesia and a lot depends on the outcome of this project. I will not beat around the bush, I want it to turn out successfully, but many of us have a huge stake in I-Tin. It comes as no surprise to you that salaries here in Indonesia are not very high. We must look to other compensation."

Mr. Subroto was from a well off though not rich family as well, and enjoyed a good education in the US. His parents were exporters of textiles including the famous batik, the best of which is hand made. He started at I-Tin in the finance department, took his turn at sales where he was quite successful, and was promoted to vice president and then president within nine years of earning his masters degree. Mr. Subroto learned to enjoy his new prosperity and wanted plenty more of it. He got it by skimming a little off the top of the government's tin industry. He and a few of his buddies owned property throughout Bangka Island and hired locals to mine tin, send it to Malaysia to be smelted, then sold on the open market.

They used phony names to hide their ownership and felt they were not likely to be caught. With the consultants on board however, and the accident bringing everything to the fore, it could get dicey—thus the meeting with Greg.

Somehow Mr. Subroto recognized that Greg was a person he could do business with. It was like the old saying, "two peas in a pod" and in this case both peas liked nice things, were aggressive in obtaining them, and were willing to take risks. Not big risks, mind you, but ones where you could undertake an action and if caught, beg for mercy.

There was an incident back in Chicago, months earlier. When Archie heard of it he was surprised, but he passed it off as pettiness.

Big deal, Archie thought at the time, Greg probably didn't realize what he was doing, or he forgot the firm's policy...not like he did it on purpose.

It was during a business trip to Singapore, Greg stayed in one of the best rooms at one of the most expensive hotels, Raffles. He knew the policy. The firm didn't condone spending client's money on expensive hotel rooms—travel expenses were charged back to the client. But Greg explained it to Archie this way,

"Sometimes it is better to seek forgiveness than to ask permission. Besides, all hotels in Singapore are expensive, and I've always wanted to stay there." It is interesting to speculate how Subroto knew Greg thought this way, perhaps it was simply that he was desperate and had to take a chance.

"I have ambition just like everyone else including, perhaps, you," Mr. Subroto leaned closer. "Certainly a minister's job is not out of the question for me and could be the next step in my career—if the right people are taken care of it is very possible—if you know what I mean."

"Not exactly," Greg looked puzzled, shifted uncomfortably in his chair and reached for his coffee. He looked up at the waiter who was refilling Subroto's cup and waited until he was through before continuing:

"I believe one should aim high, ambition is a worthwhile trait. But I am not sure, however, where anything I do is going to be of help to you. Except, of course, making sure this project is successful and giving you the credit, which, of course, you deserve." Greg tilted his head forward a little.

"Without your leadership and direction we would not be able to deliver on our commitments."

"Exactly, but you can do something even more and I can do something for you in return. This accidental death could be a problem, an opportunity for those who never wanted the project in the first place to make a fuss, hoping that now they can cancel it. Right away.

"But you and I are partners, so to speak," Subroto continued, "yes this is an important project and could be the first of many. If completed successfully it would be well received in the government and when I become minister I will make sure there are plenty more, bigger than this one. Indonesia needs your services and is willing to pay handsomely for them. But, we have

Chapter 8

to work together." The waiter returned to the table and Greg looked up at him suspiciously.

Greg's little guardian angel, fluttering gently near his right shoulder, paused and whispered softly in his ear.

"Greg, be careful, I'm worried where this conversation is going. Remember the last time you made a, should we say, 'dishonest' decision, how badly you felt—and for so long? You want to feel good about yourself, don't you Greg?"

On his left shoulder there was a little voice also, lusty and deep.

"Greg, this is your big chance. This guy wants to offer you something big, take it, who'll ever know? When do opportunities like this come along? Not very often. There's nothing dishonest here. You're smart, you work hard, you deserve whatever he's got to give. Could be just the beginning. Go ahead take what he offers. Think about how happy you'll be. Like I said, you deserve it, and besides, no one will ever know."

Greg quickly looked away from the waiter, who seemed to be taking a long time to leave the table, and back at Subroto.

"Don't worry about him," Subroto noticed the way Greg looked up, and with of a toss of his head toward the boy, "he probably doesn't even speak English."

Greg made a decision.

"Thank you for your confidence in us...in me," getting back to the subject.

"Yes, I am aware that this project has visibility and I would naturally be happy being taken care of with more and bigger projects. If there is any way I can help you in your career...or if there is a problem I don't know about?"

"There's a problem but nothing big, of course, nothing you can't handle. As I said earlier, there are many powerful people who make a good living off of tin, the people who would help me when the time comes to seek a ministerial position. They would find it inconvenient if anything were to happen to their golden goose. You can help make sure they are not unnecessarily inconvenienced."

"I do not want anyone to be inconvenienced," Greg picked up quickly, "what is it you would like me do, how can I be of help?"

"The illegal miners, they are harmless, some are good friends of mine and the little income they get ultimately helps the Indonesian economy anyway. You would be more helpful to us by spending your valuable time analyzing more profitable areas."

"Certainly," Greg took the hint but looked up with apprehension as the waiter was back to collect their dishes.

"I agree. That is not an area where there is a big payback for the time we would have to invest. You can assure your friends that their goose will remain healthy."

9

Archie was tired. The long day that began with an early wake up call in Jakarta was coming to a close—his mind was swimming. The news of Joe's accident, then Chu's bomb that Greg was planning to meet with the I-Tin President without having told Archie about it. Curtis's insensitive, offensive, ignorant report that essentially said, "take comfort, he died instantly," and most recently the disturbing account of Troy and Fiona's argument which, Archie was sure, had something to do with the accident. Would there be more?

His head was beginning to hurt and he was hungry. It was too late to visit Marapani to ask his version of what happened, so the alternative was to go back to his room, try to immerse himself in a book for a while, then have a nice quiet dinner and fall asleep early. Tomorrow he would renew the challenge.

Now walking back in his room he was thinking; the most difficult thing to deal with, especially being in this god-forsaken country in the middle of nowhere, is that there is no one I can talk to. He had his hands in his pockets; head down. The phone system prohibited calling his wife and getting her impression, which he so highly valued, of the conversation he just had with Richard about Troy. He was interested in her take on why Troy would be so upset.

When he needed her advice about something that happened, she was good at reading between the lines to discern what was going on in the talker's head, their objective betrayed through the words they chose to use, adding substance to the real message they wanted to get across—or didn't.

Why didn't Greg tell me about the meeting? What could they have met about, I'm the project manager for Christ's sake, why didn't Subroto want to meet with me, or at least ask that I be there. And Greg, it is so out of character, Greg couldn't say, "I forgot to invite you," he never forgets. He's pathological about not forgetting. He pisses me off he's so pathological. It doesn't make sense. Archie's rock was Greg, especially now, I'm reading too much into this, I know I am, but just the same....

To make matters worse he'd soon have to face his company's president, Scott Jefferson and the lawyer Michael McMillan when they arrived from Jakarta.

I know Greg will call me with a heads-up when they are expected to land, they'll probably have a million questions and I'm supposed to have the answers.

I have this funny feeling he won't tell me about his meeting.

Archie decided to get away from the Parai for dinner—alone. He hadn't eaten anything since breakfast back at the Jakarta Hilton and that was only orange juice, coffee and an English muffin—he was famished. He called Ahmed and asked if he would drive him to his favorite restaurant, the one where they all went when they first arrived on Bangka Island, the Watergarden Restauran, in Pangkalpinang. It was a forty-minute drive to there, the same back again but Archie knew Ahmed didn't mind.

He always tipped him well and, more important, treated him with respect. Archie asked if he would please come after he and his family had their dinner. He could not invite Ahmed to have dinner with him, it would not be appropriate, and Ahmed would have been mortified to even have to consider it, so he'd wait in the van or, if there were other drivers at the restaurant, they'd tell stories and talk about their charges while smoking clove cigarettes. Ahmed, though a non-smoker, liked hanging out with them.

They left for the restaurant about seven expecting to eat dinner about eight and back to the Parai and in bed by nine-thirty or ten the latest. When they arrived, however, Archie was greeted by two acquaintances from the Parai whom he couldn't ignore.

"Damm," he said under his breath, "of all nights. I should have ordered room service, they would have delivered it and both Ahmed and I would be having a well deserved sleep."

"Archie!" Hans Glos got up from the table, walked to meet him and led him back to the others who remained seated. Deirdre Cowen was there along with two people Archie had never seen before.

Chapter 9

Hans had recently purchased an old shrimp farm on the coast a mile from the hotel. He was trying to make-a-go of it but was having a terrible time. The farm had been idle for many years, so much of the plumbing and several of the pools used to raise the shrimp were in need of major repair.

Hans worked the farm as it was, believing wholeheartedly that he'd eventually make a lot of money. He was an outgoing guy, trying hard to succeed but each week brought with it a catastrophe bigger than the last. Hans, the incarnation of optimism, laughed it off and said he'd just have to work harder.

Deirdre Cowen, who remained sitting, was a regal lady in her early eighties.

"I'm British," she would state with clear, twinkling eyes, "and I'll be traveling by myself throughout all of Indonesia." She had spent the previous two months in northern Sumatra and planned to continue east through Java and to finish in Irian Jaya, at the eastern tip of the cigar shaped country. She planned to take a whole year. It was hard to believe this tall, powder puff skinned, white haired lady who walked with a cane—maybe it was a walking stick, nobody asked—would be staying primarily in wismas like the one Archie refused to sleep in for even one night.

Even more implausible was her clothing. She'd already been at the Parai two weeks before Archie had gone back to Chicago and he didn't remember seeing her in the same dress-up clothing twice. You would think she'd require a trunk...but then again, probably not. She looked the type to have a well-packed valise or two and a knack for traveling light.

She was enjoyable, full of interesting facts, had impeccable manners and immersed herself in whatever the conversation was about. She liked to tell jokes mimicking an Irish accent and was good at it, especially the risqué ones.

She extended her hand as Archie approached and with a little glisten in her eye she offered her condolences. Archie took her hand in both of his and thanked her. All that was needed to be said was said in that moment when they looked at each other.

Hans, at the right moment, put his hand on Archie's shoulder and directed him to Russ and Helen Wortly. Russ stood up, offered his hand and also gave his condolences. Sure enough,

The Bangka Inquiry

the accident was the big news on the Island. Hans introduced Russ as a consultant and in an attempt at some levity to redirect the solemn moment said,

"Russ, here, has been hired to watch over you guys." Han's thick German accent added credibility to what could have been just a smart-alack remark, an attempt at levity.

"Don't worry though, Russ is an all right guy as long as you take good care of him and his lovely wife."

Russ, who Archie immediately recognized as someone without an ounce of humor, and with no change in the expression on his face, introduced his wife Helen. She looked up, extended her hand, looking like she was copying what Deirdre did, and said, "pleased to meet you. We were saddened to hear of the loss of one of your staff."

"Thank you...is that correct, you are consultants?" Archie offered in response.

"Yes," Russ answered. "We...I mean I have been retained by one of the government ministers to make sure they get the deliverables they contracted for. You see there have been too many consultants who come to this country thinking that since the language is simple the people are simple and that is not the case. I will merely keep the government assured about your firm, as long as you remain on schedule—" lame chuckle.

This was not the time nor the place to pursue this bazaar turn of events, but since Russ and more so Helen, were instantly unlikable, Archie decided he'd make sure they had a very difficult time getting any information about the project.

"Is Mr. Thobrani the Minister you are working for by any chance? Because I've met him." Archie couldn't resist one more question.

"No, and he would prefer to remain anonymous I'm afraid, and we have to follow his explicit instructions."

Explicit my ass, thought Archie. But, I'll leave it alone for now.

"This accident," it was Hans again, "my men are telling me things like this happen all the time to Indonesians because they don't pay enough attention to safety, but foreigners are more careful. I must tell you they are troubled."

Chapter 9

"Yes," added Russ with his wife looking up at him with gooey admiration. He was still standing. "I received a call from the minister just a few hours ago and he is troubled as well. Perturbed is more like it, wants me to find out everything that happened, indicated he may launch an investigation. We don't want the project to end prematurely, do we? Well, I mean my contract would also end, wouldn't it?"

Dame Deirdre apparently noticed the fatigued expression on Archie's face and came to the rescue with her lighthearted way.

"Perhaps you all should sit down. If Joe were here, both he and I'd be agreeing that there's a time for distress and a time for pleasantries isn't there? Archie, sit here, order yourself a drink and tell me how your wife and adorable children are doing. Did they miss you or did they not even know you were away?"

"Thank you, Deirdre, I will order a drink, it's been a long day. And you look scrumptious as usual, have you behaved yourself while I was gone?" Archie picked up on Deirdre's playful wit. For a little while, he had to put Joe, his dizzying problems and his newest one, Russ, to the back of his mind.

At eleven-twenty, when he slipped into his bed he quickly fell asleep with this on his mind—tomorrow I will speak with Marapani.

The morning came too quickly but the gentle breeze and fresh smell of the sea was a wonderful way to awake. It was almost seven-thirty and Archie would have to rush to catch the tender that left at noon to bring the change of crew to Marapani's dredge. Archie needed to be on it.

First, however, he decided to ask Ahmed to take him to the office in Pangkalpinang to see the original safety film again, after which he'd have to come back to Sungailiat in order to board the tender. It was the subtle comment by Hans that his men were surprised the foreigners weren't more careful that prompted his decision to look at the film again. When he talked to Marapani he wanted to be sure he knew exactly what the dangers were and if any protocols had been breached.

The Bangka Inquiry

It isn't that there is a need to blame someone, he thought, accidents are accidents and as long as something wasn't done on purpose there is no point. However, carelessness is no accident.

Something inside Archie's head had to be appeased; he had to see the film again.

It was less than fifteen minutes long. The originators knew they would have their audience's attention only so long. Everything was presented in threes, which served to help the viewers remember important points. Archie and Curtis had been provided with a typed translation.

Be careful, watch, listen, the narrator said in Indonesian as the words flashed on the screen and the actors demonstrated. So it went on for a while. Then came the part about the buckets, the dangers one could expect. Again, the word *listen* flashed up on the screen. A bell went off in Archie's head. Curtis ordered earplugs for himself and those working on the film shoot. They were the enormous type, like those worn by the guys who direct the airplane to the gate. It was classic Curtis, impress the natives; show superiority.

Is it possible, it made Archie think, that Joe didn't hear the danger? The film made it clear that you could hear when a bucket was stuck; there was a distinctive grinding noise, like you hear when a train goes slowly around a curve. Could that have happened? Please God, no. It's bad enough, I don't want anyone else to suffer...through blame...or thinking it was their fault.

The film also warned that a bucket jam could easily cause severe damage possibly requiring the dredge to go to a workshop and the crew would not be paid while it was being repaired. The message was that nobody was to do anything unless specifically directed by the captain.

"The captain has complete *Authority,* not following his *Instruction,* is cause for immediate *Dismissal.*" The three words flashed on the screen to reinforce the announcer's point.

The trip only took a half-hour, the dredges were not too far off shore and Marapani's farmed the seabed around Sungailiat where the Parai and one of I-Tin's major workshops was located. Marapani was on deck as the tender pulled alongside. Looks like he's expecting me, thought Archie.

Chapter 9

"Good afternoon, Marapani, I hope you are well. Another beautiful day, hot and sunny."

"Yes sir," Marapani stood with his hands clasped behind his back as he gave a slight bow.

"Could I have a few minutes of your time? You know why I am here, I'm sure?"

"Certainly sir, could you follow me and watch your step the humidity has made the deck more slippery than usual." Speaking Indonesian, Marapani directed two of the crew to walk closely behind Archie, to the ready, if it looked like he might slip.

They both wore flip-flops which gave them traction but no protection. Archie always wondered which was more essential but he never did come to a conclusion.

They walked to Marapani's sparse quarters. Everything was damp to the point of wet. Archie knew he was expected to sit behind the desk, which he did, and pointed to one of the two chairs in front of the rusty colored built-in metal desk indicating Marapani should sit down if he wished.

"May I?" as he took the chair to the left. Archie nodded his head and said "Of course," and he too sat down.

"Marapani, could you tell me what happened? I've talked to Curtis and I am sure it all went so fast that he may not have seen everything. I hope you might be able to add what you or any of your crew members saw so I can get a complete picture." Marapani had a frightened look on his face.

"Mr. Archie, sir, I am sorry to inform you that I was not there when it happened. They were shooting a scene on deck when all of a sudden there was a bucket jam. Mr. Curtis told me to stop everything so he could set up to take pictures while my men freed it. Said he wanted me go to the wheelhouse and turn the dredge toward the north so he could get exactly the right light. I passed the order to my crew but Mr. Curtis said, 'no, I want you to do it...go.'

"I am sorry, Mr. Archie, sir, I thought he would wait until I returned but Mr. Curtis told my men to go ahead and free the bucket. I scolded my men, they should have known to wait for me to return. I am sorry Mr. Archie, it is my fault, I should have been there."

The Bangka Inquiry

Archie noticed that Marapani looked at him directly and did not have that typical Indonesian smile while he talked. Usually, when there is something unpleasant or difficult to say they just use more words to soften the severity of the conversation. Not this time, Marapani looked scared.

"I should not have left. If I had been there I would have seen the danger. I am to blame. When I heard my men yelling and running in all directions I knew something was wrong and ran from the wheelhouse as quickly as I could. I saw what happened immediately, the cable snapped in the bucket shaft and Mr. Joe was too close, holding the bright lights.

"Was your wife on the dredge, I understand Amulya often accompanies Curtis and the crew when they need her to translate for them, did they need her that day?"

"No Mr. Archie, she was not notified to be there."

"Marapani, it is not your fault, it was an accident and you must tell your men that it was an accident. None of them must blame themselves either."

"That is not so, Mr. Archie, I am the one who caused the accident. I should have told my men to not work on the buckets until I returned, but they do what a white man tells them...if only Mr. Joe was not behind the safety screen."

"What do you mean 'behind the safety screen?'"

"He was holding the lights. Mr. Curtis told him he would have to go inside. 'But be careful, it is slippery,' he said to him. But the screen would have stopped the broken cable, if he was not inside."

"I understand what you are saying, Marapani, but you are not to blame and I want you to tell your men also." Archie got up and touched Marapani on the shoulder. "Thank you, the tender is waiting to take me back so I must go. I appreciate your telling me what happened. No one needs to know what we discussed, agreed?"

Marapani bowed slightly and Archie quickly left the room.

So, Archie thought as the tender took him back to shore, it was an accident because no one could have known the cable would snap, but Curtis is the cause. How ignorant of him, they weren't his men, what gave him the right to order a dredge crew,

Chapter 9

what was he thinking? Every time I think of that idiot my blood boils.

Later in the evening Marapani took the same dredge back to the mainland for his scheduled two days off. When he arrived home Amulya was already in bed but had not yet fallen asleep.

"Marapani, you look worked up, is something wrong? Not another accident?"

"No, Amulya, Mr. Archie came to see me. He wanted to know exactly what occurred during the accident. I told him the truth that Mr. Curtis ordered me to the wheelhouse to turn the dredge so he could get the best light. What could I do, I could not tell him I would not do it. I should have suspected Mr. Curtis might begin filming the bucket jam without me.

"I do not like him, he is trouble and now that the truth comes out to the foreigners that I was not there I will no longer be captain. No one will trust me any more, I do not want any other job on a dredge except captain, I will have to find work someplace else, just because of him."

"Is that what Mr. Archie said? Did he say you were responsible for the accident?" Amulya swept her long black hair away from her eyes. She was truly beautiful, born in Indonesia; her parents were born in India; a relatively prosperous shopkeeper and his wife who could afford to educate her in England.

She earned a diploma and teacher's certificate sufficient to permit her to teach English at any Indonesian university. She preferred, however to work at I-Tin where the wages for someone with her credentials commanded a higher salary. She worked in Jakarta initially but was transferred to Bangka where she met the handsome Marapani and it was love at first sight.

Correction, it was lust at first sight. They knew each other only a few weeks before they decided to get married. Four months later Amulya had a miscarriage and it was no secret that it had been a marriage to save face. By now they had been married two years and Marapani believed that something happened during the miscarriage that prevented her from having children. Amulya, however, maintained the gods were angry with her and this was their punishment—at least that is what she told Marapani.

Actually, she really didn't want any, especially with him. Although she liked him, she didn't love him and it was no secret to anyone except Marapani that she fooled around in Jakarta whenever she went there for I-Tin business, which was often. It also disguised her real desire, which was to go to Australia, find a rich lover and live happily ever after.

"I think you are overreacting, Marapani." Amulya changed arms to keep her propped up as he sat on the edge of the bed.

"I don't think so. Perhaps you can talk to one of them at the office, find out more. They like how you help them and they treat you with respect so perhaps you can tell them the truth that I could not refuse Mr. Curtis when he told me to go to the wheelhouse.

"You can tell them that I had no idea he would tell my men what to do in my absence. They will listen to you, you can speak to them in their language and they will believe you. It is our only hope." He reached over and touched her cheek.

"Yes, it would not hurt to talk to them. I work closely with Mr. Troy so I will speak with him tomorrow. Now I must get some sleep, I begin work very early and I am tired. There was a lot of work today because of this accident and there is more work ahead. I don't think it will end soon because I heard that one of the ministers will be looking into what happened. Mr. Troy will help us; he treats me with respect. I think he likes me."

While Marapani and Amulya were having their discussion, Archie returned to his room to find a message. Greg called. He, Jefferson and McMillan were due next morning on the ten o'clock flight from Jakarta. Now, lying in his bed, he began mulling over the day's events. He put together the facts as he saw them and concluded that Curtis was to blame.

That nosy consultant, what was his name? Russ. And his sycophant wife, whatever her name is, I think he's trouble. He's no fool and his comment that some minister was looking into the accident was not unintentional. I'd wager his minister is knee-deep in the typical Indonesian graft and has something to hide. Finding an excuse to terminate this project would make him a happy man. I wish I knew which minister it was—I'll ask Effendi, he knows everything.

Archie couldn't fall asleep. The question was how to handle the fallout from the accident.

I'm afraid Curtis will come out clean, get away with his stupidity; the firm has a way of washing their dirty linen in private.

He eventually fell asleep thinking it would be another fretful day.

10

Suradi was beside himself with the turn of events. The accidental death of a foreigner was big news—if it happened to a local it would likely go unnoticed, except of course by the victim's family and friends. He somehow found out that the president and his lawyer were coming all the way from New York and would be arriving on the ten o'clock flight from Jakarta. To Suradi this was more important than if the President of Indonesia came.

In that scenario he would be shoved to the back of the welcoming party. This however, was going to be his show. His usual attire was creased trousers and starched shirt and this morning was no exception.

I'll bet his clothes are brand spanking new for the occasion. Archie was looking at Suradi, not wanting to be caught; it was in quick glances.

It wouldn't surprise me if he figured he'd get noticed and immediately hired to go to America to become the Head of Security for CCG with a big office, name on the door, lots of people working for him and a huge salary. Archie stole another glance.

And the smile, I think he's practicing, wants it just right when he introduces himself.

"I am Suradi, Head of Security...yes, welcome to Bangka Island...yes." If Jefferson were to say something, anything, Suradi would answer, "yes."

He answers yes to everything, even if you said, "Suradi, you're a dumb shit," he'd answer "Yes," with that shit-eating grin he is now practicing. Archie was passing time thinking about Suradi while waiting for the plane to land.

I should be thinking about what *I* will say, he snapped back to the matter at hand. For them to travel a day and a half here, same back, they are not looking at this as an exotic getaway to the South China Sea. He could see the plane; it pulled up near the gate and was turning around in a circle.

Archie thought over the probable reason for this avionic maneuver.

It is easier to turn while still moving. If the pilot just pulled in and stopped he'd have to start her up, try to get it moving from a dead stop while at the same time turning on a dime. This way he just starts it, guns it, and taxis straight away, no problem. He was convinced he had figured out the puzzling maneuver and was pleased with himself for a brief moment.

First a woman and her cute little girl appeared at the airplane door and slowly descended the stairs. Then Jefferson, then McMillan, then Greg. They walked the short distance to the terminal door that Suradi was holding open. Sure enough he delivered his ten word welcoming speech, responding "Yes" to Jefferson's "Pleased to meet you."

He's a little guy, Archie noticed.

He hoped his look of surprise at Jefferson's short, skinny stature wasn't obvious.

Hope he doesn't get blown through the door.

Jefferson couldn't have been much over five and a half feet. He probably weighed a hundred-twenty five pounds soaking wet and had pasty skin, mousy, receding hair, and looked like a brain dressed up in kaki trousers.

He had on a white shirt open at the collar and a belt that cinched his waist to the diameter of a quarter. It made his silhouette look like an ant standing up.

What a weird looking guy, thought Archie, but I bet he takes no crap from anyone.

After suitable introductions devoid of pleasantries, Jefferson gave the plan in staccato phrases:

"I want to go to our offices...meet the staff...talk to Curtis...then Troy, and then Kevin"—Kevin, the junior staff from the Chicago office.

Turning to Archie with what Archie thought was a slight look of disgust, "then you."

He had obviously been briefed on who-was-who and what their connection with the accident was.

I can't figure Kevin though, Archie thought, he wasn't there and anything he said would be based on hearsay. Something more I have to worry about. Maybe Kevin knows something that I

Chapter 10

don't and there is no way I can get to him to find out before Jefferson does. And why the look?

During the ride in the van, Jefferson monopolized the conversation. Although he didn't say it exactly this way, there was no mistaking his meaning. The firm did not take kindly to adverse publicity, would do anything to avoid it, and didn't look favorably on anyone who perpetrated it. If and when it did occur, the firm—meaning him of course—would decide precisely how to respond. It was important for him to be the firm's spokesman, no one else.

"Our reputation is our prized asset and in situations like this one, how the information is handled is critical. There are several, if not many, people in the Indonesian Government who do not want us to complete this project. Until I am assured I know all the details, I don't want anything said to anybody. I do not want someone intimating things that may not be true."

Rather enigmatic, thought Archie, what the hell is he talking about?

Jefferson spoke softly; either because he wanted to come across as more important or, more likely, didn't want Ahmed overhearing his blither.

As Ahmed turned into the driveway Curtis, who had seen the van approaching, was standing at the front door looking like the official welcoming committee. An obvious move to indicate first, he was in charge; second, that Archie was the problem; and third, he and Jefferson would save the day.

I know he's going to come out of this smelling like a rose. People like him always do, speculated Archie as he watched Jefferson's face.

I know I'm reading too much into this by thinking I'll take the hit. It's probably nothing of the sort. This accident was...is...a problem, one Jefferson doesn't need, and I understand our necessity for caution. We have to handle this just so. Even Effendi alluded to that.

Archie felt the humidity more than usual even with the van's air conditioning.

While Jefferson was spinning through the offices saying hello and shaking hands, all the while with the appropriate amount of solace, McMillan nestled closer to Archie.

"Perhaps you and I ought to chat a bit before you meet with Jefferson. He can be difficult at times and I think he woke up on the wrong side of the bed this morning. He's been unusually cranky. He's like the little boy that when he was bad he was very, very bad and when he was good...Jefferson's still bad." McMillan chuckled at his little witticism, apparently wanting to soften Archie up for what was coming next.

"Sure," Archie answered, "would you like to take a walk outside, I'll show you the grounds?"

"Let's do it, I'll tell Jefferson where I'll be in case he wants me. By now he's probably sick of me too." Another chuckle. They walked outside, turned right, and when they approached the corner of the building, McMillan began the conversation.

"Based on the current circumstances, I wanted to brief you on where we stand. It seems that according to Greg at least, there are folks in high places that are concerned about this project. They don't want us looking into their turf where we might find something that could embarrass them. You're the manager, and as manager whatever happens on your watch is your responsibility. What you say, what you do, how you look tells the full story.

"Just so you know," he continued, "Greg and Jefferson agreed that we should stick to those areas of the project's scope that do not have the potential to embarrass anyone. If Greg can assure those folks—and the I-Tin president would be a good conduit for relaying that message—all of us, the firm, the project, Greg, you—will still do what we said we would do, get results and not step on anyone's toes."

"Did Greg meet with the president while he was in Jakarta waiting for you to arrive?"

"Yes, apparently that is where the caution was delivered. I don't know anything more than that and if I did I wouldn't tell you anyway," chuckle, chuckle. "In this case, the less you know the better."

"So why did Jefferson leave me to last to talk to?"

Chapter 10

"No reason...however, although he didn't specifically tell me to talk to you, he probably knew I would. If you are forewarned about what is going on, you and he will have a more productive conversation. Sometimes it is better if he doesn't hear things he shouldn't, if you know what I mean."

"Like what, I'm afraid I don't get it." Archie was being as straightforward as possible.

"The I-Tin president specifically mentioned the illegal tin miners. Suggested we not meddle with them. Seems they are small potatoes. Whatever little they earn goes to the Indonesian economy anyway, which is what we are interested in, right? And there are a lot of them. Taking away their livelihood would cause an uproar, so lets just agree that the illegal tin miners are off limits, okay?"

Suddenly Archie got it. Sure, many of the illegal tin miners were mining on property owned by Jakarta big shots—like the old feudal system. The peasant miner got to keep a little and the property owner got to keep a lot. Jefferson figured this out; he just didn't want to hear it from anyone.

Archie nodded, but thinking to himself, this is precisely what we were supposed to get rid of, the graft that trickles down the I-Tin pipeline.

He came to the conclusion everyone knew more about this project than he did—yet he was the manager.

He felt ill.

I'm not managing anything. This project is being managed from New York and Chicago...my big opportunity to show my big ass talent, how resourceful I am, is bullshit. I'm a baby sitter. They think so highly of me they're cautious about telling me what's going on, so much for wild dreams about being rewarded with the Asia market. I'm just the belt that spins the fan.

To make matters worse, McMillan abruptly looked bored. He delivered his message and now he wanted to get back to where the action was.

This guy's another phony, Archie thought. But what came out was, "sure, we better get back, see what's going on."

"By the way, don't worry about Kevin, seems Jefferson knows his mother's family or something."

Since it was lunchtime, Jefferson decided to get into a van with the staff. Give them a thrill riding with the main man. Curtis, McMillan and the remaining staff got into the second van, which left Archie and Greg to drive alone with Ahmed.

"I don't understand, why didn't you tell me you had a meeting planned with Subroto," Archie began the conversation, quietly, so Ahmed wouldn't hear. "When was it arranged?"

"I didn't have time. There was a message at the Hilton when I arrived for me to call him first thing in the morning, so I did. You'd already gone to your room and since I didn't know what it was about I didn't want to bother you. I knew you'd have your hands full."

Archie was not impressed.

"To make matters worse, Greg, this was an accident but it was definitely Curtis' fault. Here's what I was able to piece together. Marapani wasn't on deck. Yet Curtis gave the crew orders on how he wanted them to free up the bucket. He shouldn't have done that and he knew it. He had to know it, it was black and white in the original film; they made a big deal about it.

"He sent Marapani away; he knew Marapani wouldn't approve of what he was doing just for the sake of the film. The cable snapped and killed Joe. There was no way anyone could know *that* was going to happen, but Joe shouldn't have been inside the safety cage in the first place; Marapani wouldn't have allowed that either and Joe never saw the original film so he was oblivious. Curtis needs to take responsibility for causing this accident."

"From whom did you hear all that?" Greg asked.

"I looked at the original film, saw how they specifically said don't do anything without getting direction from the captain first. Also, no one was ever allowed behind the safety cage while the dredge was running—too noisy, too slippery, too dangerous. Yet Curtis told Joe to get in behind it...to set the lighting.

"Next was Troy, who was right there when it happened. He was very upset, had an argument with his fiancé, seemingly over the impact the accident would have on their wedding plans. I saw him talking to Richard and Richie told me what he said. It wasn't anything specific, but I saw them talking. Troy's actions

Chapter 10

were those of a guy who knows full well what happened and wished he didn't. I suspect Curtis made it clear to him what the storyline was and threatened him if he said anything to the contrary.

"Lastly, I went to see Marapani. He said Curtis ordered, not asked mind you, ordered him to go to the wheelhouse and turn the dredge so it faced better lighting. Marapani said he wished Curtis would have waited until he got back before trying to free the bucket. He was being subtle with me, he knows Curtis caused the accident but he'd never say anything...at least to you or me. It wouldn't surprise me though if he told Subroto. After all, it's his dredge, he's responsible for what happens on it."

"Well, Subroto didn't say anything about Marapani," Greg let on. "And he had every opportunity...and reason to...to let me know he knew the accident may not have been entirely an accident. The fact that he didn't means he doesn't know or if he does he'll keep it to himself unless we don't play ball with the miners. That's the way it is; it's politics as usual."

Greg seemed so nonchalant about the whole thing it surprised and depressed Archie.

Who, Archie wondered, would have guessed Greg, of all people, with his preaching about how the firm would never engage in anything under the table, yet it is precisely what he is doing. Archie was watching his world collapse.

"What does play ball mean?" Archie turned to Greg. "McMillan said we were not going to look into the illegal miners, is that what this is about?"

"Yes. It was an accident. All this stuff about Curtis, forget about it, it never happened. None of us wants to give any of these Indonesians an excuse to shut us down, so forget about what happened. It was an accident, pure and simple. Let's leave it at that."

"Greg, I can't do that, it's not right."

"Sure you can. And the tin miners, they're just small fry, leave them be. They are no longer within the scope of this project, get it?"

"McMillan said the same thing, why? What happened? Is someone in high places getting rich off those miners?"

95

"The less you know the better. You only have to know that our finishing this project depends on keeping our asses out of where they don't belong...and we don't belong in the miner's business. It's that simple."

"Greg, what am I supposed to tell the staff? Analysis of the miners is clear as day on the schedule; they'll see something is up. You can't hide what you are suggesting under a rug. Even the Indonesians will see something is up. Amulya for one...Marapani obviously told her all the gory details. She's his wife for god's sake. What do I tell her about the schedule, she's not stupid, you know."

"You'll think of something, it isn't optional, we can't afford to piss off government people, we just can't."

"I'll have to think about it, Greg. You're asking me to do something that may be illegal. Certainly I have a conscience to think about too. It's easy for you to tell me what to do but you don't have to take any blame if something goes wrong and it gets out that we are protecting graft by government big-wigs."

"If I have to I'll stay here and finish the project myself, send you home. I have my orders too. Some things are just beyond our control, can't be helped. There are lots of things we don't want to do but this is the lesser of two evils. Finishing this project and getting some results is better than having it end and getting no results. There is nothing to think over, you know I'm right." Greg folded his arms and turned to look out the van's side window. He had nothing more to say.

Archie felt like shit.

Man, how could I not have seen through all that bullshit Greg gave me about always being above board, choosing to let a client go rather than do something under the table. What does that say about me if I agree to a cover-up and look the other way while someone is stealing from the company? I'm no better than the crooks who are stealing from the company; using those poor slobs who do the mining. If something goes wrong they go to jail—forever in Indonesia—while the big shots go scot-free.

Greg remained silent, continuing to look out the window. Archie gave Ahmed's face a hasty look through the rear-view mirror.

Chapter 10

That bastard knows exactly what we are talking about, I can tell on his face. He looks disgusted...at me. This is only the beginning. I'll see the same look every morning on my own face. I've got to think this through and I don't have much time, do I?

They arrived at the restaurant, took their places and commenced their festive meal, celebrating that the company's chief executive and his lawyer came all the way from New York to be with the staff.

Isn't that great, Archie thought. Did they forget that Joe's body is still in the airplane, hasn't landed in Chicago yet? In fact his wife is probably waiting at the airport, crying her eyes out while these pricks are enjoying a lunch together.

Reminds me of a book a friend of mine wants to write, he wants to name it *Feed the Meter*. It's about how when someone quits or dies in a big company, another person is immediately there to fill the empty position.

Archie ordered a glass of lemonade and sat silently, cognizant that Jefferson, McMillan and Greg were watching his behavior. Curtis kept going non-stop, that asshole.

How can anyone be so insensitive?

Driving back to the Parai, Greg didn't say much, feigning a nap, which was okay with Archie. There was nothing more to talk about, at least not right now.

However, the evening would bring another crisis...shades of things to come perhaps.

Maybe the Hindu gods really do have it in for me, giving me another message about how thoroughly disgusted they are with how I am toying with my ethics.

This is what ran through Archie's mind the next morning, after his bizarre night.

It began as he was getting ready for bed. He read a little to get his mind off things and fell asleep surprisingly quickly. He hadn't been sleeping too long when he felt something on his legs and thighs. It was a tingling feeling but it didn't wake him up suddenly. He thought it was just an itch and he scratched it away and fell back to sleep. But then it happened again. This time he bolted upright.

"What the hell." This was more than an itch. He reached over, turned on the light and threw the cover sheet up and off. Behold, there were hundreds of thousands of tiny red ants crawling over him, his legs, his stomach, his chest; moving towards his neck. The sheet was covered with them. They were making their way from the foot of the bed to his pillow.

Fortunately they had to traverse the flesh mountains and were having a difficult journey. He screamed. Not loudly, mind you, but loud enough to get his point across.

"This is disgusting, this fucked up place, what the fuck am I doing here," as he ran to the mandi to shower the little buggers off.

Of course, the next problem was what to do, they didn't go away and they didn't follow the piper to the shower and down the drain; they stayed in the bed continuing toward the pillow unimpeded now that the flesh mountain disappeared. There was a can of bug spray in every cottage, now he knew why, so he sprayed the bed. It killed the ants except the room smelled of bug spray and the bed was damp. He certainly couldn't sleep in it.

Archie looked at the clock, two a.m., no one would be in the office to complain to. He was on his own. Just what he needed, to sleep on the chair with his feet propped up on his suitcase. It was not a good night.

The next morning he told Wiranto, the Parai Manager, who listened nonchalantly.

"Yes, it happens frequently, you did the right thing, they don't like the spray. I will have someone spray around the foundation but it only works for a short time. You see, they like you, they are happy you are visiting us. They wanted to tell you how happy they are to see you. Other than that, they are harmless, we all get used to them."

Wiranto was a good guy. Whatever the crisis he laughed it off, did what he had to do and moved on to the next item on his agenda. He took everything easy.

I should take a lesson from him, Archie thought.

Chapter 10

Unfortunately I don't see anyway out of *my* problem. I either play ball or pack my ethics and go home. Either way, the miners stay, the big shots get rich, CCG gets more projects, Greg's happy and everyone wins.

"That's how it works," he mumbled.

11

People gravitate toward routine. Many work hard to avoid it and even fewer have any real success. Routine seeks out groups as its primary victims, and why not? In order to work together there needs be a schedule and that becomes a foundation for sinking into a routine.

The CCG staff arrived at their offices routinely at seven in the morning. They tried to vary the time they left—between five and six—adhering to two unwritten rules that drive consultants:

First, always arrive before your client and always stay later.

Second, you must be on the premises at least ten hours each day. Clients perceive, wrongly of course, that they are getting their money's worth by the performance indicator most obvious to them—number of hours worked.

It amused Archie at how these two rules translated into actual behavior. More times than they would care to admit, the staff spent hours each day wasting time: talking about non-work issues; staying too long in meetings or having too many meetings; inviting people to meetings who were unnecessary.

Then they would work longer in the evening, breaking with routine, and staying past seven, sometimes eight o'clock at night, in order to look good, get the real work done, and make sure they stayed on schedule—another consulting rule: don't miss a schedule date, it makes clients nervous.

It is no use, there is no way to change *consultant behavior*, it's ingrained, mused Archie.

Joe died on Wednesday, this was the following Tuesday. Things began to settle down as the staff faced the reality of their schedule for getting all the things done that were promised. The people in consulting firms who sell the projects are notorious for trying to put more into the shopping cart than it will comfortably hold. It is easier to sell a project if the client thinks he is getting a good deal on the number of hours they will provide. Consulting firms respond accordingly, knowing the staff will work ten hours for every eight billed—and the firm makes more money in the process.

The Bangka Inquiry

Russ Wortly, the consultant hired by the government minister to watch the consultants—the minister he refused to identify—made analyzing the number of staff and their hours worked his primary activity. He tried to introduce a sign-in sheet that everyone conveniently forgot to use, much to the frustration of Russ.

He and Archie had talked it over. Archie agreed to its use but through subtle hints and the ingrained aversion of professionals to being monitored, the staff promised to sign in but forgot the second day and every day thereafter.

Russ finally filled it in himself and whether the staff did it on purpose or not, they suddenly altered their routine, some arriving as early as five o'clock with a different group staying late—nine or ten. Russ finally gave up. He settled into coming in at seven and leaving a little after five each day. He filled in the time sheet himself by asking everyone the next morning what time they arrived and when they left.

The Indonesian staff was not required to follow the same long hours as the consultants—thankfully. There were times when there needed to be conversation or activities that Archie would rather the Indonesians not be a party to. Internal business was one example, how to deal with client's people who were less than cooperative was another, discussions about the Indonesian staff themselves was yet another.

Amulya was treated differently than the other Indonesians. Because she was more Indian than Indonesian, you got a straight reaction from her. She was more educated, and more like the consultants than the Indonesian clerks, so she was often included in some of the otherwise private discussions. She offered an insight into the client's people, the Indonesian attitude about working, entitlements and unquestioned loyalty to their real boss—and clearly, CCG was not their real boss.

Amulya usually walked to the office from home. She and Marapani lived about a half-mile behind the CCG offices in a nice house provided by I-Tin, and nestled among other executive's houses. She complained a lot, specifically to Troy, that it was very lonely living in a big house with Marapani away three nights at a time. She didn't have many friends and none close by.

Chapter 11

Taking a bus or riding a motor scooter to Pangkalpinang to visit Indian friends was out of the question, she considered it low class to take a bus and she'd never ride a scooter. She and Marapani owned a car but she was afraid to drive in the crazy Indonesian traffic.

This Tuesday night she and Troy stayed late. There was a lot of catching up to do.

"It's getting late, Amulya, almost eight-fifteen, we're the only ones left, shouldn't we call it a day?" Troy said to her.

"Yes, I have not had anything to eat since lunch and for some reason I am starving. You work me too hard, I will have to complain to my boss," she teased.

"I'm starving too, working with you is just as hard work, and I don't remember if I even *had* any lunch, it was so long ago," he answered.

"I have an idea, since we are both hungry, let's walk to my house. I have leftovers that I could heat up.

"Thanks for the offer, but perhaps it would be better if we went into Pangkalpinang...I'll buy," Troy said. "I don't want to disturb Marapani, he's probably asleep by now."

"No, he is working tonight. His plans changed and he went back to the dredge this morning and will not return until Thursday. Besides, by the time we get to Pangkalpinang there will be nothing open—not a restaurant I would want to go to that is. I have plenty in the refrigerator and if it doesn't get eaten tonight I will have to throw it away. It is only a short walk back to the wisma from where I live and the exercise would be good for you." It was Amulya's way of putting a little levity into the proposal. Troy knew it was closer to a mile.

"You're on," Troy answered. "Actually, I am not only hungry, I'm famished, my stomach is growling for food and a home cooked meal, even if it is left-over. Sounds wonderful."

They packed their things and Troy put the papers he was working on back into one of the locked file cabinets the consultants used to store confidential papers. There had been no incidents of anyone looking at things they shouldn't, probably because it was CCG policy to clean your desk and lock up your work papers each night.

There was never a hint that the Indonesians who worked in the offices would snoop around, it was Suradi they had to worry about. Every day, without exception, he'd have a different excuse to come to the offices, talk to the drivers and Indonesian staff, and occasionally stand over one of the consultant's desks.

It was apparent he couldn't read upside down, maybe couldn't even read, probably would not have understood if he could, and usually asked a simple question that required a simple answer as his excuse for being there. He was never there long enough to see anything. But he was there, so Archie made a rule that without exception everything was to be locked up. He even purchased new padlocks just in case Suradi had an extra key for the ones provided initially.

The thought of Suradi spying on him and Amulya entered Troy's mind as he was accepting the invitation. He didn't need to give Suradi any ammunition to bring back to his army buddies about an American bedding an Indonesian, married no less, and wife of a dredge captain to boot. However, Suradi had not been seen since four that afternoon and it was unlike him to visit the offices after five—too obvious, someone would question why he was there.

"Have you seen Suradi lately?" Troy turned to Amulya who was fixing her hair using the mirror she carried in her purse.

"No, not since this afternoon, why?"

"Just wondering, I feel uncomfortable when he is around, like he's watching me...all of us." Troy was glad he caught himself and didn't say what he was almost going to say which was: I don't want Suradi to get the wrong impression, going to your house. Troy believed saying that would have been insulting to Amulya, letting on that even the idea of something untoward occurring would enter his head...letting on that he was contemplating precisely what was never far from his mind.

Amulya was silent during the twenty-minute walk to her house. Troy tried to make conversation, talking shop, but she only answered yes or no. When she got to the house she offered Troy a drink, a beer, and she poured herself a glass of wine while she began to prepare the leftovers.

Chapter 11

"Your house is very nice," Troy stood in the middle of the room, hesitant to sit down. Instead he took a self-guided tour of the many paintings and bric-a-brac on the walls and tables.

"The only house I have been to in Indonesia is Subroto's. Of course you'd expect it to be very nice, he's the president, but I think yours has a more comfortable feel. I especially like your collection of Indian art. Have all these things been in your family a long time or have you recently acquired them?"

"A little of both. Sit, sit, this isn't much, but I think you will like what I made. Everyone says I am a good Indian cook." Amulya set a dish on the table in front of Troy. Everything looked wonderful and smelled even better—lamb, spinach and a cauliflower bean mixture.

"I love Indian food, we have some very good restaurants in Perth. I go frequently, Fiona and I, I mean." Troy's mind raced to Fiona.

What would she think, if she knew I was in this beautiful, sexy woman's house, horney as usual, late at night, her husband gone—I don't think Amulya likes him all that much anyway. Would the notion cross her mind that I might fool around? What about Marapani, what would he think?

"You must tell me about Fiona sometime, she is a lucky girl to have found you. She is coming here soon, no? I will get to meet her then. For now, eat, I hope you like it, it is only leftovers."

When they had finished eating, Troy got up, collected the dishes and brought them to the sink.

"I'll help you clean up."

Amulya carried the remaining glasses and silverware to the sink and as she deposited them into the basin she brushed against Troy's arm.

"Oh, excuse me," and put her arm around Troy's waist seemingly a gesture of, oh, I didn't mean to touch you so I'll touch you to apologize.

Troy felt a tingling as Amulya's hip proceeded to touch his, she didn't remove her hand, but instead slowly moved it down the small of his back. That was all it took.

Afterwards they both fell asleep.

Troy awoke first; it was four o'clock. He dressed quickly, shook Amulya gently and when she woke up told her he had to get back to the wisma to get ready for work.

"Thank you for the dinner. I enjoyed the evening, you are a beautiful woman and I feel like I am in a dream...that you would want to be with me. We mustn't...now it is another day. I will remember last night but we must not see each other like this again."

Amulya was waking up slowly.

"Yes, it was a wonderful evening. I too shall remember it. Marapani does not love me like you did, so I will think about you often...when I am alone. You are right, of course, we should not meet like this again even though I would look forward to it."

Troy left, walked to the Wisma Jaya and slipped into his room without being noticed. He gently closed the door thinking, I hope that asshole Curtis didn't knock on my door last night. If he finds out...first he'd say, "you got lucky," then he'd add "what the hell does anyone see in you," then he'd never let go of it. He's such an asshole.

The next day a small, private service was held for Joe in a little Christian church in Sungailiat. Jefferson warmly said a few words, admitting that he never met Joe but from what everyone had told him he felt he knew him well enough to realize how much he would be missed.

"It is a tragedy," he continued, "and we should deeply mourn. Unselfish people like Joe think of others; he would want us to move on, remembering him of course. Perhaps the lessons we learned from him about goodness can be readily applied to ourselves."

The staff and guests did not go back to work for the remainder of the day; they went to the Parai Beach Hotel's dining room where Wiranto, the hotel manager, hosted a lunch. Archie was glad to see that everyone stayed until early evening, a tribute to Joe even if it was an unorthodox way of celebrating his life and mourning his death.

Chapter 11

Throughout the day small groups took walks on the beach, others sat on lounge chairs around the pool, still others climbed out on the rocks to feel the mist from the waves crashing in. It was quiet, pensive and appropriate.

Subroto and all the top executives of I-Tin were there to offer their condolences, primarily to Archie, but then spent most of the time with Greg and Jefferson. Of course Effendi was invited and he too stayed until early evening

Archie liked Effendi. He was Chinese and dressed accordingly. He had long black hair that he tied in a single braid on the back of his head. For this occasion he wore a traditional black robe with long sleeves. It was plain but the beauty was in the simplicity and the fine quality of the fabric. Effendi was about seventy-five.

His wife had died many years ago and his four children were well educated but none lived on the Island. Two were professionals in Jakarta, another was married to a prosperous merchant in Bandung in western Java and the youngest, a girl, taught physics in Stockholm.

He was an interesting man to talk with, often synthesizing complex human behavior into simple thoughts that sounded nice. Some were easily memorable, others a little obscure, such as, "a bee collects nectar and makes honey while a raven eats carrion."

I guess it means we need bees and ravens, was Archie's profound conclusion. Effendi had so many of these little pearls you just accepted on faith that they were wise. He was well liked, therefore the staff gravitated to whichever table he was sitting at. Effendi could talk, but he could listen as well. No matter what anyone said, any topic, he listened intently, paid attention and when he commented he did so graciously.

As the afternoon unfolded only Archie and Effendi remained at the table. Archie ordered two lemonades and felt a need to discuss, cautiously of course, what he found out about the accident. Effendi was an Indonesian first and a friend to an American second so it was wiser to find out what he knew before giving him any additional information. It was not difficult. Effendi was a magnet for information yet Archie never thought of him as a gossip.

When they were alone at the table, Effendi was the first to bring up the accident.

"It is as I predicted, some in the government are feeling the heat from this consulting project. Why did they not realize, when your work began, that only a fool believes he will never get caught when he does something wrong? The fool that hurts others in the process is much more likely to get caught and more quickly."

"Caught at what, Effendi?" Archie was conscious of his tone of voice and inflection. Effendi was no fool and would be hurt if Archie was not forthcoming with him, so he had to make it sound like he knew, that each of them knew, what the other was saying, but not wanting to overtly acknowledge it, at least not right away.

"We are not looking to blame anyone for anything we find, our objective is to make proposals to change things that are not working properly, improve the value of the company to the government."

"Yes, that is true," Effendi answered, "but you certainly realize that too many government people believe they are superior because they have found a way to get rich by using the ignorance of little people who are treated like slaves to these rich people."

"I think that happens everywhere, Effendi, not only in Indonesia."

"Yes, Archie, but now these rich thieves are getting worried. You and your project are getting too close to finding out what they do not want you to find out. They are not as clever as they thought. They thought you would not find out where all the tin comes from, but you will. Now they want to end the project but they need an excuse."

"I know what you are saying, Effendi, but how is Joe's accident an excuse?"

"These foolish people are clever. They will convince themselves that consultants who are careless and have serious accidents might not be capable of helping them like they believed, now they must stop the project before something else happens. That is how they think, and since they only have to convince themselves it is like one monkey grooming another monkey."

Chapter 11

"What are they afraid we will find, Effendi? I do not want this project to end if I can help it, and I do not want to cause problems I cannot do anything about."

"Archie, the son of a very good friend of mine is a waiter at the Jakarta Hilton. He is a smart and clever boy, he speaks perfect English but he is also a good boy, he tells his father about wicked people who come to Indonesia to take advantage of the poor and ignorant ones by making deals with the rich ones.

"He told his father that Subroto was at the hotel having breakfast with a consultant. They made a deal if the consultant did not investigate the illegal tin miners, in return Subroto would convince his friends to leave the project alone. He would convince his friends that they are safe, they can continue stealing."

"Why would one of our consultants agree to such a thing, Effendi? What did Subroto promise in return?"

"My friend's boy believes the consultant was offered a lot of money if he convinces the other consultants to leave the miners alone; they will let him share in the dirty money, that is what my friend's son believes."

"Greg was at the Hilton, is he the one your friend's son is referring to?"

"It is troubling to bring you bad news, Archie. I respect you. You are a good man. In my life I have seen men who are not so good and I continue to see them. Curtis is not a good man, but Greg, he surprises me. I do not know him very well but I pride myself on being able to look into a man's soul to find out what is in there. Greg fooled me and I am sorry but I believe he fooled you too."

"Yes, Effendi, he did fool me too."

12

The afternoon of the accident Marapani took charge. He had his men wrap Joe's body in a white cloth, tie a rope around his chest, another around his knees, still another around his ankles, and had them carry him to the tender that took them to the docks in Sungailiat. Curtis and Troy, the only foreigners on board, took a place in the cabin and neither said anything during the thirty-minute trip. They were stunned. As soon as the boat docked a doctor was summoned but it was too late, Joe was dead, had been since before being carried onto the tender.

Marapani, after consulting with the doctor, and with his concurrence, decided to call Subroto, the I-Tin President, directly. Had it been a local, Marapani would have phoned his boss, the Director of Dredging Operations who would have set in motion procedures for notifying the next of kin and having the body delivered to wherever. This however was different. Joe was a foreigner, an American and Marapani immediately sensed that there could be trouble—whatever he did next could just as easily be right as be wrong.

He was responsible for his crew and any visitors and he failed. Subroto was not the type to have the rank and file telephone him directly but in this case Marapani figured the fewer who knew about it—and would speculate about it—the better, until he had instructions from the highest level.

Subroto, after grilling Marapani for the details, told him not do anything, not to say anything; leave the body where it was until further notice. When they were finished speaking Subroto had a clear understanding of how the accident happened, who was responsible and how it could have been prevented. Marapani was told to pass the message of absolute silence to the crew who witnessed the accident and direct anyone who asked—including any of the consultants—to talk to him, Subroto.

He was told to return to the dredge, leave the dead body with the doctor, remain at sea, and keep anyone on board from leaving until further notice.

Subroto then telephoned Mr. Chu, the point person for the project—the coordinator between the consultants and the

The Bangka Inquiry

government, and told him Joe Prendergast, an American, with the consulting project, was accidentally killed in a freak accident aboard one of the dredges. A cable snapped without warning and struck Mr. Prendergast. Death was immediate; there was nothing anyone could do.

He reached Mr. Chu in a matter of seconds. Chu told Subroto he would take a private plane directly to Sungailiat. He confirmed Subroto's intention to leave the body where it was until he arrived.

Chu then telephoned the government Minister, Mr. Thobrani, who was the person instrumental in arranging the contract with the consultants. Thobrani's instructions were for Chu to personally telephone the people in Chicago, get to the right person and be sure to tell them that everything possible had been done to save him, but he died instantly. He further instructed Chu to make the call himself at eight o'clock that evening which would be eight a.m. in Chicago, just as their office opened. He was to delay his trip to Bangka until the call was made and the proper authorities were contacted.

Mr. Chu returned a call to Subroto, advising him of the change in plans. He would arrive the next morning instead of that afternoon and gave explicit instructions to have the body immediately sent to Jakarta. A special plane was dispatched and Joe was brought to a mortuary in Jakarta, suitably prepared, to await further instructions from the minister, the U.S. Embassy or the Chicago office.

Shipping a dead person from Indonesia to Chicago is not without complications. For many of the things that are done in Indonesia, if you didn't know better, you'd think that whatever they were about to do had never been done before and this was the first time they were going to do it. Shipping Joe's body home was no exception. The red tape began, everyone wanting into the act.

Somehow Suradi found out within the hour about Joe. How? Probably not even Suradi knows the inner workings of army intelligence. Someone else had told the person who told Suradi, and that person was told by yet another person who was told by yet another person...and on it went. Nevertheless he

Chapter 12

sprang into action. He got Joe's passport, called his superior and relayed the information.

The superior ran it up the chain of command and the guy on top, another minister, coordinated with Minister Thobrani, his peer, and telephoned the U.S. embassy who assigned a staff officer in Chicago to visit Joe's home and inform his wife that there had been an accident, that Joe was dead, that he died instantly and where did she want his body shipped. The government of Indonesia would take care of the cost. He was sorry.

Catherine answered the door and was surprised to see a man in a suit. One always suspects trouble when a stranger, not the postman, not the milkman, not the UPS man, is at your doorstep. Her heart thumped in her chest and she felt choked. It was just after eight, the kids had eaten their breakfast and were almost ready to step outside and get on the school bus. As usual they were waiting for the last possible second.

"They are always pushing the envelope." Catherine blithered nervously to the suit. "What a silly expression, pushing the envelope, where did that come from. I'll have to find out where that expression came from."

She was at the *beginning* and she was afraid. Not of the suit. Something inside her told her to be scared and she obeyed.

Joe. It had to be, the kids are here, they could care less who is at the door, but they are here. It has to be Joe. Oh my God. Her face showed what was going on inside, the suit had seen it before.

"Are you Mrs. Prendergast?" he asked.

"Yes, I'm Mrs. Prendergast."

"Madame, I am with the U.S. State Department, can I come in?" He showed her his identification.

"Of course, please, come in," she took a step backward, opened the door a little wider, looked down for a second to watch his shoes move in, and quickly lifted her head and looked toward the kitchen.

The Bangka Inquiry

"David, Monica, it is time for the bus, please go outside and wait for the bus." Turning to the suit she gave a tenuous smile as if to say, wait, I don't want my kids to hear. Let them leave...go off to school...they are just kids...plenty of time for bad news... not now... dear God.

"Mrs. Prendergast, is Joe Prendergast your husband?"

"Yes."

"Madame, I am here to inform you that he's had a serious accident."

"Where is he, is he all right?"

"I'm afraid not, it happened in Indonesia... last evening...it was a serious accident, he didn't survive."

"An accident? Are you sure? What happened? Where is he? Please...no."

She was at the *middle* now.

"Perhaps you should sit down." The suit gently guided her to the sofa. "Is there someone you can call, a neighbor, someone close by to be with you?"

"My sister...yes, my sister...my sister lives close by, I'll call her. What happened? Mother of God, what happened?"

"I do not know any of the details, but as soon as I find out I will let you know. I don't have any further information right now. The only thing we know is that it happened on a dredge, everything was done to save him. He died instantly...can I call your sister for you?"

"No, I'll be all right. Please leave, I want to be alone."

"I can't, Madame, I am required to see that someone is here with you. It is for the best."

"Wait here then, I'll call her...I'll call my sister...I'll call her right now...just wait here." Catherine moved slowly into the kitchen and phoned her sister.

"Susan, could you please come over...right away...something's happened...to Joe. Susan, he'd dead...he's dead. For Christ sake, Susan, he's dead."

She was almost at the *end*. But the end will never really come for Catherine, will it? "Susan," she broke down, "I lost my soul," and she hung up. Her world changed in an instant.

114

Chapter 12

* * *

It was a typical clear day when Fiona arrived from Australia. She was a nice looking girl, plain, simple, didn't need makeup or nice clothing for you to notice her. She was not a raving beauty, just nice. The kind of girl every parent would wish for as a daughter-in-law. She wanted a husband to look after, have a family and viewed sex as a way to have kids, that's all.

Her mother died several years earlier, her dad worked for the city of Perth in the street department. He was a supervisor, sent crews to repair roadways. She had only an older brother, Justin, who lived in Denmark. Fiona was plain and simple from a plain and simple family, genuinely good people. She could have found someone a lot better than Troy.

They met at a wedding, Troy's friend married Fiona's friend and they had fun being attendants together. Neither of them thought much about going out with each other in the future. Troy, thinking it was expected, asked if he could see her again and she agreed. It was more a way to seal a pleasant evening than make arrangements for a rendezvous. She wasn't Troy's type.

A few weeks later she popped into his mind.

I wonder how long it will take for me to get into her knickers? It won't be on the first date I know, but it could be worth waiting for...never mind, forget it. There are plenty of them that are willing. Thus he dismissed her.

Not long after, however, she entered his mind again. He and his friend Hayward were out for a couple of beers and too quickly getting over-served. Troy brought up the strange feeling he had about Fiona. After too many "ambers" the two of them tended to revert to one of the baser levels of the Australian language.

"Damm, Hayward, I can't stop thinking about her." Hayward by now was full of wisdom too.

"Ask her out and if you don't get into her clacker, flick her off."

"She's not like that. Usually they can't wait for me to park my doodle, but not her. She's different, I know it, but that's what worries me. Why do I want to go out with her?"

The Bangka Inquiry

"Ask her out, go for a walk or something, that's all. Then you can go have a naughty with one of those other ones that thinks you're bonzer."

"Hayward, drop it." Then in a mumble, "I shouldn't have brought it up."

Fiona thought Troy was nice, stable, went to college, had a good job, made a decent living.

That says something about his character, right? She agreed. He said he'd pick her up for dinner and go to one of Perth's nicest restaurants. She was excited. She never thought about a boy like this before. Boy, what am I talking about, he's a man. And I'm a woman. I should be thinking of finding the right bloke. I think he could be, we'll see, I just have to take it as it comes.

More and more they went out together. Dinner, concerts, museums—"She even likes sports," he reported back to Hayward. "Works out great, we have a good time then it's off for a naughty with Irene and Lynette."

Fiona's father didn't like Troy and neither did her brother. Oh, the brother liked going out with him the few times he visited Perth, liked his randiness, but wasn't keen on him marrying his sister. But since he lived in Denmark, it didn't seem to matter much how he felt about Troy. In any case, neither the father nor the brother said anything. She seemed happy, looked forward to the wedding and busied herself making plans. Her father would meet the wedding couple in Bali in a few weeks. He would be Fiona's only relative invited to attend.

Troy couldn't meet her at the Pangkalpinang airport. He asked Suradi to meet her and arranged to have her go directly to the Wisma Jaya. They would share the same room for a few days, something Suradi didn't approve of but didn't say anything. He did report it though.

The day of Fiona's arrival Curtis scheduled a big film shoot and could not spare Troy. Archie, hearing all these details, suspected that Curtis was being his typical asshole self. There was something in him that needed adulation, even if it came under duress. Troy, on the other hand, wasn't moved either way. He had a good thing going. He and Amulya were going at it hard and frequently. She was the kind of woman he liked, no holds barred, loved sex, the raunchier the better.

Both were sure no one knew, and they were right, no one did know. No one knew they had sex at Amulya's house, the office, behind the office, in the van parked at the Wisma Jaya, the more varied the place and the more bizarre, the better. They were made for each other.

Things changed after Fiona arrived. She required all of Troy's non-working hours. She noticed, however, that he had changed from the last time she saw him in Perth and that was two months ago. He never was very talkative, was more of a listener and she had no trouble admitting that she was the talker.

"Perhaps the accident is on his mind constantly," she mumbled, trying to convince herself, "that's why he seems so distant, so pre-occupied." Rather than asking him she slipped into the female tendency to pay more attention to him, demand more of his attention in return, thinking that she could change him back to the way he was—or at least the way she thought he was—if she just tried harder.

Women always think they can change a man, it just takes patience and Fiona was not short on patience. This time, however, it alienated Troy. What she didn't know was that he craved Amulya. They found time to be together but not as frequently and their passion was more hurried.

One night, while they were having dinner at the Watergarden Restauran, Fiona took hold of her problem and decided to find out from Troy what was wrong.

"You seem so distant lately...actually, since I arrived here. It is like your mind is elsewhere, is something wrong? Something I've done?"

"No, of course not, we are busy that's all, there is a lot to get done and that accident put us behind."

"I think Curtis has a lot to do with it. I notice when he is around you are different, like he annoys you. If that is the case, why do you put up with him? There is nothing keeping you here. A few weeks more and we'll be married, you can quit, we'll go

The Bangka Inquiry

back to Perth and you can find something else. I've got some money to keep us going until you find something, you can take as long as you like and find something exactly perfect; I don't mean just anything. It isn't like you are unemployable, you'd find something great in no time."

"Curtis is okay, once you get used to him. It's just the job. I don't want to leave the Island; I like it here. In fact, I wanted to talk to you about this but I-Tin is going to offer me a job...to relocate here. They are going to provide a nice house; we will have a driver, a gardener, a maid, a cook. And when you have babies we'll have a nanny."

Where did all this come from, Troy thought to himself, I need to stall for time. Yeah I like Fiona, it's time to get married, but Amulya, she's hot...really hot.

"When did all this come about? How come you are telling me now, have you known this for a long time?"

"It doesn't matter, the important thing is that I found out that I am going to be asked. There is something special they have in mind for me, they are not saying what it is until they work out some details, but since I know so much about their operations I will be a senior manager in no time...no matter what department they put me in."

"I don't know. This comes as a big surprise. Does Curtis know? Would it be after the project ends so he couldn't create a fuss? I know him from back in Perth. He is not a nice person, in fact he scares me."

"It's not Curtis...well, maybe not only Curtis. I like it here that's all. You will like it here...once you get used to it. The people are great; we will work a couple of years and be set for life. The person I work with at the office told me all about what they are planning."

"Who is it, have I met him?"

"No, just one of the Indonesians who is assigned to us, went out on a limb telling me so keep it to yourself."

"Well, we can talk about it. I can't say it thrills me but a wife goes where her husband goes. I still think, for right now, Curtis is getting to you. You have to tell him one time that you

Chapter 12

cannot stay late, stand up to him and let him know he can't order you to do something you don't have to."

"I told you, Fiona," Troy snapped suddenly, "leave Curtis out of this."

Then, just as suddenly he stood up and said, "let's go, I'm tired and want to get to bed early."

13

It was still early, only seven-forty-five by the time Troy and Fiona returned to the Wisma Jaya after departing the Watergarden Restauran...without finishing their dinner...which turned unpleasant... suddenly.

Troy didn't say a word all the way home and Fiona thought it best that she be quiet as well. Of course she blamed herself for Troy's sudden foul mood.

I couldn't help it, it came as such a complete surprise; she blamed herself. That all of a sudden he's thinking we'll live here in Bangka. I ...I wonder how long he's been thinking about that. Sounds like it was a while ago, perhaps even before I got here. Why didn't he tell me sooner?

Their room was small, no place to escape when the inevitable disagreements arise. To think two people are going to live in a tiny space and not feel the walls closing in is unrealistic. This, however, was the first time it occurred so Fiona didn't know what to do.

She had thought about it one of the first days after she arrived but quickly dispelled any attempt at planning an escape because she thought, naively at best, that they were different, they were in love, they wouldn't argue. They were going to be husband and wife in a couple of weeks. She even began to think about sex.

I'm trying to think, have we ever argued before? Tonight wasn't really an argument. He has a lot going on, not only this offer... it's a big decision. I don't believe that Curtis isn't the cause of Troy's moodiness. He's probably nervous what Curtis will say, or do, when he finds out.

"I'm going back to the office. I have work to do so don't wait up, I'll be late." Without waiting, wanting nor caring about a possible response, Troy put on his shoes, grabbed a light sweater, opened the door, let it slam shut, and left.

He knew Marapani's schedule so there was no problem going directly to Amulya's house. Besides, they had arranged their story in case Marapani was home or someone—Suradi likely—saw him standing on her doorstep. Since she worked closely with the consultants it was expected that they would need her whenever one of them decided to work late.

"Those Americans," she told Marapani, "very strange. They come to work early, they leave at all hours; they come in on Saturdays...I work for them, I have to be ready to go whenever they need me." Marapani understood. He too had the impression they were an impulsive lot.

The neighbors were no problem. First of all, they are by nature not a nosey bunch. Most of them live in close quarters and learn at an early age to totally disregard something going on two feet from them if it is none of their business.

They just don't pretend, mused Troy while standing on Amulya's doorstep, they are oblivious if it doesn't concern them.

"Suradi, now he's a whole n'other jumbuck in your tucker bag." Troy was suddenly in a good mood and when he was in a good mood he enjoyed listening to himself talk Australian.

"Suradi's job is to stop, look and listen...and report. He's good at it," His knock on the door was answered promptly by Amulya. She beckoned him in, indicating she was alone.

"I can't stay long," as he stepped in, "but I had to see you. You alone?"

"Of course. Sit down, I'll get us something to drink. A beer?"

"Yes, that will be fine."

"I thought you and Fiona were going to Pangkalpinang for dinner, at the Watergarden Restauran, wasn't it?" She had a smirk in her voice. She knew why he was here and choosing her over his fiancé made it even more delicious.

"We did go but we left early. You're the one I want to be with, Amulya. It is becoming a problem, I think of you during the day when I am supposed to be working. I think of you at night when Fiona wants to talk nonsense, what are we going to do?"

"I have a similar problem. In fact mine is worse. Marapani is never home so I have a lot more time to think...about you...about us. Troy, let's go to Australia...now. I will divorce Marapani...he won't mind."

He won't mind? Isn't it interesting how people sometimes think? How ridiculously selfish can one get? How would she

Chapter 13

know? He was convenient for her so she assumed she was convenient for him. The thought that there may be any love on Marapani's part didn't enter her mind...and if it had she would have dismissed it as childish.

"Amulya, strange that you bring that up. I was thinking about the same thing. Except, instead of Australia...right away I mean...what if we stayed here, got married. I could get a very high position at I-Tin; we'd have it made. On weekends we could travel—Bali, Irian Jaya, visit the Komodo dragon; and when we tire of Indonesia and all the secluded lovers' islands we could stay at the Mandarin Oriental in Kuala Lumpur or the Pangkor Laut Resort, the place with cottages on stilts, in Malaysia. Haven't you always wanted to see all those places?"

"Troy, I've lived here and in Jakarta longer than you so I know what it is like. It is boring. The people are boring, there is no entertainment; going to the market in Pangkalpinang is like going to a flea market. There is nothing but junk, dirty stalls, overcrowded and the shopkeepers are rude, most anyway. They think they are better than everyone else, especially me; they don't like Indians.

"They are jealous because I am beautiful and they are not. That is why I don't want to stay here. I want to go to Australia, where there is plenty to do, nice shops, good restaurants. I like getting dressed up and going out. Here? You get dressed up to go to a fish market for dinner. You get home and your clothing stinks of dead fish. Yes, Troy, Australia is the place I am going to. If you want to stay here, I will go by myself. I almost have enough money saved; I've been planning it ever since I got married, so it will be very soon."

"Have you told Marapani about your plans? What about me, you always say you can't live without me...you can't get enough of me...no one satisfies you like I do. What about me?"

"Yes, what you say is true. And you will be happy you decided to come to Australia with me, you will see. Unless, of course you are having second thoughts...about Fiona. Perhaps she will make you happy, then you won't need me." Amulya was subtly fidgeting with her clothing as she was talking to Troy. Troy didn't notice he was getting aroused until it was obvious.

"Amulya. You know I can't live without you...I understand how you feel, tomorrow, at work, we can slip away and talk more about it, but right now I need you."

Amulya was right, Pangkalpinang shopping *was* an experience. Archie was sitting on the veranda outside his room unaware of what she and Troy were up to. Instead, he was thinking about all manner of things. He knew himself well enough to not get upset when he realized his mind drifted away from unpleasantries that he should have been focusing on.

Fortunately I learned...and I believe I was very young when I learned it...that you should worry about things that you can't do anything about for exactly two seconds. Then move on. Isn't that a good philosophy? Archie was beginning to challenge himself; another thing he did when there were worrisome thoughts trying to get in.

What ever possessed me to think about shopping in Pangkalpinang? But I do remember the first time. I was here only a few days and got a crash course on how the Indonesians will not say no! I asked Budi if the bank was open and he said 'yes'. I didn't know Budi that well, but I figured since he was our translator he'd know what foreigners mean when they say things or ask a question.

So I asked Ahmed to take me to the bank. He did a double take but what did I know at the time, thought it was just a little quirk.

We got to the bank and it was closed. When we got back I said to Budi, admittedly I was a little pissed off, "I thought you told me the bank was open, it wasn't, it was closed." Budi gave me a quizzically look, why was I being rude, confronting him like that, "yes" was all he answered.

Fortunately I quickly recognized I was angry and how uncomfortable I was making him feel. What did I learn from that? Don't ask a question where the person might answer no, rephrase it —"Budi, can you tell me what days the bank is open?"

The night was pleasant, Archie took advantage of his mind's total control of him, protecting him from unpleasant

Chapter 13

thoughts. So it made him continue thinking about shopping in Pangkalpinang. Essentially, the main shops were concentrated in a four-block area, a series of booths, some better constructed than others, most had four sided counters piled high with goods, mostly essentials and generally of poor quality.

Archie wanted to know, but never got around to asking, where such cheap stuff was made. It made no difference; he wasn't about to purchase anything anyway. The clothing shops had their ceilings obliterated with stuff hanging on hangers all over. When you wanted to buy something the clerk acted like you were being rude, making him or her, mostly her, get up from the tall chair where they parked themselves near their cash box.

"They are Chinese, they do not like to wait on Indonesians," was Ahmed's take on the subject many weeks later when both he and Archie felt more comfortable with each other.

The kids, Archie continued musing, teenagers standing around their motorbikes, smoking their clove cigarettes, not talking to each other, just whistling and running after anything in a skirt.

"A horney lot," Archie muttered to no one in particular.

The phone in his room rang; it was eight-thirty. It was another beautiful night. Archie had been looking up at the sky thinking—just like on the plane when he thought about Krakatoa—who would ever have guessed it, here I am sitting on a veranda, looking up at the Southern Cross.

One of the Australians, Archie didn't remember which one, pointed out…"no, actually was bragging," Archie recalled, "that you can only see the Southern Cross if you are south of the equator," which he was.

That's another thing—Archie found it soothing to reminisce. In school when he was eight or nine and learned about the two hemispheres, he remembered offering everything he owned, or ever would own, if only he could go the southern hemisphere some day. What would it be like, crossing the equator?

The Bangka Inquiry

He got it confused with sonic boom—an airplane passing the speed of sound. He thought crossing the equator would feel like a sonic boom.

He slowly got up off the chair and went in to answer the phone. The door had been left open. The breeze off the South China Sea kept any mosquitoes away and at night when it came through the windows it made him fall asleep with a smile on his face regardless of what good or bad had transpired during the day.

There is nothing like the gentle caress of the South China Sea breeze to put you to sleep.

It was the Bangka telephone operator.

"Mr. Archie, you have a call from United States but the connection no good. I am not able to connect you to the person. I could not even find out the number to call back. Only in Jakarta...tomorrow...it is a woman. I am sorry Mr. Archie, the telephones on Bangka Island are not to call far away, only here...maybe Jakarta, Mr. Archie."

* * *

Catherine had to make decisions. The U.S. State Department person left his card and asked her to phone him with the arrangements. "As soon as possible Mrs. Prendergast, I apologize, I know it is difficult, I can't even imagine how you must feel but we have to get your husband home. Could you call me tomorrow morning?"

Where does one start? Catherine's sister was a partial answer. She phoned the funeral home to find out what the procedure was to receive a body from Indonesia. It was a relief that the woman at the funeral home said she would take care of everything. She only needed to know where "the deceased was currently resting," and which airline she preferred.

Catherine's sister gave her the name of the State Department person and asked her to phone him and to let him decide which airline, seeing as they had more experience.

Catherine still had to contend with telling David and Monica.

Chapter 13

"You tell them for me, will you?" she asked her sister. "Why Joe, why did it have to happen to him; they love him so much. Monica, she idolizes him, how can I tell her that her father is dead. I couldn't bear it; you will tell her for me, please?"

Somehow Catherine got through the next few weeks. Reality returned along with the unpleasant tasks that needed to be finalized. Joe's clothing, money, the accountant, paying bills, writing thank you notes, comforting the children. Even Ginger, she noticed, unmistakably exhibited the loss in her own doggy way.

One thing that would not go away by her efforts to close the loose ends was what happened.

Why when I ask doesn't anyone know what happened? Why won't someone tell me, don't they care? He was their employee, for God's sake; you would think *they* would want to know.

Perhaps they do and they don't want to tell me...afraid I will sue them, cause trouble. It was an accident, nobody's fault. It was horrible, that's why they won't tell me. The funeral director said the casket was closed because he was laid to rest in Indonesia...laid to rest!

They did a shit poor job of embalming him, that's what she meant. Or no, was it closed because of the accident, so I wouldn't see how bad it was? Please, somebody tell me.

That night she had an unusually difficult time getting to sleep. She tossed, got up, made some tea, checked on the kids; she couldn't fall asleep. She decided to call Archie.

"First thing in the morning, I'll phone him..." she said aloud and the recurring thought again entered her consciousness:

Will there ever be an end?

14

Although both Greg and Curtis were partners in the firm, Curtis's status was that of a partner "cut down"—to use an old Irish expression. "You look just like your father, cut down."

As CCG expanded into other countries they needed to have leadership in the shortest possible time. CCG grew by buying out the owners/partners of existing consulting firms. As the former owners took their money and retired, a U.S. partner would take over the office and be charged with creating young partners from the indigenous staff. Mr. Chu, one of the original owners of the accounting and consulting firm in Jakarta was the head of the Asia market and was due to retire, hence Archie's potential dream job.

Curtis was one of two local partners in Australia. He was, however, like all the other non-U.S. partners, a partner in his office only, very cut down from where Greg was at or, for that matter, where Archie would be. If things went according to plan, like Greg, Archie would be a full partner of the worldwide firm and Curtis' superior.

Of course, Curtis wasn't standing still. He was lobbying to be the first non-U.S. worldwide partner promoted from a satellite office. He had a good thing going because he brought in a lot of work. Even though he was rather difficult and unlikable to work with, he was effective with his clients, produced results and got referrals, which he then converted into paying projects.

Jefferson and the rest of the CCG management team had already noticed him. They were, however, hesitant to open up a precedent that they might be sorry for later on—an office outgrowing its dinghy and sailing away from the mother ship was one reason. Disparity in compensation would create another problem, not insurmountable, but the firm subscribed to the saying, "if it isn't broken, don't fix it."

Greg and Curtis didn't have much contact with each other in Indonesia. It wasn't for any special reason except that a reason never came up. As long as the firm's president and his attorney were there, Curtis fawned all over *them*. He had hitched his wagon to Mr. Chu, the retiring Asian managing partner who was

The Bangka Inquiry

in a position to give the goodies; Greg's only potential was for getting in the way. Curtis figured Greg wasn't going to propel his promotion, only had the possibility of holding it back.

Therefore, a short time after the accident, when Greg let Curtis know he wanted to speak with him, he knew down deep it wasn't to announce any promotions. Furthermore, he knew he was responsible for the accident, the only thing he didn't know was who else knew.

Troy of course knew, but Curtis recognized the grip he had over him. As soon as all the commotion—that's how he put it—faded away, his plan was to discard him, send him back to Perth then fire him, in that order. Thus if Troy was to tell anyone what happened, Curtis could deny it and maintain that Troy was merely bitter over being fired and invented the story.

Marapani knew, but Curtis figured he wouldn't say anything either. To begin with since safety was his responsibility, any excuse such as "someone told me to do it"...giving the order to free the bucket, that is...would be akin to criminal behavior at I-Tin.

"Curtis, could you come to the Watergarden Restauran at seven-thirty, just yourself; there is some CCG business we need to work on as long as I am still here?" Greg's phone call was short, non-threatening and very plausible.

"Sure, Greg, I'll be there. I may be a few minutes late. We have to coordinate the vans. My driver is picking up one of the staff at the workshop in Mentok and, unless they run into traffic, will just make it back in time for me to meet you."

"Fine, if you prefer, let's make it eight o'clock, does that work out better?"

"Sure, see you at eight." Curtis spent a moment thinking about the words, the tone of voice, Greg's understanding of the van issue, firm's business...no problem. But just in case, I better have a good story ready.

* * *

Meanwhile, the afternoon after Troy and Fiona's disaster dinner at the Watergarden, she convinced herself that in fact he was

Chapter 14

working too hard, was being too closely puppeted by Curtis, and one solution was to take off the coming weekend for Bali.

Perfect, it will be a nice getaway, I can make sure all the plans for the wedding are finalized, and it will be good for Troy. He'll become more excited about the wedding...when he sees how much we are getting for such a small amount of money. Fiona had it all worked out. She only had to implement the details.

I know Troy will go for it, so there's no need to bother him at work, I'll just get Suradi to make the arrangements. Good thing Troy told me about how *that* works.

Of course Suradi was happy to oblige and came through with a nice weekend package.

I'll pay for this with my own money, a treat for Troy. Now he'll have no excuse, it won't cost him anything. She even took the scary move of calling Curtis. When she reached him on the line she said,

"Curtis, this is Fiona. Sorry to bother you but I have a favor. As you know Troy and I are getting married in Bali and I was wondering if you could give him off this afternoon. I talked to Suradi and he can get two seats all the way to Bali...for the weekend."

Curtis thought quickly and figured if Troy was not around there was less chance of him saying anything he shouldn't about the "accident."

"Sure, Fiona, that's a good idea. You know Indonesians; if there is any chance they can screw things up they will. Besides, a change of scene will do Troy good. I've been working him pretty hard. Sure, go to Bali, check on your wedding arrangements, have a nice time."

Fiona disagreed about the Indonesians screwing things up but kept it to herself. I haven't found that to be the case at all. The people in Bali have been very helpful, the only reason we are going is to get Troy away from you!

Instead she said, "thanks, Curtis, it is a surprise so if you wouldn't mind just telling him you won't need him this afternoon, nothing about going to Bali, I would appreciate it."

The last hurdle was removed, Curtis quickly said, "of course."

When Troy got home for lunch, which was the routine that developed over the few days since she arrived, Fiona was excited about the surprise. She opened a bottle of wine she brought with her from Australia, had the suitcases packed and laid out a change of clothes for him.

"We'll get something quick to eat on the way to the airport and be in Bali by seven p.m., enough time to check in and go somewhere for a nice relaxed dinner," she explained.

Troy threw a fit. "Why would you make all these plans and not even check with me? First, suppose I had to work, which I do, I've made plans to work Saturday morning."

"I wanted to surprise you, you been working too many hours, you have a lot on your mind and I thought you'd be interested in the wedding plans."

"Well, I'm not. In fact I have been seriously thinking whether this wedding is a good idea…I like you Fiona and I don't want you to be hurt, but I am in love with someone here. I was going to tell you the other night but I couldn't. First I had to make sure it's what I want."

Fiona was stunned. "How long has this been going on? You didn't just fall in love with someone else over-night. Who is it? Why?" and she started to cry.

Troy was unmoved. He had prepared himself for a reaction like this and already made plans to move to another room at the Wisma Jaya. He was hoping Fiona would take that afternoon plane…but to Perth, not Bali.

"What about our plans? If you felt like this why didn't you let me know, I would have understood, really, but the last minute?"

"I think you should go to Bali this afternoon, cancel the arrangements you made and then go back to Perth. I'm sorry." He got up and left the Wisma.

When Curtis arrived at the Watergarden Restauran Greg was seated at a table near the back of the room. There were only a few other people in the restaurant, none of whom Curtis recognized; all were Indonesians.

Chapter 14

Greg stood up as Curtis approached, "thanks for coming on such short notice."

"Sure, have you been waiting long?"

"No, well...yes, but I came early on purpose, there are some things I need to catch up on and there are no interruptions here. Jefferson is a demanding guy; if you are in his shouting distance you have to be prepared to react pronto. Have a seat. Would you like something to drink? Dinner's on me so don't be shy, order whatever you want." Greg said the latter with a slight grin, letting Curtis know it was in jest...relax, Curtis! He noticed that Curtis looked a little pale, obviously not happy to be called to a meeting where there may be trouble.

Curtis, on the other hand, did not know that Greg knew the details of the accident. He continued to figure no one knew—no one who would say anything, that is.

"Sure, Greg, thanks, I see you are having a beer, I'll have the same."

Greg got the waiter's attention and ordered another drink. "And we'll have a menu, too."

When the waiter had gone, Greg got right to the point.

"We have a problem with the accident. Just so you know, I am meeting with you on behalf of McMillan. I have orders too. It seems Subroto knows what really happened and finds it a problem for a couple of reasons."

Greg noticed the sudden change in Curtis' expression. It confirmed what Greg thought; he was malleable, would do whatever he was told. He continued.

"Whether you know or not, a number of the parcels of land where the illegal miners get tin are owned by big shots in Jakarta. Seems they are nervous that our project will interrupt their golden goose. Subroto thinks an accident that was not really an accident would give them the ammunition to close down the project. Whether we concur or not doesn't make any difference. They have obviously raised the net and the ball is in our court."

With Greg's habit of hesitating and repeating, hesitating and repeating, Curtis had sufficient time to think about what the jest of the message was. He thought he had it worked out.

"I understand, Greg, but I am not sure I know what McMillan wants me to do."

"McMillan doesn't know *all* the details of what happened and does not want to know, so first, you have to agree that what you did was not brilliant. But no one except you, me, and Subroto needs to know the details. Marapani told Subroto and Subroto will take care of him; transfer him to Timbuktu. Archie knows and I will take care of him. Does that leave anyone else?"

" Well, yes, Troy and one or two of the dredge crew."

"Subroto will handle them as well. Shipping Marapani off will send a clear message. Where does Troy stand on this?"

"Greg, first let me say I am sorry. It was stupid what I did, I didn't think, but here was a real bucket jam, right there when we were all set up. It was made-to-order, I was anxious to take advantage of it but Marapani wasn't there; I had to tell the crew to go ahead, it was an opportunity I did not want to miss."

Greg considered this last statement by Curtis. This guy is astonishing, he said to himself, Archie was right. Even now he's adjusting the story enough to shift the blame on to someone else...Marapani. You sent him away, it wasn't that he wasn't there, he would have been there if you hadn't sent him away. Oh well, go ahead, dig yourself in deeper.

"In any case, what about Troy?" Greg nodded.

"He hasn't said anything yet and I don't think he will. Do I understand that everyone would feel better if I sent him back to Perth?"

"That's your call, just so this *accident* thing doesn't become a national crisis...let's order."

* * *

On one of the mornings Archie arrived at the office at seven-thirty, he had to chuckle at the sign on the front door.

"Those Australians," he said, "where did they come up their sayings?" The sign, written with a magic marker, said "Bum The Door Gently."

It took a second to orientate himself, something was different...the furniture. In the main room when you walked in,

Chapter 14

ordinarily there were six desks, each with a file cabinet. They had seen better days of course, metal, gunship gray, but certainly serviceable. As far as Archie knew, no one had any complaints; they seemed to work fine.

This morning, however, there were six desks... new, black-wooden desks with new swivel chairs, plastic floor mats and each desk had a matching file cabinet. The original cabinets were placed next to the new ones.

"Where did these come from?" Archie said to no one in particular. Everyone looked at him and shrugged.

Makes no sense, we're on the downhill, the project will be winding down soon. The next thought was, who ordered these, and why...and who's paying?

It didn't take long to figure it out. Likely Suradi opened a furniture store and had his first customer. Archie was pissed.

The hell with formality and not confronting...Suradi doesn't count. Just to make sure, when Budi came in Archie asked him, not if he knew anything about the desks but, "please find out who ordered these desks and then let me know." No chance for a "yes" that really meant "no."

A few hours later, Budi came back affirming what Archie thought,

"Yes, Suradi ordered them and told me to tell you that they are being charged to I-Tin. They were old and needed to be replaced, so you do not have to be concerned, they will not be charged to the consultants."

"Budi, please tell Suradi that when he has a chance I would like to see him."

Later that afternoon, Suradi came to the office with his usual smile, looked very proud of himself, and stated so immediately.

"Suradi get you fine desks, Mr. Archie, consultants are doing good things for I-Tin so need good desks."

"Suradi, our job is to eliminate expenses, how does it look if we have new desks and we are supposed to be saving rupiah for I-Tin. No, Suradi, we do not want new desks, you will have to have them returned."

A tiny little change took place in Suradi's face. One would almost think it said, "you bastard." But Suradi didn't use such language, at least not in word form. But he was thinking it. He was also thinking, I'll get even, you fucker.

Following this interlude with the desks, Greg stepped into Archie's office.

"Got a minute?" was Greg's opening salvo.

"Sure, what's up?"

"What did Catherine want?"

"Catherine? I haven't talked to Catherine since way back."

"She called yesterday."

"Well, she *may* have called. Last night the phone operator rang me and said there was a call from the US; said it was a woman but the connection didn't go through. It could have been Catherine...or my wife. Why?"

"I don't know what you've done to Suradi but I don't think you are one of his favorites. He snitched, he told me a woman called last night and I figured it might be Catherine. Regardless, I just want to make sure we both understand each other and our last conversation about this accident." Greg paused longer than usual, to let Archie digest what was coming next.

"The firm has decided that it does no good to open a can of worms. No matter what, no one wanted Joe to die, maybe some bad decisions were made but it was an accident. What good would it do Catherine to think anything different?"

"Greg, he was my friend. His wife and my wife know each other. Doesn't she have a right to know? Don't we owe it to her, no matter how painful, to what really happened? Maybe she's thinking he was careless, or dumb or something. Doesn't she have the right to know that it wasn't his fault? If this is about Curtis, worried what Catherine might think or say, or do, Curtis is here, for God's sake, or Australia. Catherine is in Chicago."

"I understand what you are saying. If you stand back a bit, unemotionally, you'll see that there is no purpose served in telling her anything other than it was an accident. We have a lot to lose if the Indonesians run with this and make a crisis out of it. The landowners are threatening to do that. What happens to you, your promotion? How could someone be director of Asia with everyone knowing he works for a firm that is careless with its people? We might as well not have a director of Asia."

"So what you are telling me is that unless I keep my mouth shut I am making a career limiting move?"

"I suppose you could put it like that."

Curtis, Troy and Amulya were again on a dredge—not Marapani's—finishing up some scenes for the film. Amulya was off giving instructions to the few locals on board who were tapped to be actors. Curtis took the opportunity to talk privately to Troy.

"I talked to Greg and he wanted me to pass on how important it is to keep the discussions about Joe's accident to a minimum. He is suggesting that anything that happens to foreigners here in Indonesia is big news so they will want to talk about it forever."

"I understand, you don't have to worry about me, I'd rather not discuss it with *any* one."

"I realize. I just feel it is important that we all sing from the same song-sheet. Just one word different from what I say, you say, anyone else says gets noticed. Then the gossip begins, the story takes on heroic proportions, whispering turns to facts. Not good at all."

"Again, Curtis, you don't have to worry about me. And, I don't think you have to worry about Marapani, either. Amulya tells me he does not want to discuss it even with her. That's what she told me."

"Marapani is not going to be a problem. He is going to get transferred to the outer banks where no one will ask questions, we will not have to worry about him. Besides, his being sent away will be a message to any of the other crew who might be tempted to make up stories."

"Thanks for telling me, Curtis, but I understand, I do."

Inside, Troy was elated, and his devious mind began thinking.

If what Curtis says is true about Marapani being transferred, that makes it easier for Amulya and me. A good excuse for a divorce, I'll have her all to myself.

The horny shit even began getting an erection.

15

The "highly regarded" consulting firms recruited the smartest and the brightest directly out of "highly regarded" colleges. CCG wasn't big but it was one of the "highly regarded"—a *boutique* firm specializing in a narrow range of services. CCG was known as one of the premier high-level strategic planning consultants.

The "highly regarded" firms fought among themselves for the best by offering huge salaries. If a new consultant wanted to make a lateral move to another premier firm, he had to do so while he was still young, certainly less than thirty-five, seeing as how there was so much competition from new graduates. Older than thirty-five and there were still opportunities—second and third-tier firms coveted the few people who, for whatever reason, decided to move from the firm that recruited them initially, but they ran the risk of being considered damaged goods in terms of salary potential.

The large majority of recruits to the tier-one firms end up going with a client—directly as a high level executive or on a fast track to become one. These become the wealthy among us. Those who stay with their tier-one firms and make a long-term career out of it are not poor either.

Archie considered himself fortunate to be with CCG and whichever path he took he looked forward to becoming financially secure. His background, however, was out of the ordinary. He had been with a lesser-known consulting firm, saw what else was out there and thought, why not give it a try, what's the worst that can happen? He had a track record of developing strategic plans that were highly regarded, had good references from clients and even had the blessing of his firm's management. CCG hired him at age thirty-one.

True, he wasn't a partner but CCG was unusual in that the number of partners was limited. When he joined, however, it was clearly understood that as vacancies occurred through retirement or cashing out and assuming he performed as they expected, he would become a partner. That is why the project in Indonesia for I-Tin was so critical. It was sort of his last hurrah.

The Bangka Inquiry

* * *

Alfred Archibald Glendenning III is now thirty-seven. He and his wife Judy have two kids, Michael and Christine and live in a comfortable suburb of Chicago.

He's a family man. Weekends are spent as a family and usually there is a key event: museum, sports event, visit the grandparents; and out to dinner at least one night. Judy is a stay-at-home mom who volunteers at the senior center a few days a week, takes a philosophy class at the U of C's downtown Chicago campus and is the treasurer of the homeowners association.

Michael and Christine are in high school, study hard, and are blessed with lots of nice friends who are constantly in and out of the Glendenning house.

The family's life is predictable and includes two vacations a year; skiing in winter, northern Wisconsin cabin in summer.

Archie is a year older than Joe Prendergast, although Joe was recruited directly from Northwestern's Kellogg—third in his class no less; Archie went to Ohio State. He got teased about his name being akin to royalty but he was from an ordinary family from Akron. His parents both worked all their lives and were comfortable. He was raised in a religious and moral atmosphere; his brother was a missionary who worked in a Christian hospital in Somalia. His sister was married to a professor of music at the University of North Carolina.

Archie believed his brother and his wife were too attached to their church, "it is their only life," he often said. But inside he admired them for their outward contentment and how they were raising smart, nice, "socially with it" kids.

Archie, which he preferred over Alfred, Al or Archibald—he wasn't crazy about any of the names—considered himself average height, average weight and average looking. He liked nice clothing, not necessarily expensive, but had a sense of putting the right things together.

His male friends would tell you "the old man" acts older than his thirty-seven years but is a regular guy and fun to be with. His women friends would tell you the first thing they notice is his dark eyes; they look bright. They'd discuss among themselves

Chapter 15

why? Is it the amount of white around the pupil, just the right amount of moisture, the black eyelashes that set off the white? They also liked his sexy, kinky dark hair.

"I'll bet he has some African in his blood," one was heard to say.

His wife would tell you he notices everything. At home he will walk into a room and immediately spot the empty space where a picture frame was that fell off the table and broke. He wouldn't say anything, at least not right away, but his wife knew that he saw it and he wasn't happy that something was different. Because this annoyed her immensely, she would make a game of seeing how long it would take before he asked how it happened, but then she quickly got annoyed when he wouldn't leave it alone, wanted to know every detail.

"What are you going to do, bring it back or something? It broke. I didn't break it on purpose, let it be."

Hosts would tell you they liked to invite him to their gatherings. He would notice anyone who wasn't involved and slowly draw him or her into the conversation. But just as quickly he could walk away from any one of them—he didn't suffer fools lightly.

The people he worked with would tell you about his management style. He was honest and fair, he gave clear direction, and his non-verbals told you exactly what he was thinking. They would tell you if he crossed his arms it meant he was not buying what you were selling. If he moved closer and cocked his head he was interested. They'd tell you he never had difficulty following where the conversation was going.

People who didn't know him would tell you they noticed how he walks. Archie walked confidently. It made no difference where he was. The walk said, I am here and I am my own man.

* * *

Catherine called again. Archie was outside the office, enjoying a few minutes breather by himself, watching two chameleons getting it on.

The Bangka Inquiry

"Mr. Archie," it was Budi, "you have a phone call from United States, a person by the name of Catherine, she wants to talk to you. Please hurry." Archie suddenly felt the sting of the sun and the weight of the humidity. Not what he wanted.

"Budi, please, I can't talk to her right now. You must do me a favor and tell her I am not here and you don't know where I went. Budi, I would not ask you to do this except it is very important, do you understand?"

Now it was Budi's turn to feel the sun's sting and the humidity bear down. He was being asked to do something that went against what he believed. But Budi loved Archie, respected him, and believed him to be an honest, hard working, fair and compassionate white person who never, ever took advantage of anyone.

So, Budi had a conversation with himself.

If Mr. Archie is asking me to tell this woman that he is not here then he must have a good and important reason. Therefore, I am telling the truth; if Mr. Archie says he is not here then he is not here and I do not know where he is. Budi gave his typical little smile at having figured this all out.

"Yes, Mr. Archie, you are not here and I do not know where you are."

"Thank you, Budi, I appreciate what you are doing." Budi knew that Archie meant what he said.

Archie moved back into the shade. Better, but not by much.

I know what she wants, she wants to know what happened. She wants all the details, I know her, and she is tenacious. I also know that the firm will be cautious about giving out any official information it hasn't already given. Jefferson made it clear that *he* would decide the official line and he did...it was an accident. Period.

Archie felt like he was someplace else. It was hot and humid there also, with a lot of people circling around him, staring at him, obviously wondering what he was going to do. They were wearing white sheets, like roman senators, women wore short tunics. Some of them had their forefinger to their pursed lips, holding their elbow with their other hand. It was eerie.

Chapter 15

They are wondering what I am going to tell Catherine, I know it. If I mislead her they will know. Who are they?

For a split second Archie looked around to make sure none of the staff or the gardeners or the drivers were watching him. But only for a second.

I can't tell her, I said I wouldn't...to Greg... to Jefferson. I'd be finished at CCG. What Catherine doesn't know isn't going to make any difference anyway. In fact, she is better off not knowing how horrible it was. Let her think it was just a freak accident, he died instantly and peacefully, no pain, never knew what happened. That's the way she should think about it, for her own sake.

Get away from me, what are you looking at, you morons, go away! Archie was cognizant of the sweat forming under his armpits and on his forehead and around his waist. He took out the slice of paper towel he always carried with him for just these occasions. He wiped his forehead; there was nothing he could do about the other.

My grandmother, of all people, my grandmother, you too! Go away.

Just as suddenly, Archie was back in reality. He went inside, to the welcomed air-conditioning, stopped at the water fountain and headed for the W.C. He splashed a little water on his face and felt better. He moved quickly to his office, mindful of someone wondering why he could take a break longer than what they were permitted.

Funny I should think that, I could care less how long or how often anyone takes a break. No one here is a slacker.

He sat at his desk and thought about the screwballs walking around in a circle, looking at him.

If it were the middle ages I'd think I was Hamlet, "to be or not to be, that is the question." Well, I ain't Hamlet and there ain't no question. I've decided...I cannot throw my career away just because some old farts are walking around with their fingers up their asses.

Fiona could not figure out what to do with herself. Troy moved to another room so she spent the afternoon taking two walks but mostly slept.

I can't go back to Perth, I will have to face my family. I'll stay here, Troy is upset, many men get nervous about long commitments, he was when he told me he wanted to marry me, and he would be faithful to only me.

Troy, on the other hand, had no difficulty deciding what to do.

If Amulya wants to go to Australia then that's what we will do. I can't live without her. He realized that thought was right out of a cheap romance novel.

But that is how I feel. Things often have a way of working themselves out. Marapani is going to be sent to never-never land; a face-saving excuse for Amulya to get a divorce, we'll get married so she can get a visa to Perth as my wife, and we'll start out fresh.

Troy could not wait for lunch when they could slip away to her house, he would tell her what Curtis told him about Marapani and they could celebrate with a little quickie.

She can't get enough as it is, this will put her over the top.

Later that evening, Marapani came home exhausted, as he had been lately. He hadn't been feeling that well but figured it had to do with the turmoil inside him. He was an honest man, a good man, never ever thought he would be put in a position where he would be so diabolically tested. Now he was in such a position and he believed that is what caused him not to feel up to par. Amulya was home.

She hasn't been in a good mood lately, I think she works too hard, too many hours, but will she listen to me? No, I tell her to refuse these extra hours but she will not.

"Oh, hello, Marapani," Amulya directed the unemotional greeting from the couch where she was looking through a magazine of the latest women's fashions...from Paris no less.

"What are you reading, Amulya?" Marapani asked even though he already saw and processed the information he was asking about.

Chapter 15

Lately she is distant, not the women I am used to. Yes, she is tired, he thought, like the way she is when I-Tin sends her to Jakarta. These long hours tire her out too much, and too many trips to Jakarta.

"What time would you like to have dinner, Amulya?"

"I was hungry so I ate already, but I left yours in the refrigerator. You only need to heat it up."

Can't she do it for me? was Marapani's thoughtful reply. It is not that I want to be waited on, I would like to visit with her while she cooks...just like we used to. Everything has changed in my life. My work has changed, my home has changed, no wonder I feel so tired all the time.

"If you don't mind, I will heat it up now, I am hungry. Do you want to visit with me while I heat it up?"

"Well, I'm busy reading this magazine right now. You go ahead if you are hungry."

Marapani felt a sharp, unusual pain in his stomach.

"Yes, I am hungry. I do not feel like eating but I am hungry, my stomach is telling me I am hungry." He re-heated his dinner in silence but ate very little.

Amulya was grinning inside, but a little on edge outside. She had decided to tell Marapani the news she heard from "someone at work," no sense bringing Troy's name up right now, it would be better to soften him first.

He is much too sensitive so I will tell him a little at a time.

After Marapani finished eating, Amulya walked into their kitchen.

"I heard about your transfer today...at work...they were discussing it. Why didn't you tell me?"

"What transfer, I know nothing about any transfer." The sharp pain in his stomach returned, he felt a tingling in both of his arms; his face turned the chalk white of a Japanese actress's.

"You are going to be transferred...from dredge captain, I do not know where to. I thought you would already know... if they are already discussing it at work."

"What are they saying at work, about this transfer?"

"Didn't you know? Just that Subroto has decided that you should not be a dredge captain any more. It probably has to do with the accident. I tried to put in a word for you, and I did with the consultants. They told me there is nothing they can do, it is not their business when people are transferred or promoted into different positions in the company. Not their business to get involved."

The pain in his arm went away.

I think she is happy I'm being transferred. Marapani was stunned. All of a sudden he realized how foolish he had been, how blind.

She doesn't love me, she never did. She has a lover, they go to Jakarta, that's it...I know it. Why? Have I not been good to her? Yes, that explains everything, she is happy that I am being transferred. Amulya noticed the change in his expression.

"Amulya, will you come with me, where they send me?" Marapani already knew the answer and wondered why he was torturing himself by asking. But he needed an answer.

What else can go wrong? Amulya didn't answer; she turned and left the room. She returned to the couch and continued reading the magazine.

He had his answer.

* * *

Greg was due to leave Bangka on Friday but as he told Archie, "I think I better stay here and see this crisis through. No one wants any surprises."

"What do you mean, surprises, I have my orders and I will carry them out. No fucking with the miners, keep my fucking mouth closed, kiss Curtis' fucking ass. Don't you trust me?"

"It isn't a matter of trust, Archie. This has been a strain on all of us, and I can see where it has been particularly stressful for you. Calm down. I just think it would be better if I stayed here to take some of the burden off you, until everything gets back to normal." It took Greg forever to get all of this out, what with his stumbling, a lot of ah and eh and constant repeating.

"You are worried I might tell the truth to Catherine, aren't you. I was thinking about it, she gets Joe's trust fund, doesn't she. What else does she get? If Joe had lived and worked the usual amount of time he would have earned several million over his career. What is she left with, a few hundred thousand...to take care of her and put the kids through college. She will have to move from their big house to something tiny. Has anyone at CCG thought of that?"

"Whoa, boy. Take it easy. The firm will compensate her; take care of her. Don't worry about it; it just takes time to get all the details worked out. Yes, I'd better stay a while longer, you are too emotionally tied up in this. You surprise me, Archie. I believed you were more realistic. We can't always expect everything to work out like we want it to. Shit happens."

Greg left, satisfied that he made the right decision to stay. He would have to watch Archie very carefully.

16

Marapani got the dreaded call on his ship-to-shore radio. He was to report immediately to the I-Tin offices on Jl. Jend. Sudirman in Pangkalpinang.

He quickly changed into his best clothes, the only non-work clothes he had in his cabin, called for the tender to take him to shore, got into a company van in Sungailiat and drove as quickly as he could to Pangkalpinang.

"Why the rush?" he began the audible portion of what was going on in his mind. He was driving in the van alone. "I can talk as loudly as I want, I can scream, I can even say the bad words you are supposed to say when you are angry—piss, bastard, whore, bitch.

"Yes, I have figured it out, she is a whore. You knew that. You stupid, idiotic pig's balls. You knew it when we got married, before we got married. You knew it always, yes always." All this was said out loud.

"But did you use your head? No. You used your prick. It is her fault, the whore's fault, she knows how to attract men. She doesn't love anyone, she just wants someone to fill her stinking pussy...she is a whore." He realized he was driving too fast.

"What is my hurry?" Still out loud.

"I am stupid. Stupid dog shit. Stupid for thinking she could be a wife. Stupid to let that fat white man tell me what to do. I should have told him, 'No, I will not go to the wheelhouse, I am the captain and everyone will follow my orders. You are a stupid white man. Go to hell.'"

He unconsciously slowed down a bit. It was late morning so there was no traffic to speak of on the winding, pothole filled road from Sungailiat to Pangkalpinang.

"What am I doing? I am in a hurry to my punishment...that I deserve. That is what I am doing. All my life is ruined...because of the shit white man."

He lapsed into silence but his mind continued the conversation. It was the repeat of what he had been saying out loud, but now more logical, kinder, not thinking bad words or bad thoughts...about Amulya or about Curtis. He descended into the resignation that he had failed—himself, most of all.

* * *

How interesting that thoughts based on the same event would occur at the same time between different people on opposite sides of the globe, twelve hours apart. Catherine was lying in bed, couldn't sleep, having a conversation with herself as well. She too lapsed into logical, kinder, not thinking bad words or bad thoughts...about CCG or Archie.

All I want is answers, why is that so difficult? I know Archie will tell me what really happened. I need to know, so I can fall asleep. I stay awake thinking about Joe, it must have been horrible, to be in an accident. Then to find out you weren't going to make it. What did he think about, in those last instants? I will never know.

Yes, I will know. There is a heaven; I will see him again. David and Monica will see him again, so maybe it is not so bad. She got out of bed, turned on the light and crept into Monica's room first, checked to see she was comfortably sleeping, then on tip-toe, slowly opened David's door. The night-light was on.

"Mom?"

"Yes, David. How come you are not sleeping?"

"I'm okay, I just turned on the light, that's all." Catherine bent down, gave him a light kiss on the forehead, stroked his smooth chin, looked at him for a second... and with assurance said, "David, go to sleep. You have school tomorrow. Good night." She tiptoed out of his room, gently closed the door and screamed inside.

Why Joe? What happened? Monica's too young, she doesn't realize what happened; her father is gone. My sister doesn't realize. How could she? How could those bastards at CCG know what it is like? I want answers; I want fucking answers. Does anyone think I don't want answers? I want to know what the fuck happened. She climbed into bed, turned off the light and very, very slowly descended into a light sleep. The last thing she

Chapter 16

remembered was, I will call our Angelina tomorrow; she will know what to do.

* * *

The meeting Marapani had with the director of operations was quick, one and one-half minutes.

"Marapani, you have failed in your duty as an I-Tin dredge captain. The company has decided to send you immediately to Nais. In two days a dredge will be leaving Sungailiat for Nais and they are expecting you. You will work in the workshop in Nais. Yono is the supervisor, you will report to him as soon as you arrive and he will make arrangements. You are to go alone." The Director looked down, indicating the meeting was over.

Nias is a small but beautiful island off the western coast of Sumatra. It has rugged green hills and palm-lined coasts, famous for the waves off the southern beaches at Teluk Dalam and Lagundri. The latter is where the I-Tin workshop is located.

In June, considered winter in the southern hemisphere, Nias attracts surfers from around the world, but otherwise it just lies there.

* * *

Catherine called Angelina and set a date to meet. She went to undergrad school with Joe at Northwestern then got her law degree from DePaul in Chicago. She was on a fast track in a silk stocking law firm, a junior partner.

"Catherine, good to see you, how is my buddy Joe, how are the kids, I'll bet they are growing too fast?" Angelina was not married, correction...to a man. She was married to her profession. She loved it. She liked the cases that were tough, where she could use her ample mental acuity. She was good and she knew it.

Actually, those two things go together, don't they? Knowing you are good is a self-fulfilling prophecy—which makes you good.

"That is why I am here, Angelina, Joe is dead. It is not a long story because I do not know exactly what happened. He was

The Bangka Inquiry

on a project in Indonesia, had an accident on a tin mining dredge and that is all I know."

"When? Why didn't you call me right away," like anyone would remember she existed, what with her world-wind social life! Angelina didn't have a social life; she lived vicariously.

"When did it happen?"

"A week and a half ago, the funeral was small, our immediate family, otherwise I would have called you."

"Dear Catherine, what can I say, I am so sorry? You need help and you know I am here. I will do everything I can. No, I can't believe it. Joe? What are you telling me? Catherine, in college Joe told everyone I was his cousin from Minnesota. I'd cover with the accent. Everyone thought we were *both* hicks...he was my best buddy...I don't know what to say."

They both sat there, saying nothing, thinking, processing the information, each feeling her nerve endings. Entire pictures, scenes, days, months, years of remembrances flashed in front of their consciousness. Angelina closed her eyes... and swallowed.

"Angelina, please, I need advice," Catherine, looking down, began again, "...on how I can find out exactly what happened, I have tried calling Archie Glendening, Joe's boss who is still in Indonesia but I haven't gotten through. I am beginning to think he doesn't want to take my call."

Angelina had other matters on her mind, legal matters. Was someone to blame, someone who could be held accountable...someone to litigate? What is Joe's firm's responsibility...life insurance, annuity, settlement. She thrived on making everything right in situations like these.

"I will look into it. Give me all the particulars and let me see what I can do. Meanwhile, it is obvious to me that you will not be satisfied until you see for yourself, say good-bye to him where it happened, fix it in your mind so you can have some semblance of closure. Go there."

"Yes, now that you say it...I wasn't able...to put it into words."

"Don't wait too long, go now. I will stay with the kids if that helps. I know if you go to the spot it will be the right thing to

Chapter 16

do. I will take care of the legal matters. I will call the firm and see what their procedure is for looking after you and the kids."

"It is not about money, Angelina, that is not what I want you to do. I want you to help me get answers so when David and Monica ask me what happened I don't have to say *he had an accident*."

"Well, Catherine, looking after you and the children *is* my job and it has to be done, so I will take care of it."

Two days later Catherine was on a flight to Bangka.

She knew Joe and Archie stayed at the Parai Beach Hotel in Sungailiat, so her travel agent booked a room. When she arrived in Pangkalpinang she met Suradi. She knew of him, of course, through Joe. He helped her get a taxi and took her passport.

"It is for safekeeping, yes."

She had heard enough about Suradi, that he was Mr. Busybody, so she figured he would tell Archie she was there. Actually, Suradi now kept his distance from Archie. He had a few desks, chairs and file cabinets to unload and unfortunately he had his job at I-Tin and the airport otherwise he would devote full time to strong arming someone to take them off his hands.

I will have to raise the price to cover my troubles.

From her window she saw the van pull into the Parai parking lot and her nerves began to tingle. Now another thought quickly went through her mind.

What if there was foul play and someone is covering it up, I could be in danger. Why didn't I think about that?

No, that is foolish, they don't realize how important it is to me to find out what happened, if they knew how important it was they would certainly give me the answers, wouldn't they? There is nothing to hide.

Her window gave her the vantage point to see which unit Archie went into. She had left a message at the desk when she checked in essentially saying she was at the hotel and could they meet for dinner. She was in unit three and the phone number was 7-103.

She spent the day walking the grounds of the hotel. They were building a convention center.

A convention center, she thought, how many people are going to come to the end of the earth to have a convention at the Parai Beach Hotel?

She watched the workmen scurrying around, each looking like he had no idea what he was doing, an OSHA nightmare, shorts, no shirts, either bare feet or sandals and not a mechanized tool to be found. Only shovels, hammers and human labor, seventy-five to a hundred strong. The ladders and scaffolding were made of twigs.

In spite of it all, the building was growing and, like the remainder of the architecture of the Parai Beach Hotel, stunning in its simple, Indonesian way.

The design is quite pleasing with a surprising attention to detail, she was tenuously distancing herself from the reason she was there. She walked a little further to the Parai Beach Discothèque and was able to visualize what the Convention Center would look like.

Same architect, she cautioned a slight smile.

Back in her room, looking out the window, she wondered how long it would take for the desk to deliver the message. Would they call him; send someone; wait until he stopped by? She gave herself an hour and decided she would call Archie's room if she hadn't heard by then. Immediately, the phone rang.

"Catherine, what a...a surprise." It was unlike Archie to blither. He normally was in full control of himself at all times. "How are you, how was the trip? I am sorry I did not return your calls, I am waiting for the official report, it is due soon.

"You cannot rush the Indonesians, they have their procedures; they may not make sense to us, but they do to them. Yes, let's have dinner. If you are up to it, we can have dinner at one of Joe's favorite places. We can talk then. What do you say?"

Catherine was just as tongue-tied as Archie.

"I just arrived, this morning, about eleven o'clock and came directly here. This is a lovely place. I stayed the night in Singapore so I am slowly getting accustomed to the time change. I would love to go to that restaurant, I miss him so. I want to see

Chapter 16

where he worked. I want to see where it happened, the accident, I mean..." She was conscious of the pause in her voice. "When do you want to go, I am ready whenever you want to go," It was difficult but she got the complete sentence out.

"Give me a half hour to freshen up."

Archie hung up the phone. The scene returned and played in a flash. The old farts were walking around him with their forefingers to their lips. It was vivid. They tightened the circle and every so often one them would step out of the circle, closer to him, and point his finger in his face.

What the hell is she doing here, just what I need. He stood in the middle of the room with his left hand under his right armpit and slowly put his right fist to his lips. He stared at the phone.

No problem...it was an accident. He was working, doing the job he is paid to do, paid handsomely, I might add.

If the situation were reversed, if I was the one who had the accident, I wouldn't expect Joe to throw away *his* career. For what? What good does it do? He's dead for Christ sake, he ain't coming back. It is not my fault the world sucks. So a few big-shot mother-fuckers are fucking the company, not my fucking fault. He got more and more worked up as he started to undress.

Before Archie joined CCG he worked at another consulting firm. They had a saying, a mantra. The firm's chief service was finding ways to reduce employee expense, often resulting in wholesale terminations or "restructuring" to use the euphemism.

It was the right thing to do for the health of the company but that didn't make it easier to recommend fifteen or twenty percent of the employees get a pink slip. It was usually the younger ones who got it, men and women with families, kids, the ones who most needed the job. Years earlier the mantra was born—"it's either their kids or your kids"—to put reality into perspective when one of the consultants started having feelings of remorse about what they were being paid to do.

"It's either his kids or my kids." Archie repeated, but out loud this time. "We both have kids, his will be taken care of—very well, I might add. I need to worry about mine. This is my career we're talking about here. Those fuckers have been raping the company for years, what gives me the right to go into their playpen and take their toys? Sorry Catherine, too bad you had to make the long trip."

Archie stopped undressing and looked out the window for a second. A dredge was off in the distance, the telltale brown ribbon showing the path it took through the South China Sea.

"Greg was right," he continued out loud, "shit happens." Archie took a long, warm shower and put on a fresh shirt and trousers. As he was closing the door to meet Catherine he said with resolve,

"Besides, I'm hungry."

Ahmed drove them to the Watergarden Restauran. The forty minutes was essentially silent. Occasionally Archie singled out scenes along the way, and at one point, told Catherine about Han Glos's shrimp farm and promised she would meet him and take his "magical mystery shrimp farm" tour—which Hans morphed into the Beatle's tune.

At another point, Archie said, "I don't know what Joe told you about Indonesia, but he liked it. He often said, 'you bet, when Catherine comes to visit I am going to make sure she sees this,' when something struck his fancy. Then again, everything did. The Indonesians loved him."

At another point, he said, "he probably didn't tell you that at one of the local celebrations they had at the Parai, the staff voted him the best looking of everyone. They made him dance with the visiting dancing troupe. He loved every minute of their simple, repetitive dance that went on forever, that I thought would never end."

By the time they reached the Watergarden Restauran it was obvious that they both had been thinking about the real conversation and how each would either push forward or try stalling. Stalling would be a lose-lose situation for both of them and they seemed to have realized it at the same time.

"Catherine, I have bad news and I do not know how to tell you. I wish I did not have to tell you. I am ashamed of myself for thinking I could get by not telling you...Joe had an accident, but it

Chapter 16

didn't have to happen. It wasn't on purpose but it was preventable."

He noticed Catherine slowly inhale; he noticed her working hard to hold back the tears he realized would spill before dinner was served. He took a sip of his wine to give her pause.

"They were filming on a dredge and one of the buckets got stuck. Curtis, in charge of the filming, wanted to take advantage of the jam, how they go about freeing it and asked Joe to hold some lights. A cable snapped and struck him across the chest. It happened quickly. When I say could have been prevented, Curtis should have known better than to send Joe behind the safety cage. When a bucket gets stuck there is a lot of strain on everything. The cable snapped.

"There is more, Curtis told the captain to go to the wheelhouse, that's how come he was gone. The captain, Marapani, would not have allowed anyone behind the safety screen, but he wasn't there. In his absence Curtis ordered the crew to begin working on the bucket jam and he sent Joe behind the safety cage to position some lighting."

He noticed Catherine hadn't moved. She was looking down and suddenly her eyes were closed.

Funny, I didn't notice when she closed them, the semi-conscious thought sped through Archie's brain.

"Catherine, the firm told me not to tell anyone. There are only a few people who know what actually happened. They are afraid some Indonesian big shots will close the project unless we look the other way while they are stealing from the company. They are holding the accident over our heads…if it gets out that one of our people gave instructions to a dredge crew when the captain wasn't there and caused someone to get killed…."

Catherine looked up. "Who else knows? Greg doesn't know, he would not allow this to be swept under a rug?"

"Greg knows," Now it was Archie's turn to look down, he clasped his hands between his knees, clenched his teeth then slowly looked up at Catherine, stared at her, directly into her eyes. It said, I am ashamed for me, for us, for my associates.

"Jefferson probably knows, but not officially. The firm lawyer, McMillan probably also knows but not officially. They

The Bangka Inquiry

want to cover their asses...just Curtis, Subroto the I-Tin President, Marapani and me...and now you. Oh! And Greg and Troy."

"Troy who?"

"From Australia...Curtis' sidekick. Works with him, he saw everything but he's scared of Curtis, afraid he'll get fired if he says anything."

"What about you? You weren't going to tell me...tell anybody? This is a crime for God's sake, a crime, doesn't anyone care that someone got killed because of negligence?" That was it; she cried, he felt relief; she composed herself, he swallowed hard; each had a bowl of soup; they drove home in silence and said good night.

The next morning, Archie knocked on Catherine's door. Even though it was early he had a hunch she would be awake. She opened the door dressed for the day.

"It gets lonely here." The old Archie she knew was standing at her door. He continued, "Troy's fiancé, Fiona, is staying at the Wisma Jaya in Pangkalpinang. I think you would enjoy her company, she is very pleasant, better than being here by yourself. If you want, I can have Ahmed drive her out, perhaps an hour before lunch."

"Yes, I'd like that."

"I'll call you to confirm. I will set up a tour of the dredge for tomorrow, I cannot promise it will be the exact one, but they are similar.

"Catherine, I don't know what to do. I can't stir up the pot. All night I thought about it, there are other people, people who have had nothing to do with this, I can't let them suffer. Please don't do anything, say anything, until I get back. Tonight we will talk; I promise we will work something out."

Ahmed pulled the van up to the steps of the Parai pavilion, the open-air platform that served as the hotel's stage, dance floor, dining room and banquet area. Catherine was already sitting at a

Chapter 16

table. She had been staring for an hour at each little perfectly timed wave, its life suddenly and forever snuffed. She was the only guest in the pavilion.

They liked each other immediately. Women do that; they have an uncanny way of sizing one another up to become life-long *girl-friends*. That is another thing that is uncanny about women, they can have three, four, five, *girl-friends*, each their closest bosom buddy they tell things to they wouldn't think of telling their husband, kids...priest.

These are the people they turn to in crisis, for advice when there are life-altering events. What is the nature of this feminine phenomenon? Not even Catherine and Fiona could tell you how it just happened to them.

It did not take long before they were nose to nose, sharing their inner most secrets, knowing full well that *girl-friends* do not tell anyone else what they talk about—certainly not purposefully. A *girl-friend* might slip, inadvertently, perhaps during an emotional crisis, but they do not realize it when they slip, when they blab something they were told in absolute confidence.

Catherine and Fiona began their journey into becoming *girl-friends* by each telling the other why they were there. Why were two young women visiting Bangka Island by themselves? Catherine could not make up a story so she gave her *girl-friend* the only explanation that would be plausible. Her husband died in an accident and no one would tell her exactly what happened—she came to get answers.

As they talked, it became evident to Fiona that Troy had witnessed something about the accident and was beholding to Curtis. Catherine never told her anything specific, never compromised her promise to Archie to not say anything to anyone, but enough to allow Fiona, who was looking for reasons for Troy's sudden strange behavior, to figure out from a modicum of questions and answers about what was going on.

Naturally they both realized what each of them had discovered and with *girl-friend* logic could now discuss openly but only among themselves, without fear of compromising any promises to the contrary.

One more thing about *girl-friends*, they can be instrumental in lifting the weight of the world off each other's shoulders—perhaps in many cases the only thing that *can* lift it.

Such was the case with Fiona. Her feminine logic took over and she realized that Troy was not responsible for his actions toward her, didn't really mean that the wedding was off and he had found someone else; no, it was just a typical male reaction to a crisis. So she forgave him.

17

Ahmed was the messenger. Considering he spoke little English made it more interesting and more challenging. Effendi knew this but he also knew, as did Archie, that he was absolutely trustworthy. He would forget the message as soon as it was delivered.

Ahmed with messages was like the Indonesians who live in close proximity; they really do not hear if it is not their business. As soon as Ahmed delivered the message he absolutely forgot about it, erased it from the history folder in his mind.

"Mr. Archie," Ahmed always gave the formal slight bow when he addressed Archie or, for that matter any non-family member. Ahmed was far from subservient, but close to the manners his mother and father taught him. It had to do with civility; life is so much more enjoyable when people are civil to each other, don't get angry, work out differences and respect each other's right to think differently. A slight bow confirmed Ahmed's belief in all this.

By some means, during the course of the daily forty minute drives, when Archie always sat in the front passenger seat—a hold-over from when he was the only passenger—Ahmed communicated his philosophy in a manner that Archie could understand and appreciate. It was in this spirit Ahmed delivered the message from Effendi:

"Mr. Archie, Mr. Effendi is inviting you to join him for dinner," and Ahmed put his index finger to his lips in the universal sign of "quiet."

"Mr. Effendi wants to invite me to dinner and does not want anyone else to hear about it, is that the message, Ahmed." The beam, the shake of the head and the proverbial "yes" indicated the message was delivered and forever forgotten. You only got one chance with Ahmed so you had to get it right.

Archie wrote a note and asked Ahmed to deliver it.

"Thank you for your kind invitation. Please tell Ahmed when and where to meet. I am especially fond of your special restaurants. Thank you."

The Bangka Inquiry

The Chinese restaurants the Chinese patronized took a lot of fortitude if you were not Chinese. First, you typically walk down a narrow alley with fish stuff floating down the middle gutter. It was their garbage disposal and drainage system in one.

Next, the typical restaurant is dark, smokey from clove cigarettes and smells like rotten fish. On one end of each table there are two or three piles of maybe fifteen round bowls stacked, and in front of each place is a pair of chopsticks resting on an ornate, and very much out of place, chopstick holder. No matter how expensive or fancy the restaurant the napkins are like thin toilet tissue paper. Ordering is done beforehand by the host so except for wine if you so desire, the ten to twelve courses are delivered in measured frequency.

Each dish is placed in the center of the table; each guest, using chopsticks, grabs food out of the dish and puts it into a bowl that has been passed to him by the host. Depending on the course, you may want to put rice in the bowl first. To eat, you hold the bowl an inch from your chin and with the chopsticks shovel the food into your mouth. It is considered good form to leave a little in your bowl—a way to tell the host you are finished, do not want any more and enjoyed it.

The Cantonese have a saying, "anything that walks, swims, crawls or flies with its back to heaven is edible." At this restaurant, the courses were out of this world delicious, delicate beyond description with flavors that burst in your mouth. Portions were small so you savored each bite. Occasionally one or two looked bad and tasted worse; you wouldn't want to know what it was. Unfortunately it was rude to refuse a dish the host had ordered several hours before you arrived. But fortunately, the unpalatable ones were also small portions.

For example, take a brine made with shrimp, vegetables and salt, ferment for several months and put a piece of tofu in it for a couple of hours and you have Chou Doufu, renowned for its pungent odor. It is impossible to feel neutral about it; diners either love it or hate it.

Or what appears to be a chunk of cement but is a dried form of sea cucumber that looks like a regular cucumber with the addition of tubed feet and a ring of tentacles around its mouth.

Chapter 17

Rather bland tasting but Archie found it uncomfortable to eat...knowing what it was.

Then you have one thousand-year-old eggs. Duck eggs preserved in ash and salt for one hundred days. This turns the white of the egg darkish gray giving it an ancient appearance and definitely the need for an acquired taste.

Finally, bird's nest soup, made with the nest of the swiftlet, a tiny bird that lives in caves and makes a nest of its own saliva. The soup has a reputation both as a health tonic and an aphrodisiac.

The most bizarre, which Archie never encountered and it hopefully was hearsay—although it had to start somewhere and for a reason—required a round table with a hole in the middle. A live monkey is propped up from underneath with the crown of its head in the hole, the chef slices off the crown with one quick horizontal cut and the guests use spoons to savor the warm delicacy!

Customarily, when the host finishes his or her last bite, he or she stands up. Everyone else immediately stops eating, also stands up, bows to each other and leaves. Since Effendi and Archie were the only ones dining, instead of standing, Effendi ordered some Chinese rice wine and they commenced the business that brought them to the restaurant in the first place.

Effendi knew everyone and whether they could speak English. If the conversation was meant to be private you were assured no one else within hearing distance could understand. Effendi's English was perfect.

"I remember telling you earlier that there were many people whose livelihood depended on tin and they would not be happy if the consultants disrupted their life. There are agitators among them and they are planning to send a message to the consultants."

"What kind of message, Effendi?"

"Tomorrow night one of the gardeners, I will tell you which one because I trust you to realize he is a simple man, he does not think what I am about to tell you he is going to do is wrong. He is the brother-in-law of one of the illegal miners. This stupid man will tell his brother-in-law when your van leaves for

Sungailiat. They plan to block the road, take your driver and beat him severely...in front of you. Then they will take him away, leaving you stranded on the highway."

"Our driver? You mean Ahmed?"

"Yes. Here is what you must do. Tomorrow night you must not do anything usual. After you have pulled out of the parking lot and driven two miles toward Sungailiat, tell Ahmed you have changed your mind at the very last minute and decided to go to the Watergarden Restauran. Give the gardener enough time to make sure you are on your way, so he does not see you double back. Do not take the chance of telling any of the staff, even afterwards, after you have finished your dinner. You do not want any of them to act unusual in any way."

"Ahmed must not know anything either. Later, they will try to get the truth out of him; they have ways. If they find out he did not know anything they will leave him alone. Their ways will tell them that as well."

"But Effendi, Ahmed set up this meeting tonight, he knows you and I are meeting."

"Indonesians compartmentalize what they hear. He does not know what we are meeting about. They are able to keep certain thoughts from mingling with other thoughts. If you do not tell Ahmed the purpose of our meeting, he will not know."

"Thank you, Effendi, I will do as you say. And thank you for dinner."

It is considered bad form for the invited guest to offer to pay or split the dinner bill.

* * *

Marapani left the meeting with the director of operations resigned to his fate. He sank lower into despair, flailing himself for even presuming he could one day take over as manager of dredges.

I am a nothing. Amulya is married to a nothing...and I am calling her bad names and thinking bad thoughts...when I am nothing?

Chapter 17

She has every right to leave me. She made a mistake marrying me and it is my fault. I am nothing, why would she marry a nothing...I am the one who forced her to marry me, because of the baby. And we were punished. Now she is free. She is not permitted to come to Nais, she should leave Bangka, go to Jakarta, forget about the mistake she made marrying a nothing.

Marapani drove the van back to Sungailiat and quietly picked up the few things he kept at the dredge operations office. Fortunately no one else was there. They would know he had been demoted, was being sent to the most remote workshop in the company...as punishment.

"Which I deserve."

He got on his motorbike. He felt nauseous, the pains returned to his arms.

I do not feel well because I am dreading going home...no matter. He didn't care how he felt; he didn't care about anything.

"I am a nothing."

A passing woman on her bicycle noticed the light bounce off the rear reflector of the tipped over motorbike and stopped. She saw Marapani. She could not tell immediately if he was hurt, the way he was lying there, but when she got closer she realized he was dead. The accident did not look serious enough to kill him, there was no blood; he was thrown from the bike and landed in a soft sandy mound just behind the roadside bushes. But she was a practical woman who said to the dead man,

"I do not know about these things. I will stop at the next phone and call the police."

Amulya was at the I-Tin office when the police came to her and told her Marapani had a heart attack on his motorbike and was dead. The first thoughts through her mind were poor Marapani, he was always so good to me. He was a strong man, he was never sick. He was a young man; heart attacks are for old men. The gods punished him and now they will punish me.

Troy, of course, witnessed the exchange with the police, which only took a few minutes, and walked to her desk. He intended to console her but she whispered,

"Please, I want to be alone."

Marapani was delivered to their home. His body was ritually washed by select male relatives and wrapped in a white shroud. He was placed on the floor with his head facing the Muslim holy city of Mecca. The imam led the salat for the dead, the usual Muslim daily prayers with some special additions that relate to death.

Archie felt a visit was not only his duty but also a sign of respect for someone so closely tied to the project. Ahmed drove Curtis and him to the house. Marapani's body would not be buried until early the next morning, well within the custom of burying the deceased within twenty-four hours. When they arrived at the house, they removed their shoes and Archie immediately noticed the small arrow painted on the ceiling in the corner. The arrow pointed towards the holy city of Mecca and was on the ceiling in almost every room in the Muslim portions of Indonesia. Its purpose was to orient the faithful for daily prayers.

All the furniture was removed from the main room and replaced by a dozen hard back chairs against the four walls. Marapani's relatives took turns sitting in the room the entire time he was lying on the floor. There was a small oriental rug next to him where you could kneel down and say a prayer in the Muslim tradition. Archie did not kneel down, he stood for a moment over Marapani and said his own short prayer. He and Curtis then went around the room and offered condolences in turn to each of Marapani's relatives.

That afternoon, while his body was still lying in her house, Amulya came to the conclusion that Marapani's death was the result of foul play. CCG was responsible. They were getting even for the death of one of their people on Marapani's dredge. The police were in on the plot because there was no autopsy, yet they assured her he had a heart attack…he was poisoned. She was utterly convinced and decided to get away from Bangka as quickly as possible. She made up her mind in that few minutes to vacate their house, move to Jakarta and start a new life. She never gave a thought about Troy.

Curtis and Archie walked out of the house and were already in the van when Troy appeared. He had walked from the I-Tin offices, deciding the last minute to pay his respects. He

Chapter 17

mostly wanted to get a glimpse of Amulya, he thought about her constantly.

"Troy, I am glad you are here, Curtis and I looked for you before we left but did not find you, we can wait while you go in and pay your respects," Archie said to him as he walked past the van.

"Go on ahead," Troy answered, "it is not too hot today and the walk feels good. I will return shortly."

The van took off.

Troy noticed Effendi walking up to him from where he had been standing by himself in the shade. There were no English-speaking people in earshot and Effendi asked Troy if he could speak with him for a minute.

"Certainly, Effendi, what can I do for you?" They walked back to the shade and sat on a small rounded bench that circled the tree trunk.

"Troy, it is what I can do for you that matters right now. I have been waiting for an opportunity to tell you what you must hear. I hear everything. People come up to me and say, 'Effendi, the gods have entrusted you with a gift, you are a wise man and wise men have a duty to know everything that is going on' and then they tell me about themselves and about others.

"This is how I know what you and Amulya are doing in secret. This is how I know that you are not the only one. Amulya goes to Jakarta for her enjoyment. She is a good woman but she has a sickness that no man can satisfy.

"That is why she goes to Jakarta. I am telling you this for your own good. She wants to go to Australia and she will use you to get there, but you will not be happy. Her sickness cannot be cured and will follow her wherever she goes. You should return to Fiona. Fiona loves you and will be good for you. Amulya will only cause you pain."

Troy stared at Effendi, didn't say a word or move a muscle. He blinked twice, rapidly, as if to return to reality, got off the bench, took two steps backward, paused, turned and walked his normal pace back to his office.

18

Troy was relieved that no one asked him about his visit to the wake. A noticeable heaviness had again fallen over the CCG offices with Marapani's heart attack. No one was expected to die during the consulting project yet here were two deaths, seemingly connected, not by human bonds but by the supernatural.

Troy was distressed by Effendi's earlier remark, so he decided to leave work early and walk to the Wisma Jaya. He had not given any thought to what he would say if he ran into anyone and they asked him about the wake...he never gave a thought to how he would answer. He was unprepared.

He least expected to see Fiona, but he should not have been. He was just as likely to see her as anyone else...other than Effendi. Troy moved out of the room they were sharing within a few days of her arrival on Bangka, so she was now in her own room. No one gave it a second thought and, if in fact they had, they would conclude that Effendi preferred they have separate rooms—maybe even sealing it with a deal on the cost. In any case, she was still staying at the Wisma Jaya.

A sixth sense told him that Effendi would not be there, would still be at Marapani's house, out in the front yard, greeting some and consoling others. Effendi was like the village shepherd—everyone was in his flock.

Why is it that I believe Effendi? Troy returned a second time to processing what Effendi had told him. He already convinced himself the first time that Effendi had no reason to tell him anything about Amulya unless it was true; unless it was for his own good. Troy, although he was smart, he wasn't very deep, so he surprised himself when he murmured, "I love her. I must be crazy, but I love her."

Fiona had been sitting on the lounge chair in the garden, near Effendi's birds. Most evenings she made sure she was in her room by the time Troy usually returned from work. Since he left work early today she was sitting where he had to pass by her. There was no way out of seeing each other, Troy would enter the garden and the lounge chair was positioned on the left side just behind the thick bushes.

The Bangka Inquiry

"Oh, Fiona, I didn't expect to see anyone sitting here."

"Good evening, Troy. How are you?" It is telling how uninterested someone is in the actual answer to that question by the ease with which it follows "hello." Fiona cared about Troy immensely—she really was blind to his foibles—regardless of how *he* felt about her. Having discussed life with her *girl-friend*, she was convinced Troy's behavior was the result of navigating a storm that was whipped up by a crisis, a storm driven by the trauma of being asked to suppress its true nature.

She also believed, once the storm was over, calm and sunny would return; they'd get married, have three kids and live happily ever after.

"Do you want to have dinner?" Fiona blurted it out and quickly realized she had no idea where that came from. Actually, she immediately admonished herself for putting him in a position to say no. She was surprised to hear,

"Sounds good, fifteen minutes? Do you want to walk to that joint down the street?"

Now it was his turn to admonish himself for having answered affirmatively. Fiona got up from the lounge chair with the help of Troy's outstretched hand.

"Sure."

They looked deeply at each other for a second and walked in silence to their rooms.

The turn of events could not have been more timely. Armed with information from Catherine, Fiona believed she could reconcile her's and Troy's relationship. She certainly had no intention of telling Troy what she and Catherine discussed. However, now that she knew about the accident and how it must be what is disturbing him, she believed she could salvage their relationship and go ahead with the wedding plans.

The joint down the street was an enigma. It was a restaurant run by a middle aged man and his wife and had obviously been there a very long time; you could just tell. Yet there were never any patrons. How could they stay in business without patrons, or did

Chapter 18

the patrons suddenly stop patronizing the place once the foreigners came?

Regardless. For a long time the foreigners did not patronize it either so in either case they had no customers. The food was Indonesian and the owners had their own idea of what you wanted to eat and how you wanted it prepared. To put it another way, the menu was limited...to the extreme, and not very appetizing.

Joe was the one to change mom and pop's fortunes. One afternoon he visited and took patience to give them the recipe for Minister's Soup. Mom and pop were fairly grumpy so it took a "Joe" to get through to them.

The Parai, several weeks earlier, had hosted a convention for one of the government ministers and his entourage. It had nothing to do with CCG and their work other than it took place during dinnertime on "their" pavilion. No problem. Wironto, the Parai manager, merely invited Joe and his friends to the convention.

An item on the buffet was a bowl of one of the most delicious soups the party-crashers had tasted since arriving on the island. Later, Joe asked Wironto what kind of soup it was and quick witted Wiranto, without so much as a *by your leave*, answered "Minister's Soup."

Another communication game was invented, one of the many Joe and the Parai staff engaged in; the kind of games that develop when two parties do not fully speak the same language and use signs and facial gestures to communicate. So far the score was nothing to nothing. Wironto and the staff would not divulge the ingredients and Joe and his buddies could not guess.

At the Mom and Pop, which is the name they gave the restaurant in place of its un-pronounceable one, Joe coached the owners through a few iterations of the ingredients he thought he tasted in Minister's Soup. Together they got it right. If it wasn't exactly the same, none of the consultants could pick out the difference. Business improved immensely—but not with the locals.

The walk to the Mom and Pop was relatively silent. Troy was not a conversationalist with Fiona to begin with and the strain was obvious. After they sat down, they both ordered a beer and the day's special...Minister's Soup. Fiona got right to it.

"Troy, how could I have been so blind to not see what you are going through. Why didn't you tell me what really happened at Joe's accident? I would have understood, really, I would and this bitterness would never have happened. You know I love you and you love me. Can't we make up?"

"I don't know what you are talking about, Fiona. What do you mean, *really happened*? I told you what happened, it was an accident, pure and simple."

"Troy, I know. I understand everything. I will not tell anyone. I am only bringing it up because it has torn us apart."

"Fiona, I am afraid I have no idea what you are talking about. Has someone been feeding you bullshit? I know you don't like Curtis, a lot of people don't. In case you don't know, there are people on this island that don't want to see him make full partner. They'll go to any lengths to destroy his name. Furthermore, Fiona, I happen to like Curtis. He has been good to me and will continue to be good to me, so let's get off the subject, okay?"

"No one is trying to destroy Curtis' name. I know what happened and you do too. Curtis ordered Marapani away then ordered the crew to begin working on the buckets. The accident didn't have to happen."

The look she got from Troy affirmed what she just said and Troy knew he just affirmed it. He reverted to the normal male behavior in situations like this and got angry.

"Fiona, I just told you, it was an accident, no one was to blame, no one caused it; it was an accident, a terrible accident...but an accident."

Fiona would not give up.

"Let's leave Bangka right away, tomorrow. We can get married in Perth. I don't care about Bali. I've already worked it out. There aren't that many people coming anyway so we can call them from Perth."

Troy was no longer listening. He began to feel nervous that this situation was going to get out of hand.

Chapter 18

I could be looking at legal shit. I want no part of it. I might be covering up a crime and now Fiona knows. How many more people are going to box me in? How did she find out? Evidently Archie told her, but why, what did Archie hope to gain by telling her?

He tried to neutralize the affirmation he gave her.

"Let's change the subject." He said softly, trying very hard to control his anger and to diffuse the importance of what she just indicated she knew. "You tell me what you did today and I'll tell you what I did. You go first." Troy tried to inject some levity into the situation.

"Troy, it won't go away. Joe's wife Catherine arrived yesterday and is staying at the Parai. I drove out there, you know, two women with no one to talk to. She is a very nice woman, but sad. Naturally I asked her why she was visiting and she said she is here to find out about her husband's accident, what really happened, that is all she said. We did not discuss it any further. I just put two and two together with your sudden moodiness and I pieced together what happened. I know I am right, I understand what you are going through, please, I know I can help."

"Fiona, right about what? If she told you anything she made it up, or someone told her a bunch of lies. Nothing happened, nothing. Let's go." Troy got up, paid the bill and they left. Nothing more was said.

Fiona's undertaking would not have worked in the best of situations. Troy was not stupid, he quickly figured out that Archie must have told Catherine who told Fiona the facts about the accident.

Fiona could not have guessed, he concluded.

Fiona never had a hint that she compromised hers and Catherine's secrecy pact. Troy was also savvy enough to know this was a potential problem he could not unravel without Curtis' approval...and directive. Troy wouldn't think of acting on this stage unless the lines were scripted by Curtis.

He knew what was in store, Curtis would blame him for Fiona finding out.

But not if I tell him first, then he'll know she didn't hear anything from me.

Troy knocked on Curtis' door. He was in. He opened the door and said,

"Hello Troy, what's going on?"

"I need to talk to you for a minute, can I come in?"

"Sure. What's on your mind?"

"I think Archie knows what happened on the dredge, probably from Marapani and he told Joe's wife Catherine who is staying at the Parai."

"Whoa. Slow down. Joe's wife is here? When did she arrive?"

"Yesterday, Fiona ran into her out there, they had lunch together. Fiona knows about Marapani and the crew. The only way she could know that is if Joe's wife told her. And the only way Joe's wife would know is if Archie told her."

It was at this moment that Curtis decided.

This guy is going back to Perth.

"Thanks for telling me Troy, not to worry, I'll take care of it. Just go about your normal business and don't give it another thought." It was the signal for Troy to leave and he read it correctly.

"OK, I just thought I better let you know."

"Thanks, I'll see you in the morning, good night."

Curtis closed the door but worry slowly began creeping into his mind.

If Catherine is here, found out I had something to do with her husband's death—even though it was an accident, pure and simple, someone caused that cable to be stretched too tightly, I'll have to find out who it was—there is a chance she might make trouble. Americans sue for the most trivial reasons; when they stub their toe for Christ's sake, think nothing of it for every minor accident.

He was slowly working himself into a lather.

She just wants money, she will probably just sue the firm, they will settle for enough to make her happy and things will return to normal, and that will be the end of it. Meanwhile, Troy I have to watch. He's intelligent but not street smart; he's also a push-over with women and Fiona is a goody-two-shoes. Yeah, that Fiona can figure things out real quick. Troy, he can be made

Chapter 18

to say anything within reason. Yes sir, it's back to Perth for him, but with the promise of a promotion right away as long as he keeps things in perspective.

19

Heeding Effendi's suggestion, Archie and the Parai contingent left work at their normal time and headed towards Sungailiat. Everyone in the van, Archie, the two Americans along with Richie, the Aussie, was more jovial as they headed off.

They were dealt a double-dose of crap, Joe and now Marapani's heart attack. Fortunately the passing of time tends to put things back into perspective. They were looking forward to their world returning to normal and were happy that it was beginning to show positive signs.

After about a mile, Archie said, "I'm hungry and don't feel like eating at the Parai, who wants to go to the Watergarden—it is on me."

Richie, the smart-alec of the bunch said, "why ask, we bloody always have to go wherever *you* want."

Archie responded with a pretend hurt, "wait just a moment, it's only a suggestion, you guys decide. What always happens is I ask what you want to do, give you the opportunity to suggest something, what do you do, you come up with the lame 'you decide' or, 'you always do what you want to do, anyway.'" Archie feigned a whine. "The problem is none of you wimps can make a decision so you defer to me. So, here we go again, what's it going to be?"

Richie was up to the challenge, "ok, the Parai is bonkers."

"Really," answered Archie, and without waiting for another response said, "Ahmed, turn around, we are going to the Watergarden."

They all chuckled. It was a typical tête-à-tête. It didn't make any difference whatsoever to them—but it was crucial to Archie, he wanted to make sure there were no hints of anything being askew. They were hungry and thirsty and ready to relax after a long week. When people go through intense situations together, they develop their own rules of engagement. That is where the Parai group was at; poised to lighten up and it served as a way to hide the real reason why they were not taking the road to Sungailiat.

When they arrived at the Watergarden, Deirdre was there with Hans Glos. Archie ordered some food to be taken out to Ahmed and walked over to say hello to his two friends.

"Fancy meeting both of you here, people are beginning to talk about the secret romance between you two. Hello Deirdre, hello Hans." Hans got up to shake Archie's hand; Deirdre remained seated and said,

"Hello to you too, give an old girl a kiss. Hans here smells like shrimp so I won't let him kiss me and at my age I need all the kissing I can get." Hans chuckled; all three of them knew Hans did not smell like shrimp, he was persnickety about his personal hygiene, unlike many of the German tourists that visited the Parai.

"What's going on?" Deirdre continued but Hans answered with another question.

"Russ, that consultant they hired to watch you consultants, is he still bothering you or have you sent him off on wild goose chases?"

"Russ is doing a splendid job. He takes attendance, reads all the reports before he delivers them to I-Tin and makes sure there is always fresh coffee and tea in the office. He is a very busy guy. Do you run into him very often?"

"No, I don't, but I was just telling Deirdre here that I am hearing snippets from my workers, seems there are some agitators around who don't like you, Archie. If I ask my men what they are talking about they become mum but I'd watch my rear if I were you."

"Yes, Archie," Deirdre chimed in, "I was with some of the I-Tin wives the other day and they too brought up rumors there may be trouble brewing. Again, they didn't have anything specific, at least that they were willing to share with me."

"Not to worry," Archie said, "I've heard talk as well. It happens occasionally in our line of work, usually nothing dramatic, someone always thinks they are getting the short end of the stick when consultants do their job. But thanks for the warning.

"I'd better get back to the boys, they are thirsty from all that road dust and won't start drinking in earnest without me.

Chapter 19

Looks like we may be in for a long night so we better get started early. Fortunately things are beginning to return to normal. And it's Friday, the beginning of another weekend, what more excuse do we need to get a little hammered? Deirdre, make sure this guy gets you home early, I don't want people talking."

Good, Archie thought, they won't suspect that I had advanced warning either.

* * *

After Troy left Curtis' room, having told him the news about Catherine and Fiona, Curtis called Greg who was still at the office. He was having dinner later that evening with Subroto in the president's compound and the plan was for one of Subroto's drivers to take him back to Sungailiat afterwards. It was to be a more-work meeting of sorts.

"To talk about some additional projects," Greg had announced earlier to Curtis and Archie. "There is no need for you to come, I'll fill you in. Could be big; could be just talk. I'll let you know."

Greg answered his phone.

"Greg, Curtis here, how are you?"

"I'm good, Curtis, I'm headed over to Subroto's in a few minutes, what's up?"

"You know Joe's wife Catherine is here?"

"Yes, I know."

"According to Troy she is here to inquire about the accident. From what Troy tells me, it would appear Archie told her all the details and she told Fiona. I suppose if she just returns to the States that will be the end of it, but I thought you wanted to know. You may want to remind Archie of the potential problems with the locals if some cock-and-bull story other than just an accident gets out."

"Thanks for the info. I'll speak to him."

"Okay, give my regards to Mr. Subroto."

Greg hung up the phone and said to himself,

Give your regards to Subroto, what makes you think he wants your regards. He thinks you are a pompous ass for embarrassing him in front of the minister.

With that Greg cleared his desk and walked down the street to the president's compound.

On the other end of the phone, Curtis felt elated.

What is Archie doing to himself? Doesn't he realize he is toying with one of the firm's largest clients? Is he crazy or something? Talk about sending your career down the poop-shoot; not my problem, it just makes it easier for me to get the Asia directorship, and for that I'd have to be a worldwide partner. Keep up the good work, Archie my lad!

Greg was shown into the great room of Subroto's house. There were two other guests, both of whom Greg had never met. I-Tin did not skimp on the amenities provided to their executives. The low table was set with fruit drinks and enough hors d'oeuvres for a dozen people, and good too.

"Greg, I will not waste time with formalities. These two gentlemen, like me, are owners of land where tin is mined. If any of our miners feel their livelihood is threatened they will cause trouble and that is not good for you or us. If they do cause trouble and are found out they will be jailed, then there will be investigations. None of us want investigations. We are trying to find the instigator of the trouble and more details about what they are planning but so far we have not been able. You must be careful, we don't want anything to happen, do we?"

"I appreciate your telling me. We are no longer looking into the land mine operations, what else can we do to get the word out that nothing will happen to them?"

"That is not as easy as you may think. They do not always believe what *we* tell them. They only believe in the money they get—how much they get right now—and they compare that to what could happen with the consultants looking too closely into their business. Nevertheless, we will see what we can do. Let's have dinner and discuss the next lucrative project for Greg and company."

During dinner, Greg only half participated in the small talk between himself and the three of them. He responded when

Chapter 19

he had to but evidently whatever he said didn't add or detract from the conversation. Like in most business meetings, the exchange that takes place during the meal is only fodder for the real discussions before and after. He was deep in thought.

This accident is becoming way too visible. It should not be taking center stage and becoming the catalyst for making dramatic changes in what we were contracted to do. I think Subroto and the others only recently realized their golden gooses are in jeopardy and are looking for something, anything to excite the natives. I wouldn't be surprised if they weren't orchestrating the stirring up of the agitators.

Greg decided what to do. He confirmed it in his mind while the others reverted to Indonesian for a joke or something.

My dear friend Archie, he concluded to himself, is becoming a liability. This stuff was beginning to die down now Archie's resurrected it again. He told Joe's wife, she told Troy's girlfriend, fiancé, whatever she is, and Curtis is nervous again. No wonder the natives are getting restless, we are our own worst enemies. Archie has got to go...quickly.

Since Troy had gone to dinner earlier with Fiona and wasn't part of the Parai contingent, Curtis, after hanging up the phone from talking with Greg, found him in his room when he knocked on the door.

"Got a minute?"

"Sure, come on in. I just opened some wine...it isn't plonk. Fiona brought it with her from back home, would you like a glass?"

"Sounds good."

Troy poured a glass just below the rim for Curtis and a half for himself—all the while thinking, Curtis coming to my room, this could be good news...or...this could be bad news.

He wants me to work tonight. Nope, he would have refused the wine. The sparrow-fart doesn't drink when he's got an important film shoot. Then it's got to be bad news, he wants to pester me about Catherine...wants to know what she said, what Fiona said. Worse, he's found out about me and

Amulya...probably from Suradi, more likely that ding-a-ling Effendi.

Probably wants to go over the "story" again, he's bonkers about it. It was an accident, for bloody sake, he stuck his nose where it didn't belong, caused an accident.

Well, let's get on with it, I don't feel like amusing you all night.

"So, what's happening," Troy asked as he handed the wine to Curtis.

"I just got off the phone with Greg, he's on his way to see Subroto...about more work. This might be our lucky day, you and me. Archie's being stubborn about this accident thing, I'm sure he wants to make it a monumental case, help Catherine sue the firm for big bucks."

"What makes you say that?" Troy asked.

"I just have a feeling. What did you get from Fiona, did she say anything about why Catherine wanted to know things."

"No, nothing specific," Troy lied, "said Catherine just wanted to find out what happened...but she knows what happened, Fiona knows what happened, she was upset about it, probably Catherine is too."

"I have a question," Curtis said, "am I getting the feeling you and Fiona are going through some difficult times? Not unusual just before the final commitment.

"Unless of course there is something more troublesome. I am not prying but if you need someone to talk to, I'm married, been there, done that." Curtis managed a little cluck, cluck sound.

"No, we're dinky-di, just some details to work out. But I am worried about this accident. I do not want to be caught in the middle of one side saying one thing and another side saying something else. I have a career to think about and do not want it dashed."

"I am glad you brought that up," Curtis butt in, "I am pretty sure I am going to take over managing this project. This conversation stays between you and me, but it looks pretty good. If that happens, you get promoted to Australian partner within a few months, I promise.

Chapter 19

"I see you more or less locating permanently in Jakarta; you would be the Jakarta office manager. Old man Chu is getting ready to retire, he'll be gone soon and Jakarta is going to be merged with the Perth office. I get the feeling there will be a lot more work. Greg is talking to Subroto right now about that very thing. The Americans will not stay in Indonesia indefinitely. They've done a good job of filling in where we needed it, but it is too far for them to travel."

Curtis could not read Troy's reaction. He thought he'd show at least a little excitement; his career solidly on the right track, but there was nothing. Curtis put it down to a manifestation of wedding worries.

Troy on the other hand was elated and was trying hard to suppress showing it. Amulya was always on his mind, now more than ever. He decided to reject what Effendi told him. They were truly in love and she would be faithful; clearly she was ready to settle down now that she found him.

I am different from the others, she is ready to settle down, he told himself.

True, she wanted to move away from Bangka, he only had to convince her to wait a short while, a few months on the outside, and he would be stationed in Jakarta. They could find a nice house with gardeners, cooks, maids, and he'd have enough money so she could shop to her heart's content.

He couldn't wait until Curtis left. He was planning on walking over to Amulya's in any case, under the guise of paying his respects seeing as how Marapani was still lying on the floor. The thought of a quickie entered his mind as well.

Curtis dashed all that with his next volley.

"What are you and Fiona doing tonight, I thought we'd go to the Watergarden Restauran, if you haven't eaten we can grab something and then have a few drinks to celebrate the promotion I guarantee is coming real soon. If she is not up to it you and I will go."

"Let me check with Fiona." Troy realized there was no way he could refuse Curtis right after essentially getting his promise of the promotion he was looking forward to. Besides, he saw no good coming from Curtis and Fiona at the same table.

"Actually, she and I just had some soup...over at Mom and Pop's. She said she was rather tired and wanted to get to sleep early, so my guess is she won't want to go. I won't bother her... how about just you and I going. I'll have a beer while you have dinner. I want to hear more about what you said about Greg and more work in Indonesia."

"Give me five minutes," Curtis answered, "we'll meet in the lobby."

20

Archie and the boys were still at the Watergarden Restauran when Curtis and Troy arrived. The timing could not have been worse. Both Archie and Curtis looked at each other, surprised more than anything, which quickly degraded to:

"I was having a great time forgetting for a moment what an asshole you are and now you show up to spoil it"—that from Archie's side.

"This guy has just ruined his career and he doesn't realize it...it couldn't happen to a nicer guy"—that from Curtis' side.

They both quickly thought of a way to avoid any conversation between them but just as quickly realized that that would have spoken volumes to the other patrons, some of whom were I-Tin people, not to mention the staff still sitting there. It wouldn't work, they would have to at least say hello. Archie first...

"Hi Curtis, Troy. We were just getting ready to leave, but if you want to pull up a couple of chairs we'll have one more for the road together."

"Sure, sounds good," answered Curtis.

Everyone said their hellos, ordered a round, chit-chatted and after a few minutes of small talk, Kevin and Ritchie, both of whom had too many beers and who constantly ribbed each other on the merits of Kevin's America versus Ritchie's Australia, said they had enough to drink and were going to stagger outside and duke it out for their respective countries.

Tim and his fiancé had been engaged a little over a year and Tim wanted to hear more about Bali from Troy. "Got a minute? I've got some questions about Bali, we are thinking of going there on our honeymoon?"

Troy would rather not discuss his wedding plans, afraid he'd let on that he and Fiona were in the process of splitting up...and even more afraid he'd let drop that he and Amulya were seeing each other and were making plans to move to Jakarta as soon as Curtis took over from Archie and gave Troy his promotion. But he had no choice. They excused themselves from Archie and Curtis, who were now the only two left at the table, and walked over to stand at the makeshift bar together.

Archie, trying hard to control his contempt for this creature sitting across from him said,

"Was it something I said or do we have B.O. or something...they all left."

Curtis, trying hard to contain his elation over what he thought would be Archie's impending dismissal, chuckled,

"Probably both."

He intended to add some levity before continuing. "Actually, it is a good opportunity for me to bring up a matter I wish I didn't have to discuss with you. Even though I am not yet a worldwide partner, I am still a partner, so I outrank you, but I've never interfered with how you are directing this project. We are in Asia you know, and my office calls the shots in Asia; you are merely a visitor...but you are playing with trouble, insisting on spreading rumors about how I caused Joe Prendergast's death."

"First of all, Curtis, you may be a partner and I am not, but it was clearly determined that I am the project manager, and you are not...so we can quickly clear this up by talking to whomever you think has the authority to clarify that decision. Second, Curtis," and Archie realized he was quickly losing self-control and was powerless to prevent it,

"No rumors are being spread, at least not by me. If there are rumors perhaps you may want to rethink *your* story, perhaps *your* story is the rumor and what actually happened is the fact."

"Just what are you getting at, *my* story?" Curtis recognized that he also was losing it, "someone stretched a cable too tightly or it was rusted and should have been replaced, or it was just a freak accident that it broke. That is the fact and I had no control over that cable. There was no way in hell I could possibly know the cable would break. Period, end of story."

"You are forgetting one little piece." Out of the corner of his eye—you know how that happens, you realize something is going on in your surroundings but it is processed too deeply inside your brain. Whatever is happening in the forefront takes precedence and obscures what is occurring at the periphery. This happened to Archie. Deep inside his brain he saw people at several other tables glancing their way, drawn by the gradual increase in his and Curtis's voice.

Chapter 20

They know we can't stand each other, it shows.

Archie processed the thought but it was too deep in his brain for him to do anything about, so he continued, his voice getting louder.

"You are forgetting one little piece," he repeated, "you told Marapani, no, you *ordered* Marapani to the bridge. Then you *ordered* his crew to work on the bucket."

That same deep part of his brain realized his eyes were narrowing, a symbol of impending anger welling up...but he was just as powerless to bring this cognizance forward.

"I looked again at the original film. In case you conveniently forgot, Curtis, it explicitly states that no work on jammed buckets shall take place unless the captain is present because it is an extremely dangerous undertaking. Furthermore, Curtis, the film states that under no circumstances should anyone be behind the bucket fence while the dredge is moving. Recall, Curtis, our discussion about the film and how putting things in three's helps the Indonesians to remember? Recall, Curtis, the three words: Authority, Instruction, Dismissal? In case you conveniently forgot, the film said, 'the captain has complete *Authority* and not following his *Instruction* is cause for immediate *Dismissal*' or is that a rumor also?" As soon as the words were out of his mouth, Archie realized how stupid *that* last comment was.

"You are interpreting the facts to suit your own idea of what happened. Jefferson, McMillan, Greg and Subroto have each said it was an accident. Let it rest, Archie, continuing to tell people your interpretation will only get you into trouble. You are on thin ice to begin with. I know what you told Catherine. The firm is not going to sit by and let people like you, people who should know better, put them at risk with hysterical wives of people who have had an accident and they think they can get rich by proving that it was intentional...or preventable.

"But then again, you won't be here much longer so we don't have to worry, do we, Archie?" As soon as the words were out of *his* mouth, Curtis realized how stupid *that* last comment was.

The Bangka Inquiry

At the same time, both of them became aware of the volume of their voices and the glances people at other tables were giving them. They did not know which, if any of them spoke English and hoped their volume, although loud, was not loud enough to enable any of them to understand exactly what they were arguing about. They had been nose to nose, and that helped, but still they were not sure.

A few of the people in the restaurant, if they were not able to figure out exactly what was being said, certainly recognized that Archie and Curtis were arguing about the project. People I guess are inherently gossips. Often it is not done intentionally but seems to be a natural supplement when a conversation takes place about the particular event. Such was the case here. Unbeknown to Archie and Curtis, the I-Tin sales vice president who was visiting Bangka from his headquarters in London, was seated at a table behind them and witnessed the altercation.

The next morning during a meeting with Subroto the VP innocently asked if there was any problem with the project that he should be aware of. Subroto answered no, and naturally asked why.

"Why do you ask, what would make you think there is anything wrong?" Subroto was on guard, no one knew of his ownership of tin-producing property except the several others who also owned property.

"Last evening, at the Watergarden Restauran two project men from CCG were arguing...quite loudly, I might add. Everyone in the restaurant noticed. I was not able to overhear precisely what they were talking about but I did hear the words 'accident' and 'Marapani' and I have heard about the accident aboard Marapani's dredge."

"Yes, there was an accident, and I am not aware of any details that you would not have heard about. I do not know why they were arguing, perhaps something internal. I have heard of friction between two of them and up until now it was never in public. We do not want that sort of behavior, I will talk to the person in charge and advise him that behavior like that will not be tolerated."

Chapter 20

"I would not have brought it up except that everyone in the restaurant saw what was going on; it is not the Indonesian way. Thank you for taking care of it," responded the VP.

That same afternoon Archie was still provoked from his encounter with Curtis; he was embarrassed that he lost his composure over someone who, in his mind, was not worth it. It affected him so greatly he could not concentrate on the monthly meeting coming up in one-half hour with the I-Tin senior management.

The meeting would take place in the I-Tin conference room, which was a holdover from when the Dutch controlled almost everything in Indonesia through the Dutch East India Company. The VOC, as it was known (*Verenigde Oostindische Compagnie*), colonized Indonesia and were not very nice about it. Their primary aim was maintaining their monopoly of the spice trade. VOC did this through the use and threatened use of violence against the peoples of the spice-producing islands, and against non-Dutch outsiders who attempted to trade with them.

For example, when the people of the Banda Islands, on the Eastern tip of Java, continued to sell nutmeg to English merchants, the Dutch killed or deported virtually the entire population and repopulated the islands with VOC indentured servants and slaves who worked in the nutmeg groves. The Dutch were not nice people.

The conference room was large, the focus being the egg-shaped table in the center of the room, which could seat thirty-one people, fifteen on each side and one at the head. Modernity was introduced in the nineteen-fifties with a microphone positioned in front of each leather-backed chair in order that everyone could hear each other without shouting—the room was big and filled with echoes from the poor acoustics.

During a meeting the room smelled from a combination of clove cigarettes and pungent coffee. When one of the persons sitting at a microphone indicated he or she would like to say something, or if a question was directed at anyone, that person would first have to switch on their microphone and shut it off when they were finished talking.

This little procedure was enhanced with a slight but annoying crackle when a switch was either turned on or off. Not all microphones had the crackle but it happened enough times to present a challenge to stay focused when a meeting was long or not interesting.

Subroto, the I-Tin president, sat at the head of the table and Archie sat in his usual seat, fourth from Subroto's right side. Six managers were seated on Subroto's left side. The position of each person was determined by his rank in the company. Who determined the ranking system is unknown but the obviously important were sales to the right of Subroto and accounting to his left. The smelter operations manager sat just before Archie and to Archie's right, Budi, the official translator.

Budi probably didn't count on the importance scale but clearly they looked to him to make sure the translations were accurately understood on both sides. Russ Wortly was the last person on Subroto's left side and thus across from Archie. Archie eventually found out from Effendi that Russ was appointed by the minister of political, legal and security affairs to monitor the consultants. Yet, if distance from the head of the table mattered, he was the least important person in the room...although he managed to consume the most talking time with his prolix style that could quickly make you wish you were dead.

Today's meeting, like all the others, was an update on where Archie and his team stood based on the project schedule. The agenda entailed reporting on the number of man-days that had been spent to date on each of the forty-three detailed key events that comprised the scope of the engagement.

One of the key events for example, was to "determine the cost of repairing a certain dredge"; another was "to analyze the staffing level of one of the workshops." The project manager was always constrained by the number of man-days he could spend to complete the project because that is what determined the fees, the costs, and the profits for his firm.

In a typical project with a large number of key events the actual number of man-days allocated to each key event was,

Chapter 20

however, flexible, and the project manager could juggle how many were spent on each—some key events requiring less and others requiring more.

Not so with I-Tin. Perhaps because they had been burned in the past or because it was the only means they believed they had in which to monitor progress, regardless of what was presented in these status review meetings, it boiled down to actual vs. planned man-days for each key event.

This is where Russ came in. The Minister of Political, Legal And Security Affairs was savvy enough to also want to know if the percentage of man-days used for each key event matched Archie's estimate of the percentage of that key event that was satisfactorily completed.

The minister did not want to find out, for example, that after ninety percent of the allocated man-days were spent on a particular key event, that perhaps only sixty percent of it had been completed.

Of course, Archie's estimate was exactly that, a reasonable estimate, but still an estimate. Not good enough for Russ, however. He had to question each estimate because if he merely agreed with Archie, how could he justify his existence? Thus he could go on for fifteen minutes questioning Archie's rational for how he arrived at the estimate.

Archie realized that once he gave in and changed his estimate as a result of this diatribe, his entire credibility would be at risk. Therein lay Russ's verbosity.

This particular meeting was dicey because of Subroto's insistence—during his meeting in Jakarta with Greg—that the consultants merely do a cursory look at the land miners. Of course he could not communicate his insistence to his management team…and certainly not to Russ, so this put Archie into the position of having to justify using less man-days for the land mine key event and justifying using more elsewhere.

To complicate matters, Archie had to convince Russ and the I-Tin managers that there was no value in spending any more man-days looking any further into this issue. His rationale was that spending any more time would accomplish nothing because if a mine were to be shut down it would eventually reopen. Too much money was at stake.

He was proud of his ability to sway people's minds with his presentation skills. "It would be like trying to stop a river from reaching the sea; it would find a way even if it had to go underground," was how Archie put it.

Of course, he didn't believe what he was selling but he hoped the analogy would convince the others of what he was forced by his own lack of compunction to present.

Too much money at stake—refers to me. Too bad, but it's either my kids or your kids, went through Archie's mind as he was mouthing the words to the assembled group.

The I-Tin managers were convinced of the merits of this conclusion, as was Russ, because the total income to the country would not change.

Where Russ was going to pay for himself was to insist on a rebate from Archie's firm for the number of key event man-days they would not have to use. Archie, on the other hand, had to use the entire allocation if he wanted this project to be financially successful in his firm's eyes. The meeting went on and on.

21

When the meeting finally ended, with Archie and Russ no closer to agreeing on any one single thing, ever—just as in all previous update meetings—they walked out of the building; Russ first, Archie following a few steps behind, thinking,

I'm amazed at how, week after week, we dance around an issue for five minutes, neither of us budges, then we move on to the next one. Doesn't he get it?

Archie knew exactly why and how they were able to dance around and not agree. *He wanted it that way.* For Archie to agree with Russ just one time would give Russ a power over the project that would be disastrous. In order to justify his existence, he could second-guess everything: every move, every decision, every conclusion. The way Archie maintained control over him was by capitalizing on a bad habit Russ had of never looking directly at you while he was talking. Instead, while sitting at the conference table, whenever it was his turn at the microphone, he never looked up from his notes and didn't look directly at Archie, Subroto, or anyone else for that matter—a non-verbal message that he was not a hundred percent sure of himself.

Across the table, Archie capitalized on this weakness, making it clear he conveyed the opposite picture—that he was unquestionably correct and completely sure of his position on whatever issue they were discussing. He did this by staring at Russ all the while he was blithering. Obviously Russ, without an ounce of self-confidence, could feel the stare and it unnerved him.

Fortunately everyone got the picture, even if Russ didn't.

After spending excessive time "beating a dead horse," believing he had made it perfectly clear that he was performing a valuable service by, for example, grilling Archie on the fine points of an *estimate* of percent complete, he capitulated, ending by saying something to the effect:

"We can revisit this issue at the next meeting," or:

"I will monitor this carefully," or the best one:

"Let me go on record that I do not agree with Mr. Archie's estimate." He didn't realize that he hadn't convinced anyone of anything.

Incidentally, all the Indonesians, including Subroto, called Archie by the formal, Mr. Archie. Calling someone Mr. and using only the first name was not all that unusual. Many Indonesians, in fact, only have one name.

As Archie and Russ walked out of the building and were about to go down the couple of steps to the driveway, Russ abruptly stopped, turned around and asked Archie if he could speak with him for a moment...privately. They walked a short distance to a little gazebo that sat under a large tree in the gravel parking lot. It was a strange looking structure in that its little round shape didn't fit with the rest of the surroundings. It was constructed with a low wall of white bricks, had a red tile roof and a small fountain in the middle. Just looking at it had a cooling effect and the tree's branches provided welcomed shade. Perhaps that was why it was there. Being out in the sun for just a few minutes felt like your skin was burning.

"What's up?" Archie began.

"I wanted to finish the meeting before bringing up an unpleasant subject. Mr. Subroto asked me to pass along his concern about you and Curtis having an argument last evening at the Watergarden Restauran." Russ didn't look at Archie, obviously uncomfortable at having been directed by Subroto to be the messenger.

"It seems one of his friends, I am not at liberty to tell you who it is, was sitting at a table near you and witnessed your 'inappropriate' behavior."

Archie could feel his face getting red. He immediately got on the defensive. He began by thinking, who the hell are you to criticize my *inappropriate* behavior. Where do you get off, you mealy-mouthed lackey? Doesn't Subroto have the balls to tell me himself; he has to use an idiot like you? And furthermore, "*I am not at liberty to tell you,*" Archie mimicked to himself. What, does keeping your little stupid secrets to yourself turn you on, or is the only thing you can do? Besides you smell like piss, don't you ever take a bath...when are you going to wash your greasy hair? And polish your shoes once in a while, for Christ sake, you look and smell like crap.

Chapter 21

Because this made him feel a modicum better, a little superior, Archie realized he was losing his composure and immediately tried in vain to keep it in check.

"I hear you," was his only response, said with a pronounced scowl, and he got up and walked to the van that Ahmed had running to cool the inside.

"Take me back to the office," he barked. As he mouthed the words he realized that he was descending into the pits.

Ahmed of all people, why should I take out my frustration with myself on him?

Troy had not seen Amulya for a whole day and did not go to the burial, he was not invited; no one from the office was. He missed her immensely. Today, however, she was back at work. She informed Archie that she would only work for a few hours because she was upset due to the suddenness of Marapani's death. Although she never said anything to anyone, she was firmly convinced that he didn't have a heart attack at all; he was killed in retaliation for the American's death.

She was afraid for her own well being, figuring that whoever was involved in Marapani's death would be afraid she would expose the truth, how he really died—although she admitted to herself that she didn't know how it was done.

She had to get away from Bangka as soon as possible. Her excuse to Archie that she was upset, which was why she could only work for a few hours this morning, was a cover-up for the real reason; she needed to make arrangements to get to Jakarta without Suradi knowing or suspecting until the very last minute, in case he was implicated in Marapani's death. Or, more likely, she thought, so he couldn't sell the information.

Troy was happy to see her and during a minute alone asked if it was all right if he came over to her house that evening. Amulya had already decided that Troy was of no consequence to her future plans but realized that any answer other than "yes" could possibly create a scene that she could not afford. Especially with anyone looking for signs that she knew the real reason for her husband's death.

Now that Curtis brought up the apparent conflict between Troy and Fiona, the cat was out of the bag, so to speak so Troy had to be extra careful to not let anyone suspect that the reason was his love for Amulya. Therefore Troy waited until after everyone went to the Parai for dinner—he had excused himself saying that he wasn't hungry—and made his way to Amulya's house.

When she opened the door Troy did not notice that Amulya was in a housedress. She usually wore something sexy when Troy was expected but tonight it was anything but sexy; matronly would be a more appropriate description. Troy did not notice the dress but he did feel something was strange.

Amulya offered Troy his usual beer, poured herself a glass of wine and sat across from him. She began the conversation.

"I am very upset about Marapani. I believe he may have found out about you and me and that is what caused his heart attack, we were very much in love and he could not live without me."

Troy did a double take.

This is not like the Amulya I know, she told me many times that they got married for convenience and that she was in love with me. She must be going through a stage, that's it, remorse, or guilt or something, a normal part of grieving, especially since it was so sudden. She couldn't prepare for it. She'll get over it; I have to be her support, be understanding, was Troy's interpretation to himself.

"I understand, Amulya. I understand what you are saying even though I could never feel the pain you must be going through. But you know you can count on me, I will be here whenever you need me," Troy droned on.

"No, Troy, it is over. I cannot see you any more. I will mourn my dead husband. I will quit work and stay here in our house, where we lived together. I will spend every day missing him."

"Amulya, I understand. Please, understand me as well. I love you; I cannot live without you. You will get over this eventually, then we can resume our plans; move to Jakarta. I haven't told you this, but I am going to get the promotion and an

Chapter 21

assignment to Jakarta sooner than I expected. We will find a nice house; have servants, a driver to take you wherever you want to go, just like we planned. Change takes time, I understand."

"No Troy, you don't understand. I am not in love with you. I never was so if I gave you that impression, I am sorry. I do not want to see you anymore. Tonight must be the last time."

"Of course you are in love with me, how could you have said it so many times if you didn't mean it?" Troy was beginning to get angry; beginning to wonder what was happening, why was she acting this way.

Perhaps Effendi was right, he thought, perhaps she does have a sickness, a weakness for men. She doesn't want to settle down with only one man, she wants variety, Effendi was right.

Troy, as everyone knew, was a bright guy but not necessarily street savvy. However, he was starting to realize that the world is made up of many different kinds of people, some people with unusual needs. It was slowly beginning to seep in that Amulya is one of those people. The fact that *he* had unusual needs had not crossed his mind.

Well, Troy considered, if that is the case, why not make the best of it...forget about love. We both want the same thing, like the same things, that doesn't go away because she doesn't love me. Fiona might love me...but Fiona doesn't like the same things Amulya does. After a few seconds to process this, Troy said,

"Amulya, I do understand. I was mistaken about you loving me but you do not have to worry, I understand. We had a good time together, perhaps that doesn't have to end...we can still have a good time once in a while, let's remain friends." Troy got up, walked over to Amulya with his hand outstretched to shake hands on the deal.

Amulya stood up, they shook hands for a long enough time to get the juices flowing and did it right there on the floor.

A few hours after Russ delivered Subroto's message to Archie, Subroto convinced himself that Archie was a liability he could do without. He had an inkling that Archie was going to tell someone that he and the others were stealing from the company.

Well no, he thought, not stealing, I pay to have the tin removed from *my* land so it isn't really stealing. But that is not how others will look at it, will they? Officially all tin in Indonesia belongs to the government, not to individuals even if it is found on their land. That is why any one who mines tin on their own land is considered stealing it. I do not agree, it is not right, but what does *that* matter?

Yes, he continued thinking, Mr. Archie is a liability and we must get him out of Indonesia without his suspecting the reason. With that, Subroto called one of his English-speaking clerks in and told him,

"Go across the road to Mr. Greg's office and invite him to my office to discuss some ideas regarding a dinner out at the Parai for the VP from London." It was a ruse, sending the clerk with a verbal message, anyone overhearing it would not suspect anything unusual.

Greg was not very busy when the clerk arrived and, in fact, welcomed the diversion of walking a block to the I-Tin office. He was shown into Subroto's office immediately. The clerk took advantage of his mission and stayed awhile to gossip with his friends who were working at the CCG office.

"Thank you for walking over," Subroto looked at Greg's wide brimmed hat. It usually meant the person was going to be out in the sun longer than a few minutes. "Or did you have one of the drivers drive you, the heat is very intense today and you can get burned even though it is only a short distance."

"Yes, I walked. For some reason, even though my skin is light, I do not burn easily so I can walk short distances. Besides, the long-sleeved shirt and this wide-brimmed hat keep the direct sun off me. I have very little skin exposed. Thank you for asking."

Following the worldwide corporate way, there was a lot of small talk before getting to the meatier subject. The pleasantries over with, Subroto dove right in.

"I continue to have concerns about Mr. Archie. It is difficult for me to have this conversation with you because your staff is none of my business to get involved. You heard about the

Chapter 21

argument last evening between Mr. Archie and Mr. Curtis at the Watergarden Restauran?"

"No, I have not heard anything. What happened?" Greg answered. "Perhaps it was merely a personal argument and no one bothered to inform me. Am I correct, or do you believe there is a larger problem?"

"It is as I thought. None of the other consultants were present to witness the argument. That is why you have not heard anything. However, the I-Tin VP of Sales is here visiting us from his office in London, and he made a point of telling me that although he did not hear the complete argument, it seemed to him 'two project men from CCG' is how he put it, were of a different mind and the VP believed it concerned the accident, which he obviously had heard about." Subroto paused a second and continued.

"He asked me why the two project men would be arguing about the accident...I would feel more comfortable if the entire subject of the accident were put into the past. Now the private owners are going to hear more talk of accidents. They are fearful of Mr. Archie. They told me so. They are fearful this man is—how do you put it—on a hunt. He does not understand the trouble he will cause on this hunt. He is hunting very cunning people."

Subroto never referred to the activity as illegal tin mining, it was *private* tin mining.

"Perhaps one of the ministers involved in private tin mining will make it difficult for Mr. Archie to have his visa renewed. His visa is due to expire soon. He will be forced to leave the country and not allowed back in. Did you know that? Yes, I have been informed. That means someone is afraid of your Mr. Archie, to go to the trouble to find out when his visa expires. Don't you agree, Mr. Greg?"

"I will take care of it," Greg decided quickly, "I will re-assign him back to the United States. Thank you, Mr. Subroto, for letting me know all of this. You can count on me."

They resumed pleasantries, Subroto offering to host a buffet between the I-Tin managers and the consultants in honor of the visiting VP from London. It was arranged and Greg walked back to the office. It seems no one realized he had been gone.

22

Archie was standing in his favorite place outside the consultant's offices across and down the street from the I-Tin headquarters. He was drinking from a bottle of water and watched as Suradi got out of his company van and walked inside.

What made Suradi who he is?
Why did his wife marry him?
Who are his friends?
Why do they value his friendship?
Do they?

Of course they do, or they wouldn't be his friends. The real question then is how many does he have?

I don't think he saw me standing here Archie thought...has important business!

Suradi's VW microbus was white (all the others in the company were either olive green or beige) and had SECURITY written on both the driver and passenger side doors. The single word was printed in gold letters.

What a strange person, Archie continued thinking. He's tall for an Indonesian, not tall by American or Australian standards, but by Indonesian standards. Must have some Dutch in his blood...from way back.

He uses his height to intimidate people, that's it, I just figured that out. That "throw back your head with the smirky smile," that helps. He reminds me of a kid's plastic alligator. You wouldn't call a plastic alligator cuddly, or maybe not even cute. If you put it on your pillow along with the stuffed ones you had, it would be for security...yes sir, security. You'd sleep better knowing there was an alligator in your collection.

Archie was enjoying his little thoughts even though he wasn't completely aware what he was thinking about; wasn't aware he was thinking specifically about Suradi. He just felt content, drinking his water and enjoying the day. So he continued.

His wife, I've met her, don't remember her name, but I was surprised when I saw her. Nice looking, a little on the heavy side...traditionally built...I've read elsewhere someone described

The Bangka Inquiry

like that...well groomed, gold rim glasses, thicker than average lenses. A little matronly.

How did they meet, I wish I knew. I can't imagine Suradi saying "will you marry me?" Looking into her eyes with passion. Nope, can't imagine it. But he said something to that effect, maybe he just said "show up at the church on Sunday, and wear white." On second thought, probably not, he's Muslim.

He always wears a uniform. I've been in Indonesia eight months and the only other uniforms like that I've seen are on the security men at the Jakarta airport who carry Uzi machine guns across their chests. I wonder if Suradi ever told his wife that the Uzi was invented by Uziel Gal right after the 1948 Arab-Israeli war. No, probably not. He'd keep that secret from her, I know he would, but I wish I knew why he would.

Archie was beginning to really enjoy himself. Suradi was a study and, one should take a few minutes when he finds "a study" to think about him, see if there is a lesson there. After all, in the final analysis aren't people the most important thing? Archie took a another sip from his bottle of water.

I'd like to see where he lives, his house. I can picture it, clean and neat, somewhat minimalist, not loaded with any unnecessary stuff, but what is there is the best. Suradi cannot tolerate the ordinary. Like his VW, he takes pride in his *white* VW, the only one in Pangkalpinang; takes pride in his house...and his kids. How will they turn out? Wait till he finds out he can't control that!

Perhaps I should quit my job and just study people, that would be worthwhile, learn from them. But how would you apply it. As soon as you tried to reengineer someone you'd destroy him.

Suradi's spit and polish stands for here's who I am, and what I stand for, and what I value. I don't think he wants material things in order to bring him comfort; no, they give the right impression, just like his fake smile.

Oh, he's happy all right, people look up to him, (many are afraid of him). That is what is important to Suradi. Archie snapped back to reality, screwed the cap on his water bottle and walked back inside, content that he now understood Suradi better.

Chapter 22

Suradi had come to see Tim Snyder, the American staff person who was getting married the following year, and who, after talking to Troy, definitely decided he and his new bride would honeymoon in Bali. Tim's visa would expire in two days so he had to leave the country and return in order to go through passport control to get a fresh two-month stamp on his passport. Ever since the new desks and file cabinets debacle Suradi kept his distance from Archie. He would deal directly with Tim.

"Yes, Mr. Tim, I have made arrangements for you on Friday three o'clock flight to Jakarta and reservations I made at Le Meridien, you will be happy. I will meet you at the airport with your passport with the visa expired so you have to leave the country. I make these arrangements for all the consultants who are here helping us." Throw head back, smile...ain't I just cuddly?

Since there were thirty-five consultants, this was a frequent occurrence and Suradi was getting rich with all the commissions. Tim, like the others, took it all in stride. When everyone ran out of more fascinating things to talk about they discussed how Suradi was able to keep track of so many passports. Most thought he could not write. No one ever saw him do it and if he needed something written he would hand you a pencil and paper, smile, and assume you would just write it down for him.

When Tim saw Archie, he told him he'd be going to Singapore over the weekend (two nights, Friday and Saturday, Suradi got more commission from the Le Meridien that way) and did he want him to bring anything back. Archie, after having dissected Suradi just a short time earlier, brought up the subject how does he keep track?

"Perhaps his wife...or a secretary whom he secretly puts the make on?"

"No," answered Tim, "Suradi is not the type to put the make on anyone, there you are mistaken, Archie."

"Perhaps, but all the same, I sometimes worry; what if he screws up? I'd wager if I asked anyone what day their visa expired, maybe there would be one of us who would know; I don't know when mine expires. I should have assigned someone to keep a chart...too late now...the project is winding down. I guess we'll have to hope for the best. I wouldn't want to be on the way home and find out I overstayed my visa. Depressing notion"

* * *

Ahmed did not live far from where Archie and the others stayed at the Parai on beautiful Tenggiri Beach. He lived closer to Sungailiat. It usually took him ten minutes to get home. No matter what time it was he would have a cup of tea with his wife and they would discuss how their respective day went.

This night was average, about eight p.m. when Ahmed dropped Archie and the others off...they had stopped for carryout at one of the joints on the main highway. They needed variety even though the food was exactly the same—same menu for breakfast, lunch, dinner...regardless where you ate it. Except the Watergarden Restauran, their menu was a little more robust.

For Ahmed to get to his house he had to drive about a half mile off the main road, turn left and drive about five-hundred feet to his house. They were waiting for him at the intersection. They formed a line across the street, knowing Ahmed would slow, stop and ask what the problem was.

They dragged him out of the van, and beat and kicked him everywhere. Ahmed's wife heard the commotion and came over to see what the problem was. She gasped as one of the men held her around the waist. She had to see it; there was nothing else she could do.

It was over in about five minutes. They left.

Ahmed's wife bent down to see how badly Ahmed was hurt.

"Why would anyone want to do this to Ahmed, of all people. Ahmed, he never hurt anyone." She just stared; his eyes were open but lifeless, his face black and blue, bleeding from his nose and mouth, his crotch wet, his right leg broken.

Chapter 22

Ahmed was average height and weight, nicely put together. You immediately noticed how each of his body parts fitted with the rest; his twinkly eyes. He looked like a cuddly, stuffed teddy bear. He dressed nicely, had a sense of what went with what; shoes always clean; looked good no matter what he wore. The fact that he didn't particularly care what others thought of his appearance was the key, the signature of why he looked good.

Neither was he interested in expensive clothes, didn't wear jewelry or a watch, nothing around his neck as so many of the local men did—for them some sort of status. He didn't wear cologne, you knew he was squeaky clean...the essence of contentment with who he was; utterly comfortable.

Archie had been to Ahmed's house several times. His wife was a short pleasant but not beautiful woman. Her mother who looked ancient lived with them. "She is ninety-five," Ahmed informed Archie. They had a daughter and two boys. The boys, typical of their age...ten or twelve, couldn't speak any English but spoke volumes by running around, doing tricks like climbing a coconut tree, putting their pet moonson around their necks (their furry, black civet) and generally not sitting still; acting like boys.

Ahmed just smiled, they are just boys, his smile said, but everyone assembled knew those boys knew their limit. Not because they were afraid of their father but because they respected him and he respected them.

Ahmed was not a "patsy," an "easy mark." He was aware that he was a nice person, a good person, but he would not let others take advantage of that, like so many other "goody-two-shoes" do. Somehow he transmitted, "that is not something you should ask of me," so no one did. By the same token, if you did ask Ahmed for help you could count on it.

Ahmed was proud of his family, his house, his mother-in-law; proud that he was a Muslim, proud that he was an Indonesian, and content because there was nothing Ahmed, or the others in his family for that matter, wanted that they couldn't afford and nothing they couldn't afford that they wanted. It was written all over each of them.

Wiranto, the Parai manager knocked on Archie's door to bring him the bad news.

"Why?" was Archie's question although he knew the answer. "Why did they have to kill him? What is it that makes people do things like that, how can they live with themselves?"

In situations like this there aren't a myriad of thoughts, just the same few over and over. That is where Archie was.

Why? Why did they have to kill him? What is it that makes people do things like that, how can they live with themselves?

In truth, Archie was beginning to fall apart. He recognized it and the others recognized it. Greg felt he had to take charge. He walked into Archie's office the next day, closed the door and suggested Archie go to Singapore for a few days, a week.

"Curtis will take over your responsibilities, I am putting him in charge of the project... you are too distraught. It is not that I blame you, you have been through a lot, but I have the project to think of, I believe you understand and agree that it would be best for you and the firm, no?"

This is the last straw, where the rubber hits the road, the final nail in the coffin, the point of no return, over the horizon, the end of the line...where did these phrases originate was Archie's first thought. Shouldn't I be coming up with something new, something original, like this is the shits, I can't handle adversity, I'm screwed?

Greg continued, "what do you say? Take a break; you know you need to get away for a little while. When you come back we will see where things stand. You could work from your hotel room. You are good at writing reports, you can start on the final report. What do you say?"

Archie just looked at Greg. What could he say? He was smart enough to know that Greg's choice of words indicated it was a done deal, any attempt to change his mind would be futile. But defensiveness was a way out.

"What if I don't agree, what if I do not want to take off a few days? I am the project manager, not Curtis, that's the arrangement. Curtis is a liability, Subroto doesn't like him, the staff, except for Troy, can't stand him, how will he be able to get

Chapter 22

anything accomplished. This is my project and no one is going to give it away, is that clear?"

Greg got up off the chair and walked to the window. He opened the shutter a little, looked out and thought, he needs time for this to sink in. It shouldn't come as a surprise; he doesn't understand that some things are bigger than ego.

He had the opportunity to play ball but no, he has a warped notion of what is right and what is wrong. Sometimes you have to be flexible, what is right for some people isn't necessarily right for other people. Or wrong, for that matter.

Archie, meanwhile, given a few seconds to process what transpired, resigned himself that the decision was made.

Oh, I could continue to fight it, I could threaten that I will expose what I knew about Greg and Subroto's arrangement, I could go to the minister, who is my friend, I could write a letter to the Wall Street Journal.

Archie pursed his lips together at the last stage of descent into resignation, steepled his fingers, put them to his lips and said, softly,

"Perhaps you are right, but I do not feel like going anywhere, I'll take some days off and stay here on the Island."

If you looked carefully you would see a little tiny smile form on Greg's face.

23

People don't change that easily. That is, their fortunes don't change. Everyone is born into a slot and most remain in that slot all their lives. Slots are tendencies...he has the tendency to be obese; she has the tendency to be a leader; those two have the tendency to be on stage.

That one is in the *good at sports* slot, and this one is in the *going to be rich* slot. Oh, the slot may get wider, even may narrow, but it is extraordinary to transcend your slot. It is not quite pre-destination but there is an element in the human makeup that you could call pre-destination.

If someone accomplishes something big, changes their condition, their fortune, you say, "that person is special" or that person was "lucky."

But what makes them special...lucky? Maybe it's their slot. How many little girls who love to sing, perhaps take lessons from the best teachers; they perfect their voice, they have the desire to perform on T.V. or Broadway, they are accomplished, very good, plenty good for T.V. or Broadway...how many make it big? The few who were born into that slot, the "make it big slot" that's who. Not very many other accomplished little girls achieve greatness, fortune. When they do they may say, "it's my karma, my luck."

But it is also their slot. Good fortune doesn't come to the majority. On the other hand there are those who do make it even though they aren't that good and you say to yourself, how did that happen, why them? What gods were smiling on them? How can I get the gods to smile on me? If someone transcends their slot, we say, "they were at the right place at the right time."

Is that it? Is that the only explanation?

Archie gradually came to the conclusion that he had reached the outer edge of the slot he was born into.

There is no way I am going anywhere, no matter how I try or wish for it. I am not special. I am destined to remain where I am. It's my karma. True, I will make a comfortable living—through hard work and dedication, but it is not ordained for me to become a "major success," nothing more than just comfortable. But that is what I want...to be a major success, make a lot of money, be important. I want people to say, look at him, he was born into the *successful* slot.

I don't mean super rich. I dream of a house on the South China Sea, taking vacations, driving a nice car, being able to afford to buy my family nice things, never having to worry where the next dime is coming from.

Why isn't it in the cards for me? What makes Greg different, or Curtis? Greg is destined to become a high roller; that is his slot. Is he smarter than I am? Is he a better person, does he have skills I don't have? And Curtis, who borders on evil, he gets the gold ring. People like him were born into the *gold-ring* slot.

Look at Suradi and Ahmed, poor Ahmed. Suradi, who is devious, dishonest, mean and spiteful, was born into the *powerful* slot. There is something in him that will propel him upward, it is only a matter of time, he will become powerful, and rich by Bangka standards, it is written. Ahmed, who was wholesome, good, honest, he got dealt a lousy hand, murdered as a message to me—don't mess with the miners; the *martyr* slot.

It is more than just happenstance, it's in the cards, people like Ahmed, like me. If we are lucky we may reach the outer edges of our slot, but that is as far as we go.

I may as well quit the firm, I'm finished, my career is finished. What is it in me that I can't overlook what is not in my power to control no matter what? Sure, Joe had an accident, sure it could have been prevented, sure it was Curtis' doing. Why didn't I just leave it alone? Why didn't I just roll with it? Why didn't I merely tell Catherine it was an accident; leave it there? Who did it profit when I told Curtis I knew what happened? Yes, it made me feel good at his expense. "Look at me, I'm superior to you"...whom did it hurt...me...my career...*my* kids.

Greg was right when he said I should look at the big picture, when he told me to leave the miners be. Did I listen? I can't change the world. The rich and powerful will win, they will always win because either they were born into the *winners* slot or they were pre-destined to escape the one they were born into.

Chapter 23

Following Greg's instruction, Archie, took a few days off and stayed at the Parai. The two days consisted of sleeping in, reading the book he had wanted to finish and taking walks down the beach. One of his favorite places was a fishing village; a fishing harbor would be a more likely description. There were a few small buildings where fishermen kept their things. Some nights probably slept in them. Their boats were moored a short distance off the sandy beach.

Archie was thinking about his lot in life, the slot he was destined to remain in. The sky was exceptionally clear, the water very still. The fishermen usually go out after dark so you cannot see them or their boats when they are out, just the lantern they have hanging from the mast bobbing up and down in the gentle waves.

Early in the morning the boats were tied on buoys. They were large rowboats with a mast. Their bright colors: red, blue, green, yellow reflected in the still water...so clean you could see the floor of the sea under the boats. You could see hundreds of multi-colored fish, each one different, swimming among boats of the same colors.

"It would be nice to be able to paint, be able to spend quality time painting beautiful scenes like these fish, boats, shoreline," Archie mumbled to no one; he was alone on the beach.

Who am I kidding...it is over. Curtis will stay on as the project manager. I will have to quit the firm—if I don't get fired first. My career is through, and for what? In the process of adhering to my "holier than thou" attitude I've screwed myself. Will Catherine care? Will anyone care? Of course not. Oh, she will thank me for giving her the information she will need to sue the firm but what does that do for me? What can you buy with "thanks for telling me the truth, for helping me out"?

He walked back to the Parai, surprised to see Greg there, sitting at one of the tables drinking a glass of lemonade. When he saw him, still at a distance, Archie stopped short. He exhaled, resigned himself that what he was just thinking was now going to become reality.

"I guess it's too late to quit," he mumbled out of earshot.

Greg didn't say "hello" or "how are you." He went right to the point.

"Archie, the firm has made a decision. You are to go back to Chicago. I have already contacted Suradi and he is making reservations. It may be as early as this afternoon. You can stay at the Jakarta Hilton tonight and if Suradi cannot get you on a flight out of Jakarta tomorrow, stay tomorrow night as well. I am sure you know it is in your best interest...and the firm's."

Greg stood up, extended his hand and said,

"I'll say goodbye now, I have to get back to Pangkalpinang, but I will see you in Chicago, in a couple of weeks. I believe I will not have to stay here beyond that. Give my regards to your wife."

He shook Archie's hand and left.

That was quick and easy, you bastard. Archie stood long enough to watch Greg get into the van, then sat down and looked out at the horizon.

Goodbye, South China Sea, it was great while it lasted. After a few minutes—turned out to be an hour, actually—Archie got up, walked to his room to pack his things.

While he was packing, the phone rang. It was Suradi's travel agent, his cousin or daughter, perhaps his wife.

"Mr. Archie, we have a reservation for you this afternoon at three o'clock to Jakarta and we were lucky to get you a seat on the five-thirty to Singapore where you are booked at the Le Meridien. Then tomorrow, your flight leaves at seven forty-five a.m. to Amsterdam, connecting directly to Chicago. Your tickets will be waiting for you at the airport. I hope you have a pleasant journey. Thank you."

Archie thought about how perfectly scripted whichever of Suradi's relatives called him.

He thought, yes, they learned their job fast, they must have been trained by the airlines, a requirement to become a travel agent, seeing as how there was no travel agency on the island just a short while ago.

This is nuts, I won't even get a chance to say goodbye to the crew. Sure, I'll see Tim and Kevin back at the Chicago office,

Chapter 23

but I'll never see Richard, or Troy again, not even Russ, my "favorite" consultant.

Effendi, or Budi either...no one has any use for someone who fails. It is probably better that I don't see them. They won't be put on the spot for something to say.

"Sorry you screwed up, sorry to hear you couldn't manage a large project, sorry you aren't going to get the promotion you hoped for. Sorry, but it just wasn't your slot."

At the Pangkalpinang airport, sure enough, Archie's tickets and passport were at the counter. Suradi, still angry that Archie wouldn't play ball with the new desks, made himself scarce.

Big powerful man...right...afraid to see me, thought Archie. In truth, I screwed up there too. What makes me think I am so holy, so righteous?

So what, the cost of the desks would have gotten lost in the millions I-Tin wastes each year, yet it was a big deal for Suradi and I had to interfere. What is it about me that I think I am the morals chairman? Who the hell do I think I am?

The flight from Bangka to Jakarta went quickly. Once at the Jakarta airport, the itinerary called for Archie to board about five-fifteen for the five-thirty flight to Singapore. Since he was leaving the country he had to go through passport control. The officer looked at Archie's passport, then looked at Archie.

"Step aside," he said, "someone will be with you in a moment." He pointed to a spot just to the right of the line.

Archie moved to where the officer pointed, wondering what could be wrong. Everyone else, it seemed, breezed through. After a few minutes another officer walked up to Archie.

"Come with me," he said.

"Where are we going?" Archie asked.

"Come with me," the officer repeated.

He led Archie to a small office and told him to sit down, then he left. Archie looked at his watch. It was forty-five minutes until takeoff. He looked at his watch every minute for the next seven.

Finally a third officer came into the room. This one looked like he was all business.

The Bangka Inquiry

"Your visa has expired, the penalties are severe for anyone who is in the country illegally. You will have to go into Jakarta and they will decide what to do with you." The officer was not friendly.

You know the type, dress them in a uniform and the power goes to their head. The bigger the fish you can boss around, the bigger the man that makes you. This passport control officer thought he was *huge*. Archie asked to look at his passport; he handed it over reluctantly.

"My visa expired yesterday and I will be leaving in a few minutes, can't you bend the rule just a little?"

All of that was code for "what will it cost me?" No one in Jakarta was above bending the rules for a little cash. But not this huge guy, he was wallowing in the power detaining an American gave him.

"No, you will have to go to Jakarta and get a temporary visa."

"But Jakarta is at least an hour away, I will miss my flight."

"That is the rule."

"Can't you do it here, I will pay the fee," another code for "make is as much as you want." Nothing doing with huge guy.

The standard procedure was to go to the ministry of state transportation located in downtown Jakarta. What with the traffic, at any time of day except midnight, that would be at least an hour each way. There was no telling how long they would make you wait at the ministry...to stamp your passport.

Why, Archie thought, what's the purpose, just stamp the damn thing, or don't...kick me out of the country instead.

Well, I guess Suradi showed me. I knew when I first met him he was diabolically clever, serves me right for nixing his desk deal.

All the alternatives went through Archie's head. He'd miss his flight causing him to stay overnight at the Jakarta Hilton, assuming they had a room; it was a very busy hotel. That wasn't the worst part—it was, at least, a luxury hotel. Flights out of Jakarta were usually full, getting a seat on short notice was not the norm. The worst was when you get geared up to get home and

Chapter 23

there is an unexpected delay, the time goes by very slowly. Every minute you think, I could have prevented this...here it is twenty-four, forty-eight hours taken out of my life, completely wasted...I'll never get it back.

The Indonesian government knew that this was a severe penalty, that's why the desk wasn't at the airport; you had to go downtown, guaranteed to miss your flight.

The question is why...you are going to leave...and if you come back at all it is in the interest of improving the Indonesian economy—whether business or pleasure you are going to spend money. Who gains by this punitive procedure was Archie's musings as he just stood there looking distastefully at huge guy.

Suddenly Archie remembered his meeting several weeks ago with Thobrani.

We seemed to hit it off, didn't we? Didn't he tell me, "if there is anything you need, just let me know?"

Now I need him, Archie thought. To huge guy he said,

"Please call Minister Thobrani, the Economic Minister, I know him and want to talk to him. He will take care of this problem."

The officer stiffened slightly, looked at Archie while making his momentous decision, and said,

"We do not have time for playing games, you must go to the office in Jakarta. The Minister cannot help you. If, like you say, you know the Economic Minister it will not help; the State Transportation Minister is in charge here."

Archie thought quickly.

"But the State Transportation Minister and the Economic Minister are very good friends, they are often together," hoping they weren't bitter enemies and hoping huge guy wouldn't ask the Transportation Minister's name because Archie had no idea what it was.

It worked.

"Yes, in that case I will place a call through to Minister Thobrani, wait here." Huge guy was not about to take the chance that Archie wasn't for real.

A few minutes later he returned.

"Come with me."

The Bangka Inquiry

They walked to the second office down the hall and a woman indicated Archie should sit. Her attitude was similar to huge guy's; powerful, didn't she tell the American to "sit here?" She dialed the phone with pursed lips and a few seconds later the Minister was on the phone, which she thrust at Archie, visibly annoyed that this low-life would be talking to one of *her* ministers.

"Minister Thobrani, this is Mr. Archie, the consultant from CCG, we met a few weeks ago...in Pangkalpinang...at I-Tin." Archie paused, hoping the Minister would say, "yes, I remember you," which is exactly what he did say.

"How are you and what can I do for you?"

"I am afraid I let my visa expire and I am scheduled to leave the country in a few minutes. Perhaps you can help me?"

"They consider that a serious offense. How did it happen? Has this happened before to any of your people? I have no authority over the transportation ministry; there is nothing I can do. However, I can call their office, I know Minister Mahmood, I am not sure I will be able to reach him but if I do I will talk to him. Other than that I cannot help, their rules are very strict," which was code for, "that was a stupid thing to do, let your visa expire."

"Thank you sir, my plane leaves in one half hour so I would appreciate what you can do." The Minister said goodbye and hung up the phone. Archie said to huge guy,

"I am supposed to wait here, the Minister will call back." What else could he say? The woman glared. Archie figured she hated him.

Fortunately only a few minutes went by and the phone rang. It was the Transportation Minister who asked to speak to the passport control officer on duty. Huge guy took the phone, immediately stood at full attention—Archie thought for a moment he might even salute—and said "yes" six times in a row. When he hung up the phone there was a definite change in his attitude. Now he was bowing and fawning like a sycophant. It worked, Archie got on the flight with full VIP treatment.

Perhaps I *can* make it, Archie thought. Perhaps being honest, upstanding, does have its rewards. I bet Minister

Chapter 23

Thobrani, and probably Mahmood as well, aren't power hungry and devious, yet they are successful. Was it luck, was it their slot or did they work hard at it...maybe get a break or two along the way? I'll never know.

24

Subroto was in Jakarta for I-Tin business. He called Chu to request a meeting; they arranged lunch at Chu's club. Subroto could not resist a free meal at the best private club in Jakarta—you had to be Chinese to be a member.

"The reason I wanted to talk to you was my concern over the miners' restlessness with the I-Tin project," Subroto began. "You probably heard that they beat up one of the consultant's drivers. I do not think they meant to kill him, they are basically good people, but they apparently got carried away. Their livelihood is at stake, you know."

"Yes," Chu answered, "I have heard. I met that man, the driver, his name is Ahmed. It is an unfortunate situation. What are you going to do to help his family?"

Chu's question was a subtle message to Subroto that Ahmed's family should be taken care of. The subtly was not lost on Subroto; he knew Chu; knew he had a reputation for being savvy about how the world works yet a proponent of anyone he thought may have been taken advantage of...and he had the resources and network to get what he wanted, whatever it took. Subroto knew this and was forced to make a commitment.

"I will personally see that his family receives his full salary until their youngest is fifteen."

"Good," was all Chu had to say to let Subroto know he would make sure it happened.

"Yes," Chu continued, "I understand the miners are concerned, but they are engaged in an illegal business. They cannot believe they are immune from the law, can they? They are destroying their property, our valuable Indonesia will be destroyed forever."

"Yes, the miners must be stopped, or at least regulated, but I believe it will take time. Things will have to settle down first. I am here to inform you that we, the I-Tin managers, believe this project was initially a good idea but it has deteriorated. It should be ended right away. We do not want any more trouble. Why, one of the consultants could be next, beat up, that is."

Chu quickly responded.

"Am I not correct in understanding that the consultants agreed to merely put together a timetable for the illegal miners...that is all they would do? They would design a procedure that, over time, would allow some land mining but would hold them responsible for restoring their land to its original condition? Isn't that all they were going to do? If so, what is the problem with the miners, what are they concerned about?"

The question was rhetorical; Chu did not expect an answer from Subroto. Chu paused, then posed this question to Subroto,

"Should they not be able to finish that valuable piece of their charter?"

Subroto believed Chu had no idea who the landowners were, probably never suspected some who owned the land were not the miners; he would have used an entirely different approach, different words. Subroto and his buddies had been successful in hiding the real ownership through layers of paperwork. However, the key to maintaining the secrecy was very simple—the fact that no one suspected also meant there was no reason to investigate. Yet he also knew it would only be a matter of time if the consultants continued their work that someone would stumble across the truth and let it out. The project had to be cancelled...the sooner the better.

"I believe enough work has been done so we, the managers of I-Tin, can finish the timetable started by the consultants. This way, if the miners see that the consultants have gone away they will return to normal. It will give us enough time to not only complete the timetable but begin implementing it...slowly, with alternative jobs for any miners put out of work...good jobs."

"It is not my decision," Chu responded, "why are you coming to me? I did not authorize the project, Minister Thobrani is the one you need to talk to."

"Because Mr. Thobrani, who authorized it, will be influenced by what you think. We, the I-Tin managers, need to have your concurrence before we approach the Minister. Do we have it?"

"As I said, it is not my decision. However, whatever the Minister decides I will support. I will not try to influence him in any way."

Chapter 24

Subroto was pleased with himself. Besides, it was a delicious lunch.

* * *

Archie called his wife from Amsterdam to let her know what time he was arriving at O'Hare airport so she could pick him up. When she innocently asked why he was coming home, he said,

"I'll tell you everything when I see you."

She tried unsuccessfully to put that to the back of her mind. It wasn't unusual for Archie to be called to the office for meetings. Yet she had a strange feeling.

This is not the reason this time, she told herself.

He would have said he was coming home for a meeting. Something is wrong. It has to be connected with Joe's death. I can feel it.

As soon as she hung up with Archie, she decided to telephone Catherine. They had not talked since Catherine left for Indonesia and Catherine, after she returned, saw no good in discussing what she found out, so she decided not to talk to anyone, no matter who it was.

She was aware of the position her trip put Archie in and prepared herself for what could happen to him, but excused it,

I had to know, I had to know how Joe died.

In order not have to vindicate herself, she kept everything she learned inside, talked to no one except Angelina.

Since Angelina was instrumental in getting Catherine to travel to Bangka Island to inquire what happened, she knew Catherine's travel plans and called her immediately upon her return. She wanted to know what transpired. She had begun working on the lawsuit and needed specifics to finalize it. She was doing the legal work on her own time.

Joe and I go back enough years, it's the least I can do.

Initially, getting Catherine's concurrence was not easy. However, once Catherine thought about David and Monica's welfare, she agreed.

Catherine picked up Archie's wife's phone call on the third ring. She recognized the voice immediately when she heard,

The Bangka Inquiry

"Catherine, this is Archie's wife, how are you? I think of you often but I did not want to bother you by telephoning. You are going through a difficult time and I knew that if you needed anything from me you would not hesitate to call."

"Thank you, yes it is difficult but each day is a little better. It was such a shock."

"I know you went to Indonesia," Archie's wife continued, "to...to speak with Archie...but he and I have not discussed it. The reason I am calling...well, I just got off the phone with him, he is in Amsterdam...he is on the way home. I am worried. I have a strange feeling something is wrong, something to do with the accident. I am sorry to bother you, but *is* there something wrong?"

"Yes, I'm afraid there is," Catherine answered. "Do you know Angelina, Joe's friend from college, the lawyer? Archie does and may have mentioned her to you. She is looking into Joe's accident and has told me not to discuss my trip with anyone. I am sorry...but she made me promise."

Catherine continued,

"*Anyone*, is what Angelina said, 'that includes your sister, your children, Archie and his wife, no one, understand?' She was that specific and made me promise." Archie's wife did not respond so Catherine went on.

"I do know, however, that she wants to speak with Archie, as soon as possible. She asked me if I knew when he was coming back to Chicago, she said it was important to talk to him. I told her I did not know. If he is coming home it may be best for all of us if he talks with Angelina right away. I will get her phone number for you."

So I am right, Archie's wife reflected while waiting for Catherine to get the phone number, he is coming home because something has gone wrong. Is he being blamed for Angelina's lawsuit? When she returned to the phone Catherine could sense a bitterness in Archie's wife's answer to Catherine's,

"I have it, do you have a pencil?"

"Yes, I've got one, go ahead."

Catherine gave her the phone number then added,

Chapter 24

"We do not know anything, we won't know anything until he gets home. That is why I am telling you what Angelina said, she wants to talk to him. I do not want anything to happen to him…or you…because of me. He needs to contact Angelina, can you understand that?" Catherine gave Archie's wife the phone number again.

"Yes, I will tell him that I talked to you and will give him your message. I am sorry to have bothered you…but I am worried. Thank you for the information. Goodbye." She hung up the phone and looked at Angelina's phone number she had written on the notepaper.

* * *

After much consideration, Curtis decided to renege on his earlier decision to send Troy home. He figured that now that he was project manager he could give Troy his promotion, demonstrate that the Jakarta position was forthcoming as well, and have Troy where he could watch him.

"Troy is not likely to bite the hand that feeds him." Curtis murmured before calling Troy into the office to tell him the good news.

"Troy, thanks for coming in so quickly." Troy blinked twice; why the sudden change, what was up? Wasn't this the first time ever since they knew each other that Curtis said the word "thanks" to him?

"Have a seat," Curtis continued.

"I have good news, hopefully what you have been waiting for. I've cleared it with headquarters in New York…congratulations, you are now a Perth Partner; effective immediately." Curtis stood up, walked over to Troy and shook his hand.

Whew, Troy said to himself but quickly thought,

What brought this on? It makes me nervous…I want the promotion, sure, but it makes me nervous. Curtis does not glad-hand for nothing; he's getting something in return. Keep my mouth shut, that's what it is. Okay, I can do that.

"Thanks," was all that Troy could think to say, "thanks a lot, I've been looking forward to this day. You will not be sorry; I will do my best. Thanks again." He hoped that signaled to Curtis that he knew what was going on and could be trusted to cooperate.

The promotion meant a pay increase, the respect of his fellow workers, except of course Richard, who saw something "smelly going on" but didn't say anything, and most important, Amulya.

But Amulya would have none of it. Not only did she tell Troy several nights earlier when they were together that it was over, she refused to speak to him other than what was necessary for work. She told him he could carry on about it, tell anyone he wished, she didn't care who found out about them; it was over.

Fortunately for Troy there was still Fiona.

Fiona had gone back to Perth and hung on to the hope that Troy was going through a phase, she would be able to change him; she merely had to give him time. She was convinced her plan worked when he called her with the news.

"I am sorry, Fiona, you know I love only you. I was infatuated but when I thought about who I want to spend the rest of my life with, it is you." He told her about the promotion and asked if they could resurrect the wedding plans...in Bali. They would have to work fast but it could be done.

Fiona fell for all this B.S. She congratulated herself on her patience and her understanding of Troy. The wedding would take place as planned. Fiona was pleased with herself.

The next call Troy made was also to Perth, to his friend Haywood. He told him the good news about his promotion and made arrangements to tip a few ambers the next time he got home. He never mentioned the wedding but did ask about Irene and Lynette and wanted to know if they were still a threesome with Haywood.

"Sure," he answered, "and they ask about you all the time, they like it when the four of us get naughty." Troy was happy to know they would be there when he needed them.

* * *

Chapter 24

When Archie arrived in Chicago after the long journey, his wife was waiting for him. It was a twenty-four hour ordeal to go half way around the earth. Before his first trip to Indonesia, when his kids asked where he was going, Archie pointed straight down.

"If you dig straight down you will end up popping up on Bangka Island. Most people believe you will end up in China, not so, from Chicago it would be Indonesia, exactly where your dad is going."

Archie wasn't sure they believed him. After all, he was only their father, their teacher said "China." In any case it was a moot question; it couldn't be done anyway.

Naturally everyone was happy to see him when he arrived back at his house. He had not spoken at length to his wife to let her know what was going on, telling her instead to wait until he unpacked, until the kids were in bed and they could relax.

"But don't worry, everything is okay," he assured her.

However, he wasn't sure himself how okay things were. Everything depended on what Catherine would do.

"If she sues," Archie told his wife while they were in bed, their usual place for talking things through, "the firm will blame me for telling her what I was told to keep to myself. If she doesn't sue, and is satisfied with what they would consider 'reasonable compensation', perhaps my job can be saved. It depends on her."

"I was waiting to tell you," his wife answered, "I talked to her today, right after you called me from Amsterdam. I knew there was something wrong, something to do with Joe and Catherine. She told me to tell you to call Angelina, you know, Joe's friend, the lawyer?"

"Of course I know her, is she going to sue?"

"Catherine wouldn't tell me, she said she had instructions from Angelina not to talk to anyone, even her sister, David and Monica, us, no one."

"That sounds like a lawsuit is brewing. When am I supposed to call?" Archie realized this was a silly question. Was the answer two o'clock or ten thirty-eight or nine twenty-two? He recovered, "I mean, I will call her first thing tomorrow morning." Archie figured the future didn't look good.

"Let's get some sleep. We will see what tomorrow brings."

Archie's phone call to Angelina resulted in a conference later between the three of them, Angelina, Archie and Catherine. It was to take place that afternoon in Angelina's office. It was a short meeting. After pleasantries, Angelina spoke first.

"Catherine, this is about Joe, and you, and the kids. Joe was a great guy, always ready to forgive and forget, but not this time. He would be concerned about you and David and Monica, and I respect him for that. This isn't about forgiveness, we can forgive whoever was responsible for the accident, but we can't just leave it be. You and the kids need to consider your future. Everyone will tell you compensation is no substitute, but it is reality. Joe has to provide for David and Monica...and you, as if he were still here, working at CCG. Do you understand, do I have agreement on this?"

Both Catherine and Archie nodded, realizing Angelina was not through.

"Archie, the case hinges a great deal on you. I do not think we will have too much difficulty getting a settlement, more than if we did not threaten a lawsuit, but if we can show culpability and the Firm's desire to sweep it under the rug, cover it up, we will have a better case. And Archie, that is where you come in."

Archie spoke his piece.

"I am not proud of my firm. True there are other circumstances, others who will suffer because of this, and I need to consider them."

"Who," Angelina butted in, "who will suffer more than Catherine, David and Monica? No one will. Joe paid the ultimate price, any other monetary considerations pale." She got worked up fast.

"Who will suffer? You have a point," Archie reconsidered, "Marapani the dredge captain would be held responsible but he's dead. He had a heart attack. His crew probably will get a slap on the wrist, maybe fired...which is what they deserve. The landowners, some will probably go to jail...me." Archie was sorry he included himself; it didn't come across like he expected.

"I am sorry, I didn't mean that," he said.

Chapter 24

Angelina had them both where she wanted. She was good and she knew it. Inside she was a softie, but she hated it, hated it when someone tried to run away from his or her responsibility. If you do something wrong, apologize, seek forgiveness, take the punishment. In her experience, in the long run, the people that do this come out better than those who run away from what they have done.

"Okay, lets get started. Archie, start from the beginning, Catherine, I want you to go to the lounge and get yourself a cup of coffee. I'll call you when I want you." There was no bullshit with Angelina.

* * *

After covering his bases with Chu, Subroto talked to Minister Thobrani to get his concurrence that the project should be ended immediately. This is how he made his case:

"Three people have died as a result of this project, it is time it ended. Problems have surfaced with the illegal tin miners, they are more entrenched than we initially thought and it will take time to dislodge them. But the work of the consultants was not in vain. To date we got what we paid for, the dredges will be repaired to the consultants' specifications, the workshops will be restructured, new procedures will be put in place, that is what we have paid for to date.

"And I will see that the illegal mining is handled. Slowly, to give everyone time to make alternative plans. It will take months, perhaps a year, but it will be done on my watch."

To his surprise Thobrani agreed, saying to Subroto,

"Your reasoning is sound, I agree."

The meeting was short. Subroto thanked the Minister for his wise decision then figured he better get out of there before he got into a conversation he would not relish. He returned to Bangka and immediately contacted Greg to schedule a meeting.

25

Subroto sent his messenger to ask Greg if they could meet. A few hours later Subroto welcomed Greg into his office and began the conversation.

"Mr. Greg, I appreciate your taking the time to visit, especially on short notice. I hope everything is going well?"

"Yes, Mr. Subroto," Greg answered, "for the most part everything is going well." He sat in the chair indicated by Subroto's outstretched arm and continued.

"Yes, the project manager transition has gone smoothly. Mr. Curtis will be fully prepared at the next review meeting that, of course, I will attend as well. As you know, Mr. Archie has left Indonesia and is now in Chicago.

"Yes, I understand he had some difficulty at the airport...with passport control." Subroto slowly sat down in a chair across from Greg.

"That is true," Greg acknowledged, paused to let the comment wither—there being nothing gained from discussing it further—and reverted to the previous topic.

"When I received your message I was in the process of preparing the *formal* announcement of the change in project management. I feel it is important to communicate the correct message. I do not want to give the impression that the project is experiencing difficulties or delays or is in any other way in trouble."

"Yes, it is always important to send the correct message," Subroto nodded in agreement and immediately continued, wanting to seize the moment to make his announcement.

"Yesterday, while I was in Jakarta, I met with Minister Thobrani. I must be frank with you, the landowners are nervous with the developments that have occurred. They asked me...told me would be more precise...they want the project to end immediately."

Subroto looked carefully to see the reaction on Greg's face. What he saw would determine what he would say and do next: offer another project, or money, and if so how much—or both. He continued.

The Bangka Inquiry

"I discussed with Minister Thobrani the situation here on Bangka and he agreed the project should end immediately. We discussed the three deaths that have occurred during the project. He too is beginning to sense pressure...from the government...to take action." Subroto paused to let his message sink in, and then continued.

"It seems the government does not want any excuse for unrest on Bangka Island. Subroto extended his arms with palms up, a signal of helplessness.

"As you can surmise, I do not know who all the landowners are; some could be ministers, I don't know...and if they are they could also be putting pressure on Thobrani."

"I see," Greg answered. "Frankly I will admit your message does not come as a surprise. We have been getting subtle hints and, more worrisome, threats of additional violence. Greg searched for an explanation of what Subroto just told him.

"Based on what you are saying, it may not have been a good idea to send Mr. Archie home. Perhaps that sent the wrong message. In anything we do, the news travels fast."

"Yes," Subroto agreed, "it travels fast.

Greg continued. "The men who work the mines, they may be fearful that a new project manager will resurrect the plan to investigate them, take their livelihood away."

"You could have a point," Subroto answered. "In any case we must end the project immediately," getting back to the purpose of the meeting. "I am sorry to have to bring you this distressing news." Subroto paused to more closely watch Greg's reaction and then continued after determining the minimum it would take to get Greg's collaboration.

"Of course, Mr. Greg, you will be given another project, even more lucrative than this one. It will be in Surabaya, in central Java, in the tobacco industry. It will be officially announced shortly. In the meantime, the Minister would like to know if one week is sufficient to have all the consultants off the Island?"

Greg thought of many things he could say to change Subroto's and Thobrani's mind but quickly rejected them. He believed, and rightly so, in the consulting business, once you get a

Chapter 25

"no" to anything, it is very difficult, if not impossible to get it changed to "yes."

Even though I saw the possibility that this could happen, Greg thought, in retrospect it would have been better to have gotten Minister Thobrani into the decision to send Archie home. Perhaps we could have collected the entire fee.

Greg was conscious not to show his displeasure. The Firm did not look kindly at projects that ended before the full fee was paid. However, Greg thought, there was one way to recover the balance of the fees, so he quickly acquiesced.

"I understand, Mr. Subroto, and I agree," Greg went on, "we do not want any more incidents." He crossed one leg over the other knee to signify that his next comment should be considered fact, not a request,

"We can be off Bangka Island in a week. We will find suitable temporary office space in Jakarta to finish the final report and complete our agreement with you."

Subroto saw this as a reasonable compromise, realizing the position he put Greg into. "Yes, that will be suitable," he stood up and walked over to the credenza to get two cups of coffee, signaling that the worst part of the meeting was over.

"We will also be able to keep in contact that way."

Both Subroto and Greg felt it was a win-win agreement.

Greg added to himself, "before long I will be a landowner as well; Subroto will see to that."

* * *

After the initial meeting with Archie, Angelina felt comfortable that there was enough material to file a lawsuit, which she had every intention of settling out of court. Archie was in her office again, the second visit in as many days.

"Based on the information I have, I will file a wrongful death immediately. I am confident that we have a very good case. It may necessitate my traveling to New York to depose Jefferson and McMillan. Company presidents and their lawyers do not like being put on the witness stand. That alone should make them want to settle rather than succumb to a long trial," she said lightly.

Archie nodded in agreement with what Angelina was getting at.

"He often talks about the necessity of keeping a low profile in matters like this. He reverts to his oft-stated expression, 'let's wash our dirty linen in private.'"

Angelina continued,

"I am including Greg and Curtis in the lawsuit as well. We have an office in Australia and they do work in Indonesia. Greg is due back to the US in a few weeks, correct?"

"Yes," Archie answered. Then he looked directly at Angelina, as if to seek answers.

"I do not know how he could have fooled me. I've known Greg for years, known him to be above board, instilling the firm's ethical values into each of us. Could he have changed in just a short time?" Archie was still looking for an explanation of what changed Greg from a person concerned about doing the right thing to one easily corrupted by the first opportunity to come along.

"Yes, Archie," Angelina said, "human behavior does not surprise me any longer. I see things like this quite often. Easy money makes people change. It has always been like that; money and greed make the world go around, as the old saying goes. Greg, unfortunately, is not all that unusual."

"I suppose you are right. However, I do not think Joe would ever be like that. There are honest people, unfortunately they often get hurt for their honesty."

"Yes," Angelina answered...then changed the subject.

"What about you, what will you do? This lawsuit is going to reflect badly on your career and there is nothing much I can do about it. Oh, I could include in the settlement that there is no recourse to you, but that is not a satisfactory solution. They could make it hell for you."

"You are correct," Archie looked directly at Angelina again.

"I have decided not to stay with the firm. I want to enjoy my work, not wake up each morning expecting to do battle.

Chapter 25

Unfortunately there are co-workers I shall miss, people I enjoy working with."

"I figured you'd come to that conclusion," Angelina said softly, "I do not want to make excuses for bringing suit on behalf of Catherine, but I think you realize that with Joe's accident, things would never be the same between you and CCG. Whether I bring suit or not, things have changed. I know it is difficult, but you are making the right decision. You will not have any difficulty moving on."

"Angelina, it is more than that. I am as guilty as Greg and Curtis. I originally decided to cover up the real reason for Joe's accident. Yes, I changed my mind, but I was tempted not to. I think Catherine knows. I refused to speak with her when she phoned. It was only when she was there in person did I decide to tell her the truth."

Archie paused a moment, Angelina said nothing, realizing that he had to let it out, had to talk about what was so obviously bothering him.

"I try to excuse myself by saying it wasn't money or greed, I was just protecting my family, my kids. But that excuse doesn't work and I have to live with it. I am no better than Greg and that is a difficult thing to come to terms with."

Angelina saw that she was in no position to agree or disagree with him. This was something he had to work out himself. She did, however, try to lessen his turmoil.

"In any case, you did do the right thing, exposing the cover-up. Being tempted is a long way from actually going through with it. Maybe that helps, maybe it doesn't, but it is worth remembering."

Archie looked at her, she could tell he was weighing what she said. She figured she would get back to the matter at hand, take his mind off what could or couldn't have been.

"I think it would be better for you to hand in your resignation."

"Yes, I already decided that, and thank you for what you are doing for Joe...and Catherine. This didn't have to happen, that is what constantly goes through my mind. My problems are nothing compared to that...it didn't have to happen."

A few days later, Archie and Angelina were shocked when they read in the Wall Street Journal that Greg quit CCG and took a position with another consulting firm. It wasn't immediately clear under what circumstances he made the change. However, a small announcement several days later in the business section of the same newspaper announced that Greg was being sent to Indonesia to work on a project for the tobacco industry. The article indicated he was recently hired as an executive vice president.

Angelina telephoned Archie with the news only to find out he had already read it.

"He got that project for keeping quiet about the landowners," Angelina surmised, "and changing firms was his way of collecting the reward, no?"

"Yes, I believe you are correct." Archie answered, and then asked, "if this case settles out of court, Greg wins; is that how it works?" It was a rhetorical question...what could Angelina answer?

"That's not all," Archie continued. "Yesterday I found out that Curtis Morgan is the first non-US partner in CCG. And speaking of rewards, CCG announced that he will be the director for all of the firm's interests in Asia."

Angelina responded.

"The system isn't perfect, but my interest is not in fixing the world, only making sure Catherine and Joe's kids never have to worry about finances." Then she added,

"Don't fret Archie, you'll do okay as well. There is some justice left." She wanted to encourage him. She knew this nightmare affected him greatly.

26

Evidently the project team saw the shadows on the wall because everyone took the move to Jakarta in stride. It was an easy move. The project was due to wind down shortly so the staff had begun tying up loose ends, culling and packing files and organizing the support materials needed for the final report.

When they arrived in Jakarta they decided to use conference rooms that the Hilton provided rather than rent short-term office space. Only the staff critical to finalizing the report stayed, the rest were sent back to their respective offices. The final crew included Greg and Curtis; Troy Eastwood and Richard Rowland from Perth; Kevin Buscome and Tim Snyder from Chicago and Budi, the single-named Indonesian translator appointed by I-Tin.

Budi was particularly savvy in the workings of the company—he knew the procedures, was familiar with the workshops, knew each of the dredges and the cast of characters that was I-Tin. He had a working knowledge of most of I-Tin's other holdings—the schools, clinics, hospital, T.V. station and so forth. His contribution to the Jakarta team was to answer questions that might come up. He was like a human transcript the jury could call for while they were deliberating.

He was a likeable, regular guy, short height, rather long wavy hair for an Indonesian, and a dark, ruddy complexion. There was no question that his mind was quick. He had two unusual characteristics going for him. If he walked into a room for a few minutes then left and you asked him what was in the room he could list just about everything down to the number of pencils in a holder. If he looked at a document and had some familiarity with whatever the document was about, he could recall it almost word for word. If it was something he did not know anything about, he might remember a little of it, but certainly would be able to tell you how many paragraphs were on the page.

His second characteristic was his instant likeability. Most Indonesians have a constant smile but his was infectious. He did not normally make himself the center of attention, but somehow his presence was felt. You knew when he was there and when he

The Bangka Inquiry

was not. He was like the schoolyard monitor, you were aware he was watching you, making sure you didn't get into trouble. When he laughed, everyone laughed, when he did not think something was particularly funny no one did. He listened intently and if he did not know an answer he would tell you so; but if he did, it was precise.

How he did not know about the miners, that the owners were wealthy big shots rather than the little guys living on the land and doing the work, was an enigma...or if he did know he was not about to discuss it. On the other hand, the subject never came up. Very few were privy to the arrangements and there was no reason to suspect anything other than what you saw on the surface.

The plan was to spend two weeks together working on the report at the Hilton in Jakarta then return to Chicago to finalize and publish the report. Only Curtis and Budi would travel to Chicago with the Americans. There the rough report would be finalized and sent to the firm's readers who would "wordsmith" the document to check grammar, spelling and sentence structure to make sure it was clear and concise. Graphs and diagrams would be professionally drawn, a cover designed, given one final review, and several copies beautifully printed and bound.

Greg and Curtis would return to Indonesia and formally present the report to the government minister Thobrani with Subroto the I-Tin president and Mr. Chu from the firm's Jakarta office in attendance.

Changes happened quickly.

First concerned Greg. He phoned Curtis' room soon after they left Bangka Island for good and had arrived at the Jakarta Hilton. He announced that he was returning to Chicago immediately. He explained that something had come up that required his presence. Curtis knew that if Greg did not volunteer the reason it was not appropriate to ask so the question was left open. Other than being short one person—Greg's job was to review sections as they were completed—no one gave the reason a second thought.

Chapter 26

Unbeknown to the staff, Greg had telephoned an acquaintance in another well known but smaller consulting firm. His friend's name was Michael Power.

"Michael, Greg Manning here, how's it going?" The phone call from his room at the Jakarta Hilton went through immediately and Greg was happy he found Mike in his office. He had to be careful how he handled this phone call. The trick was to offer a series of profitable projects in return for a position in Mike's firm but not make it sound like a quid pro quo.

Mike remembered Greg immediately. They first met at a black tie dinner to raise money for Children's Memorial Hospital. Both their firms were sponsors and Greg, Mike and their wives sat at the same table. All four hit it off right away so Mike was not surprised to hear Greg's voice on the phone.

"Where are you, I thought you were in Indonesia?"

"I am," Greg answered, "sitting in my room in the beautiful Jakarta Hilton. I keep telling you and your wife to come visit, it is an experience one should not miss if one has the opportunity."

"Would be great," Mike responded. "The problem is getting away. I'm not complaining though, I subscribe to the cliché 'make hay while the sun shines'…just like you do except your hay is in Indonesia, mine is here…."

"So you are busy, that's great," Greg answered. "There is nothing more depressing than to have guys sitting on the bench hoping for the next project to be approved. Backlog is a good thing," Greg added.

"You can say that again," said Mike. "When are you getting back, we should arrange lunch. I want to hear all about Indonesia."

"Actually," Greg answered, "something big has come up. That's the reason I am calling you. I was offered a lucrative project but I am not sure my firm is all that enamored with doing it…there are some internal politics getting in the way." Greg stretched the truth. "Naturally I thought about you."

"I'm always interested in lucrative work," Mike's interest perked up. "Tell me more."

The Bangka Inquiry

It was a long phone call. Greg went through the specifics of the project, as much as he could gather from talking to Subroto. It was a big enough project to perk Mike's interest. As he was explaining the details, Greg was confident that Mike was accurately reading between the lines, picking up Greg's subtle hints about the part he, Greg, would play in it—it was critical that he lead it, he had proven himself, he was the known entity.

So, he took a chance and presented his scenario to Mike.

"Frankly, I would not mind living here. I like the people, they like me and I have the contacts. If I stay with CCG, which I am not married to, there is a problem with the local office. There is no way they want another high-priced consultant to mix things up—they don't particularly want a foreigner telling them how to do their work. Yet getting this project is not a certainty if I am not involved. So, I have and idea..."

Greg presented a plan whereby he would join Mike's firm as a senior executive, work out of Jakarta and take a percentage of the work generated there—almost like a sub-contractor.

Mike was one of the founders of his firm so he had the authority to decide if this was a good arrangement. He liked Greg, recognized his abilities and decided then and there to accept Greg's plan. Greg's compensation package would be based on the increase in revenue so there was little downside to the arrangement other than an initial, relatively small out-of-pocket expense.

"What is the timing of all this?" Mike asked.

"I am coming back to Chicago tomorrow," Greg said, "what does your schedule look like? Let's meet and discuss the details."

"Sounds good," Mike answered, "how about Friday for lunch?"

The second change for the project team happened a week later. Greg was in Chicago, had resigned from CCG and finalized his position with Mike's firm. The tobacco project was announced in Jakarta where Greg was successful in getting it awarded to his new employer. Everything looked perfect.

Then the plans went awry. Everyone—the CCG staff still in Jakarta, Greg, the I-Tin employees—were surprised; no one saw it

Chapter 26

coming, but Minister Thobrani announced that he was "promoting" Subroto to President of I-Tin Exports, Ltd, the wholly owned subsidiary located in London. Most in the know considered it a step above a lateral move because there were perks involved in living in London that were not available in Jakarta...and certainly not in Pangkalpinang on Bangka Island.

The Chicago team planned to present their report to Subroto. However, not being president any longer he would have little interest and certainly not be in any position to implement recommendations. Similarly, the new president would not be anxious to implement either; newly appointed executives want to spray their territory before taking someone else's advice. Who would they report to?

When Greg heard the news he speculated, and rightly so it turned out, that Subroto lobbied for the move to London. He was too cosmopolitan to be satisfied with Pangkalpinang.

He and Greg had an opportunity to meet during a layover Greg had in London on his way back to Indonesia.

"Mr. Subroto," Greg began over lunch at one of the finer hotels, "it pleases me to hear about your promotion. Your experience back on the island will serve you well and I salute the foresight of Minister Thobrani to select the perfect candidate to lead I-Tin Exports, Ltd. After all," Greg continued, "I-Tin needs brisk sales to make the mining operations profitable and you are the perfect person to lead the sales effort."

"Yes," Subroto answered. Modesty was not something you would normally use to describe Subroto.

"I am looking forward to achieving the level of sales the government requires." Then Subroto switched subjects. He wanted to make sure his arrangement with Greg and the illegal mining situation remained intact so he offered a little pearl to Greg.

"One of the reasons I looked forward to this meeting was to let you know there is some property that will be available shortly and I wanted to make it possible for you to take advantage of a very good bargain."

The Bangka Inquiry

"I am always interested in bargains," said Greg

"There is a property being sold by a friend of mine and he would rather it not be sold on the open market, if you know what I am getting at. My friend is selling because he is in poor health and would like to get his estate in order. He does not want his family burdened by things they have no knowledge of...mining, for instance."

"I am very interested," Greg picked up, "but could I afford it? With all due respect, I am not in the same league as some of your friends, Mr. Subroto, but I appreciate the offer."

"You are lucky, Greg. My friend is anxious to complete a sale in the shortest possible time. He is very sick and knows he does not have much time left and wants to leave his estate liquid. He asked me to help him with the transfer so I am confident your budget could handle an investment like this."

Wow, this is perfect, thought Greg, I get to do the easy tobacco project, I answer to hardly anybody, and I get a golden goose thrown at me for good measure. I must have died and went to heaven.

He did not think convincing his wife of the arrangement would present any problem. She had her career, which was extremely important to her, they had no kids and didn't want any, and there would be enough money to meet each other anywhere, anytime. She would approve any arrangement, including his being absent for extended periods, as long as their treasury got bigger.

When Archie heard through his CCG contacts about the changes in Greg's fortune, all except the mine ownership, of course, he couldn't help thinking, sure enough, he was born into the right slot!

Chapter 27

Troy and Fiona's wedding was a rowdy party. As long as Troy was enjoying himself, Fiona ignored the missing parts she had always hoped would be the hallmark of her wedding. She always dreamed of a solemn ceremony, attended by friends whose friendship they would maintain for a lifetime, a sophisticated reception—it did not have to be elaborate or costly, she merely wanted it to be formal, in keeping with her notion of what getting married meant.

She also knew enough about her countrymen not to be deceived.

They don't refer to Australians as rowdy for nothing, she thought, especially from Perth. It was her way of excusing the deterioration of the event that turned out differently than the way she dreamed of it.

Haywood was Troy's best man. Fiona knew Troy acted differently when he was around Haywood. The two of them went back a long way—since they were eight years old—and learned early on that acting foolish, bawdy and disrespectful did not have any negative consequences, in fact, they thought, it set them apart, made them the life of the party.

"I like Troy so much better when Haywood is not around," Fiona confided to her maid of honor, her best friend, "I wish he had picked some-one else."

Then she continued, "but he didn't, so we will make the most of it, won't we?"

Troy invited Amulya to the ceremony and even though it was in Bali, not exactly down the road from Pangkalpinang, he truly believed she would attend.

Why do I want her to attend, he asked himself? It is not to show her that I survived her rejection. No, that has nothing to do with it. I just want to see her again, talk to her, dance with her. He was conscious that he spent a considerable amount of time looking over the assemblage, trying to spot her.

I know she'll come, he convinced himself.

Fiona was conscious also.

"Who are you looking for...Archie?" she asked him. "It's strange that he is not here yet, did he miss his flight?" Evidently Fiona had no idea that Archie was back in Chicago, and didn't know—or if she had been told, didn't care—that Curtis was now the main man and that the team was working out of a hotel in Jakarta. She arrived in Bali directly from Perth on Friday evening and here it was Saturday afternoon. She of course had not seen Troy. She considered it bad luck for a bride and groom to see each other just before their wedding, so they did not have a chance to talk since her arrival.

"He is not coming," answered Troy. "He is not coming so don't worry about him."

"Then who are you looking for? Why is he not coming? I wish I would have known he wasn't coming, when did you find out?"

"Questions, questions, Fiona, Let's not get started off with questions. You ask too many questions. I can't answer them as fast as you ask them." Fiona noticed Troy was getting agitated...on our wedding day! Over who is here and who is not. She kept quiet for a while but then could not resist one more.

"Could you at least tell me why Archie did not come, I thought he was a good friend?"

"It is not important, Fiona, let's not worry about Archie today. This is our day so let's go have a good time, let's party."

Fiona became pensive. She looked down at the ground, squeezed her lips together and blinked a few times. Was she trying to hold back some tears? There is something wrong, she thought, this entire accident thing has been difficult for Troy. Catherine was on to something and it gives me a bad feeling. She decided to leave the topic alone on their wedding day but she hoped she would eventually find out what really happened and why Troy was so taken with it.

True, Fiona did not know Archie was sent back to Chicago, and she also did not know that Angelina had filed a lawsuit in Perth naming Curtis as a defendant and that Troy would be involved. It happened quickly. Angelina believed in striking while everything

Chapter 27

was still fresh in everyone's mind. Her experience was that you could settle more quickly and for more that way.

Fiona, having a difficult enough time coping with this her most important day, had no idea of the turmoil going on inside Archie. He quit the firm and sent out some feelers to other firms he thought might be interested in him, but he did not do it wholeheartedly.

I'm in a funk, he realized, I am not sure I want anything to do with consulting anymore. But what would I do instead?

Thoughts like these were going through his mind more and more frequently. There was no question that the entire Bangka ordeal had an impact on him, a negative impact.

"Mostly, it brought out my true nature, hidden from myself to begin with," he mumbled to himself while sitting in his car.

Archie was on the way to a meeting with Angelina. She had called the previous day saying there were a few loose ends she wanted to tie up, bring him up to date. She's ecstatic, Archie thought, nothing like a juicy case to get her all lathered up.

When he arrived Angelina was waiting for him and he was shown directly into her office. After a few pleasantries she got right to the point.

"Suit has been filed in Perth naming Curtis and Troy; I decided to throw him in as well, a party to the wrongful death. It is you, however, that I am worried about and one of the reasons I asked you to come here today. I got a call from Catherine yesterday and she is worried. She told me she does not want any litigation to go forward if it means causing you problems...and she is worried; she believes that is what is going on. So, my question to you is, 'what *is* going on?' I need to know."

Archie was taken aback. She certainly doesn't beat around the bush, does she?

Archie's wide eyes indicated what he was thinking. He had no idea the turmoil inside him was so visible to strangers...and Catherine was essentially a stranger. True they knew each other socially, had recently been to several meetings in this office together, but that was the extent of it.

"It is me, Angelina, it has nothing to do with what you are doing. My world has collapsed, I've collapsed, I no longer know what I stand for, what I want out of life, where to go from here." Archie surprised himself how quickly he opened himself to her.

"Take it easy on yourself," Angelina put in, "I cannot feel what you are going through but I can understand and sympathize. First of all, you have got to get rid of the notion that you did something wrong. You may have thought about not telling Catherine everything, but you eventually did tell her. Isn't that what matters?

"Secondly, you have wonderful prospects for moving on, you have an entire career to count on. With your experience...and don't short change what you've learned about handling crisis from this experience, you could be snapped up in a moment."

"Angelina, I've been through all of that, it hasn't helped. There is more. I feel like I contributed to Joe's death. I know it wasn't my fault, I know it. But deep inside I also know that I failed. If I had just seen Greg for who he is, if I hadn't trusted him, believed him to be an above board person who was more concerned about the project and the staff than himself and his position....

"If I had seen Greg and Curtis for what they are, what they stand for, Joe would never have even gone to Indonesia. I wouldn't have gone to Indonesia. I sent him there...he trusted my judgment, I was blind to the real Greg and it contributed to his death, not directly but I am no better than Greg and Curtis, I too considered putting myself above the truth and I am having trouble coming to terms with that."

"Like I said, I can understand, Archie," Angelina answered, "but you need to get a hold of yourself...for your own sake; your wife and kids. Go see a priest, a rabbi, whatever, but get counseling. I can help you find someone...but you must get help."

Angelina took a deep breath, waited a moment, and continued.

"The second reason I wanted to see you was to brief you on the timetable for settling the case, either out of court, which looks likely, or bringing the case to trial. I want you to be aware of

Chapter 27

the extent of your participation so you can make arrangements in any new position you decide to take.

"I believe," Angelina continued, "that you will get over this, my only hope is that it happens before the case comes to trial—if it does. I don't want you moping around. I need you steady, upbeat, in control, like the Archie I know." She tried to add a little levity.

"Seriously, get some professional help...and don't hesitate to call me if you need me."

As he was going down the elevator he thought, she is right of course, I need to get over this. I am feeling sorry for myself when I should be feeling sorry for Joe and Catherine. There are a lot of opportunities out there.

As the elevator door opened and he stepped out into the huge, depressing marble lobby he slipped back into melancholia. It is no use. What am I supposed to do, call Greg and tell him, hey Greg, you are my boss, friend, mentor; person I look up to, so give me a position with your new firm...or get me back into CCG...anything, I promise I'll be good? Is that what she wants me to do?

By the time he got to the revolving door he convinced himself that there are other firms, I will just have to put together a plan how to approach them. Is the methodology any different than solving an operational problem for a client?

I will be the client. So, Mr. Client, this is what I found and this is what I propose.

I will come up with key events, put them into a timetable, create a process for measuring how well the project is going...simple. I can't wait to get home to get started!

He stepped out into the dreary, cloudy, windy Chicago day.

I am sick of "what we found, what we propose," sick of "key events" and "timetables" and "performance tracking." I am done with consulting I need to find something else, my own business perhaps, attend a franchise fair; see what franchises are out there. My friend, Bernie, he opened a "Curves for Women,"

The Bangka Inquiry

he loves it. A franchise is hard work, but the chances of success are greater than starting something on your own.

Three months later, Archie was doing part time teaching at the community college. It took him a long time to decide what he wanted to do with himself but he was sure...pretty sure...that he was on the right track. The teaching job was a vehicle for getting him back into the academic groove. He was taking night and weekend courses for his master's degree. His short-term goal was to get a teaching certificate along with his degree so he could eventually teach at the university level. Longer term he wanted a PhD.

I can see the whole thing. Obviously students need ethics courses, who knows better than I do? Isn't it better for a person who had a brush with ethics...me...to teach it? I will do research, case studies, teach from experience, consult, write a text book...dedicate it to Joe Prendergast.

Fortunately Archie and his wife had saved enough money to see them through. She was supportive of the plan, agreeing to refinance their house if what they put away ran out, to take out the built up equity so they did not have to change their lifestyle. Besides, she told him, she was ready for working outside the home now that the kids were in school most of the day; even more to cover their living expenses.

* * *

On the morning Angelina called, Archie was studying for a test on Saturday.

"Hello," Archie said into the phone.

"This is Angelina, Archie, I've got good news, they settled."

"Great. Did everything turn out like you expected?"

"Yes, I got exactly what I wanted. The reason for this call is to let you know, and I will go through the details in a moment, but I want to thank you for everything you did. I am sure Catherine will be calling you to thank you as well. I know it was difficult but we've suffered the beginning, got through the middle, this is the end...as much as it can ever be the end."

"Great news. It is a relief knowing that Catherine and the kids will be safe...from worries about finances, that is."

"Here's the deal, Catherine gets Joe's salary for ten years, a lump sum payment of five-hundred thousand...a lump-sum has been set up in trust to cover everything, I am not taking any chances...two-hundred thousand for each kid and another trust fund to pay medical insurance for Catherine for life and the kids until they are twenty-five. At the last minute I threw in a life insurance policy on Catherine so if anything happens to her, the kids get a million each."

Angelina was out of breath.

"Angelina," Archie said, "well done. You don't know what relief I feel...selfishly because I did not look forward to a trial, but for Joe's family. I congratulate you."

"Thanks," Angelina said, "but I am a little selfish too, I thrive on wining cases. I think I will go out and buy new shoes or something."

They both chuckled, which was a good thing.

On the other side of the globe, Amulya too was the recipient of good news. Although what she got was not nearly as financially rewarding as what Catherine and the kids got, it was something she dreamed about, even though she was never really sure she would ever attain it. So from her view, she was elated.

She had applied to Gadjah Mada University in Jogyakarta and was accepted as an assistant professor of English. She got the good news the same morning that Angelina called Archie.

Eventually, because Archie kept in contact with Richard Rowland, "my favorite Aussie," he found out about Amulya's good fortune. He never stopped thinking, however, how insignificant his entire part in the Indonesian project actually was. It was a rude yet cleansing, liberating, emancipating awakening; but with Amulya taken care of, poor Amulya, the case was closed.

This is a work of fiction. Although there are people—good, wholesome, ethical people, who serve as the template for some of the characters, in the end they are fictional. No real person acted in any way like the characters in the story. And the story itself—it too is fiction. Some of the location is based on reality, some incidents are based on actual experiences; but most of it is made up to fit the plot. Any similarity to actual persons, events, and places is a figment of my imagination.

...Author